DOUBLEDAY | new york london toronto sydney auckland

SHACKLING | WATER

adam mansbach

PUBLISHED BY DOUBLEDAY
a division of Random House, Inc.
1540 Broadway, New York, New York 10036

DOUBLEDAY and the portrayal of an anchor with a dolphin are trademarks of
Doubleday, a division of Random House, Inc.

This book is a work of fiction. Names, characters, businesses, organizations,
places, events, and incidents either are the product of the author's imagination
or are used fictitiously. Any resemblance to actual persons, living or dead, events,
or locales is entirely coincidental.

Book design by Gretchen Achilles

Library of Congress Cataloging-in-Publication Data

Mansbach, Adam, 1976–
     Shackling water / by Adam Mansbach.—1st ed.
         p. cm.
         1. African American men—Fiction.   2. New York (N.Y.)—Fiction.
     3. Jazz musicians—Fiction.   4. Saxophonists—Fiction.   5. Drug abuse—
     Fiction.   6. Young men—Fiction.   7. Hip-hop—Fiction.   I. Title.

     PS3613.A363 S53 2002
     813'.6—dc21

                                                             2001047398

PRINTED IN THE UNITED STATES OF AMERICA

MARCH 2001
FIRST EDITION

10   9   8   7   6   5   4   3   2   1

For my grandmother, Felicia Lamport Kaplan

SHACKLING WATER

The fire music soul cascade was Latif's first serenade, clawing its way out of the family stereo and swirling round his head. He was fourteen years of age, and the dull metal tenor sax on his lap hummed suddenly electric as the redhot blue notes spiraled through it, bouncing like frenzied molecules against the instrument's interior. He had never heard anything like it in his life, this muscular horn spiking holes in the air with every honk and scream, puncturing time as it dove through a cresting tidal wave of drums. The horn dipped and bobbed above the amniotic ocean on winged ankles, shrieked and spiral-dive plummeted into it, vanishing inside the grave of Icarus only to reanimate ichthyoid, a toothy green sea monster undulating over brimstone waves.

Latif rocked and jerked in shifting rhythm, soaking in the serenity and tumult of creation. His music teacher watched and knew he'd made his point and then some. The song ended with bass strings thrumming, drum thunder rumbling in vicious summary and one clear ray of intense light, a horn line so clear it ripped a path from the sun straight through the ocean to the bottom and lit the water from within. The whole sea shimmered tranquil, and suddenly the concordance of these pushing pulling elements was clear: the purposed unity beneath the conflict and the probing and the play.

Mr. Gates relaxed his jaw and waited for Latif to speak. The boy had been his student three years now, and Gates knew without being told that Leda James-Pearson had hired him to give her son weekly lessons out of much more than a simple cultured wish to fill a child's head with music. It was preventive surgery, the desire to graft a saxophone on to an idle hand and innocent mouth before they grew so strong and eloquent that other neighborhood teachers, lounging on trafficked corners and in dusky poolhalls, might find them useful. Latif was bending the corner of that age, strong-wristed and beginning to walk home from school the long way. Obligation to his mother and tacit friendship with his teacher conspired to keep the music lessons coming, but until that afternoon Latif had merely been out to do what everyone he knew was out to do: hustle, push a rap star car through the small radius of Roxbury, Massachusetts, and out into the world beyond, do what had to be done to make a killing.

A killer in the making, his mother thought in darkest moments, watching Latif jaywalk the block to cross the players' paths. Nothing sheathed his interest save a fourteen-year-old's transparent cool, one that fell away at the first acknowledging headnod, phrase, or shoulder-bang embrace. But in the minutes between the delicate dusty touch of stylus to vinyl and the record arm's automatic click, rise, end-of-side glide back into standby—in the song's white spaces, the stolen moments between the saxophone's very notes—Latif's vague aspirations froze and shattered in midair like liquid nitrogen confections.

The truculent truncated boom-kick headbanger boogie of hip hop drums seemed frozen too, all of a moment, like ice chips hacked from glaciers. Hip hop was the indigenous attitude of Latif's ninety decca ecosystem, a malaproper melange of tired braggadocio and quickdraw innovation, pimpology and brother-sisterhood. America not as melting pot but mixing board, wedged between two turntables and a microphone, amalgamating tortured newness from the scraps of dying sonic dynasties, postmodern like a motherfucker. The inheritor of Amiri Baraka's poetry-of-new-jazz ploy of cleaving words and letting separate juices flow from each linguistic chunk, hip hop was rap/id, dis/missive, a now/here neighbor/hood, u/n/i/verse the world. Hip hop was rugged drumsounds dredged from the diamond-laden mine of recorded history and reverse-processed into blunt lumps of coal that left your ears sootstreaked with funk.

But the rigidity of sampled sounds was child's play against the mathematics of what Latif had just heard. This drummer's accents shed their skin and slithered; his cymbals hissed with minute tonal variations, and his sticks lunged deadly at the floor toms.

And the horn shining on this record eclipsed every lyrical ass-whipping ever spit, burned through the cloudy local soundscape with pure raw open honesty, so emotional yet so precise, so far removed from any kind of pose. After three years laboring in service to an unseen master, working his indifferent lazy-fingered way through the simple melodies his teacher gave him, Latif reached consciousness together with conclusion. He understood upon hearing the record that he must learn to blow this climbing angular tangle of ministry, of history, mystery, and misery in syn-chronicity—knew it like his mother's hands before he knew what it was or why.

His limbs felt heavier, more profound, as if the knowledge had filled some hollowness within his bones. Latif stared at the bronze of his horn until his eyes softened and unfocused, letting the color melt across his field of vision, then blinked it back to clarity and looked up at Mr. Gates, suddenly the second most im-portant person in Latif's life: the conduit to the tenor player on the record, Albert Van Horn.

They saw each other every day from then on, playing and lis-tening, learning and teaching, talking as musicians. Mr. Gates, Wessel, strained and stuttered to tell everything he could, to hand down ritual and technique, mechanics and folklore, as Latif sat with his head wide open and eyes wired wild with desire. Wessel studied him, amazed, gazing from Latif's ears to his hands and wondering if there was anything inside him, any bone or blood or flesh to slow the flow of knowledge, because it seemed that there was not. Wessel's words and music's sounds entered Latif's ears and tumbled out his horn with freefall speed.

The kid got bad so fast. Things Wess had played at twenty-six, a grown and traveled man, Latif was figuring out by seventeen. Snatches of frenetic luminosity punctuated his solos; he wrapped superstrong infant hands around the language and spoke by squeezing, snapping, and tapping at its joints. He learned to think in diverse signatures and became a black cat flitting underfoot across the regimented path of America's music marathon parade.

By eighteen Latif was ballplayer lanky and clean headed, with intelligent hands and an undated bus ticket to Manhattan. His soft darkbrown gaze rolled across the inert latenight street outside his bedroom window, but his fingers never strayed from the saxophone balanced in his knee-crook. He traced the rimtop with a thumbnail, pressed his heartshaped lips together flat and imagined meeting Van Horn, firm in the resolution that the musician should know nothing of his existence until he was worth Van Horn's knowing. He imagined himself tiptoeing in the great man's shadow, learning secretly by slow degrees, then springing from the darkness fully formed into the light. Night after night Latif in his bedroom listened at Van Horn honk wail scream lament and chastise, stayed up until weak watery sunlight trickled through the window crimebars and striped the walls. He huddled in a tiny energetic ball, or shadowboxed, or paced the room with long unfurling strides as Van Horn played. Sometimes Latif drifted, letting his mind graze and wander fields of fourleaf clover and deadly hemlock, and other times he balled his hands and bowed his head, concentrating on the music note for note.

He left for New York suddenly one morning, two weeks before his nineteenth birthday, redeeming his dogeared ticket and boarding the Bonzai Bus at six A.M. after a final night of study.

Something had surged over his bedroom in the small morning hours, a wellspring of adrenaline Latif had never felt before. It was as if a python cord of energy had looped through him, turned

Latif into a needle's eye, connected him to others in a chain, and lifted him until he dangled legs akimbo. Albert Van Horn was in the chain too, and Wessel Gates; Latif felt them both distinctly within the rich black rope of the tradition. Below it was the music, awesome and ordered perfect like life from an airplane window.

Latif touched down still weightless and jumped into the struggle like a soldier from a chopper. He gathered up his saxophone and soloed with the Van Horn solo that was playing; over and under and around it, answering its questions and questioning its answers, covering Van Horn with bursts of protective gunfire when he charged through open battlefields and sprinting in his wake to safety when there was some. When the music ended Latif laid down his horn, feeling spent and ready. He stuffed a duffel bag, tucked a stack of records underneath his arm and lifted the crimebars from his window, vaulted the ledge and clambered down the fire escape, horn in hand. He ran to the bus station in a crazy hopscotch pattern, the sound and rhythm of his footfalls reprising the solo he'd just played. The metronome of his breathing stayed sure and true as Latif ran, sneakers slapping color onto empty streets.

New York was two places. There was Dutchman's, five night a week host to the Albert Van Horn Quartet, and there was the hothouse Harlem block on which Latif's boardinghouse crouched, fifteen degrees warmer than life all year round. In a furnished corner room Latif slept, played his horn, and heated breakfast: cans of hash and instant oatmeal on a hotplate he'd set up against the rules. It was either that or clothes-iron grilled cheese, an entrée too degenerate to contemplate.

Uptown radiated flavors he knew well. It was depressing and comforting to think that black folks were stuck in the same trifling neighborhoods both here and there, the Apple and the Bean. More shit was open late here, ten 24/7 bodegas for everyone back home, and malt liquor was cheaper in the Bean though advertised as prominently in both cities—as though dudes on their way to work or school or church just up and impulse-copped a forty of Olde English because they saw a poster of a woman with some big titties cradling a bottle in her arms—skidded to a halt in front of the store like *Hmm, yes, come to think of it I have been meaning to get inebriated as fuck and thus temporarily forget my plight as a walking crime suspect and police shooting target. I believe I shall get me some drank, forsooth.*

Same iambic rhythms to the convo on the streetcorners and same trochaic laughter spearing and reshuffling the rhythms. Same predatory glances shooting from brothers' eyes to sisters' asses and same anger and fear falling from women's downcast eyes onto the pavement. Same churches, same bums. Same deep-frying grease, same chicken and whitefish joints, same snipes for rap albums and gospel shows pasted to the scaffolding of buildings. Same McDonald's and Popeyes crowding out the mom-and-pop joints, same corporate philosophies mandating that eateries in black neighborhoods be short on seating space lest customers get comfortable. Same urban-renewal in the form of trendy clothing chainstores, same keep-the-money-in-the-neighborhood backlash fading before the bottom line.

Only major neighborhood difference Latif noticed off the muscle was the Spanish population, the Puerto Ricans, Dominicans, Colombians, and Cubans in the spot. Busybody blockparty mamis held down sidestreet stoops and watched their squealing brightfaced children twist the remote controls of toy monster cars, which zipped circles around the midblock summer domino tables peopled by foursomes of sixty-something caballeros holding ivory bones against their paunches, computations running through their heads. Empty cervezas frías jutted from the pavement like stalagmites, and arroz con pollo mingled in the air with yerba. Merengue lit up some apartments, James Brown others. Hip hop drowned everything when Jeeps rolled by, and teenage smoke ciphers chorused their approval when somebody crept through bumping something hot.

Local Spanish businesses were just as raggedy as the black ones, Latif noticed. The boutique some muñeca had opened up next to the roti spot was as empty as papi's corner deli, tragically understocked with nothing but overripe plátanos, stale Dutchies and Private Stock. The TV repair shop was full, but only with electronic junkheaps and the laughter of four mujeres gordas watching telenovelas and playing hearts in the backroom.

The sole independent business on its feet appeared to be Good Buddy Chinese Takeout Kitchen, which in addition to flipping sweet-and-sour chicken and pork fried rice had diversified in order to better serve its customers, embracing a wide multicultural variety of shit you could fry. Folks were particularly open off the mofungo and the Szechuan-style yucca con ajio, dished up hot out the wok with a little soy sauce. Cheap and generous, the spot had garnered a devoted clientele: The young hustlers on the block ate there so much, people joked, that the staff knew everybody's name, address, and diet. *If he notice you ain orderin enough iron, money throw some spinach in with your Kung Pao Shrimp no extra charge. Even got free delivery for when you too treed up to walk a half a street up.* Styrofoam combination plate containers lined with emptysqueezed packets of duck sauce blew across the sidewalks of the block, slapping Latif's ankles as he made his journey to the downtown train station each evening.

At Dutchman's Latif studied, ate a liquid dinner, worked his hustle. Everyone has one, he'd realized soon after stepping off the bus and into New York's radiant midday. A dream and a hustle. He thought it now, months later, to reassure himself, repeated it to calm the bile simmering in him over what he was and what he feared he wasn't. Latif sat in bed watching calligraphs of smoke rise from the cigarette between his fingertips, left arm locked flat atop the triangle's peak of his knee like the scales of justice. Outside one window: kids playing stickball. Down below the other: an apparent dice game he could only hear, ears tuned to the clicks of red and green cubes tumbling against the buildingside and to the shittalk of the players, which escalated into threats of violence with parabolic predictability. Latif's eyes, agile beneath awnings that hovered a hairsbreadth nearer to the curves of his irises than they used to, were learning to slide across whole spaces rather than dart from A to B.

The kid got bad so fast. Three months off the bus and he was twice the musician he remembered having been, that vague kid who sat up every night inhaling sounds until he hyperventilated himself into a cosmic meditative frenzy, and three times the man. He'd been all nerve endings then, so soaked in the kerosene of his own sweat that a single distant spark could set him thoroughly aflame. Now Latif was firewalking every evening.

The sudden ducats in his wallet burned holes not through his pocket but his patience; the thirst for confrontation had been mounting in Latif for weeks, tickling the back of his parched throat. The fact that he was a jazz world baby, an infant swimming on mere instinct in a reservoir of untapped knowledge, didn't mean shit anymore. He'd slapboxed the thought into submission.

Latif's mind had tightened and toughened with resentment for his hero, for the crystal ocean clarity with which life shimmied from his horn. Albert uncoiled every night like Satchel Paige, free for whole unbroken moments at a time. Latif watched Van Horn from a dark lookout near the barstools, letting the notes prick his skin like acupuncture needles. Their points were tipped with a potent truth serum. And one in ten, Latif had begun to think in recent weeks, was dipped in venom, screeching at him *Clumsy sucker! Every black motherfucker in here knows exactly what I'm saying loud and long. I'm playing inside your melon, breaking shit down past halfnotes, quarters, eighthnotes, sixteens thirtytwos sixtyfours, cleaving infinitesimal lesions in your brain with surgical eloquence and firetruck delivery—and you ain't done shit but hustle skag in back wall shadows, calling yourself a musician. The burden of proof is to your chest, jim. Stick and move, show and prove, give me something I can feel.*

How had this happened? Nothing had mocked him when he first came to Dutchman's, a jumpy kangaroo of a kid padding down the stairs at midnight after two wrong trains, an hour's journey from Harlem. The place was packed and every head was nodding: saxophones trombones and trumpets gleaming with refracted stagelight energy and Van Horn blooming into solo. A poreless mass of cymbals coated the air, canvas for the splatterstrut impressions of the sage, and Latif could hear it all in the pockets of time and air between the phrases, life and all sorts of pain, migration, love and death and war, piss, lava, moonlight, fucking. Musicians lining the back wall moved like marionettes to what Van Horn was doing and Latif looked out over the room, this vibrant humming creature, and felt himself melt into it and become gloriously anonymous, one more swaying synchronized appendage. His mind hovered just outside the moment and he peeped himself with satisfaction, thrilled with his own hipness in navigating time and space and landing in the place to be. He couldn't have felt more privileged if jazz had been illegal and Dutchman's a speakeasy. There was no need to talk with his fellow patrons; just sharing this same dark space, touching these same gleaming brass bannisters and hardwood tables, finding his dim reflection in these same wall mirrors, was dialogue enough.

The club was a universe in miniature, a fractal broken off and wedged discreetly between two unassuming buildings on a quiet Village block, down a flight of stairs and soundproof until the moment you opened the thick walnut door and music wrapped you in its warm embrace. Ahistoricality was some shit you left at the coatcheck when you came in; Dutchman's kept the past warm like a petri dish and everyplace you stepped something had happened that the old Russian cook could storytell in sprained English with his arms wrist-deep in bread dough.

Fifty years the spot had stood, through bop and free and fusion, staring down police raids and the periodic Death of Jazz. A portrait gallery hung on each of two long walls. One was a hall of fame, the other one a cemetery. When there was only one gallery left, the owner always said as he performed the solemn ritual of moving a portrait—most recently those of Joe Williams, Jackie Byard, Kenny Kirkland, Leon Thomas, Don Pullen, and Milt Jackson—he would close the club.

Already Dutchman's was a throwback, the only joint in town which still booked longterm gigs. Van Horn was in week two of a six-month run, a prize equivalent to acceptance at an artists' colony and the closest thing to woodshedding in public. For aficionados and audience musicians, too, longterm gigs were precious opportunities. Only by hearing the same band night after night could you really begin to get inside of what was going on up there.

It wasn't long before everywhere but Dutchman's seemed dead to Latif; the streets of New York, manic with the noise of commerce and industry, furious with crosscurrents of talk, were a windswept desert by comparison. Everything and everybody was inside the club, where time was not linear and rigid but elastic, something one could borrow, bend, return, and tickle. Van Horn's drummer Murray Higgins did it all and every night. He sat high on his drumstool, grimacing and growling like an ocean god and pounding tridents against drums. Latif sat entrenched and entranced at the nearest corner of the bracket-shaped bar, where there was no cover charge and he could jiggle the same drink until it was nothing but melted ice, and tried to follow along. Higgins' conception of time was so advanced that had he so chosen Latif believed the drummer could have been a mathematician or physicist par excellence. Higgins played time without ever bowing to it, without time ever seeming to confine him. He transformed it like a showman's prop: In Murray's nimble overmuscled hands the beat was a vaudevillian's handkerchief, becoming first a veil and then a hat and then a stick-up man's bandanna.

There was no single focus, no trusty fingersnapping accent on the two and four to keep the audience clued in; instead, Higgins conducted a sometimes smirking, sometimes clenchingly serious flirtation with the beat. He sprinted ahead of it like Jesse Owens, searing ground with speed and power, then turned around annoyed and tapped his foot and waited for the beat to catch up. He followed behind it like a child mimicking a friend, copying its walk in subtle parody with an off-cadence doubletime rhythm on the hi-hat or an aggressive tempo-pushing pattern on the bass drum. Sometimes Murray played the beat where it should be for

11

an instant, like a three-card molly hustler flipping up the money card, and Latif seized upon the moment, tapped a metronome-hand on his leg and compared Murray's forays and reconfigurations to the point of origin. It was at such times, when Latif could lasso a context, that the drummer's genius, the way he pushed the band, was clear.

Or was Higgins being pushed? Was there a leader, or did the whole room pulse together? Latif left Dutchman's each night wondering a million things, replaying scenes and sounds nonmusical and musical, retrospectively choreographing an elaborate dance. Was it coincidence that a couple at a side table had argued fiercely during Murray's solo, a hotspiced polyrhythmic stew he'd stirred and churned with mallets—mallets whose soft white heads flew up and down against the sock cymbal so fast that they blurred and streaked through the red of the stagelights like bolts of lightning?

Was it coincidence that when Albert reentered on tenor the couple grew quiet, the man hunching shoulders over elbows and the woman resting her chin on her fist? When Van Horn's trilled opening curlicues engorged and deepened, grew mournful and low, was it coincidence that the couple stopped bickering and stared into each other's eyes? When Sonny Burma layered meditative velvet chords behind the horn and Amir Abdul walked the bass beneath it all like a man ice skating underneath a bridge and a full moon, was it coincidence that the man took the woman's hand, pressed it to his face, and kissed it?

Music danced lead with life in here, and when it was time to go Latif shimmied up the staircase underneath a slategray predawn sky. Weariness tugged at his muscles but his mind was never tired, and Latif walked to the train each night resolved to devote himself only to breath and sound, tightening his fists against the rush of adrenaline which surged through him whenever he thought about his music and the future. It was liquid impatience and he knew he had to beat it back, control it, this hip hop desire to break through the woodshed door and sprint into the world. He reminded himself that he would only stagger like a mad scientist's creation, alive but half-formed and unviable, if he left the laboratory too early in search of companionship, love, whatever it was that made monsters break out of their masters' labs.

Latif woke up each morning fiending for nightfall so he could journey back downtown; it was his reward for a day's work. His saxophone looked dull, unglinting, against the morning washout of the room, but Latif closed his eyes and slid the reed between his lips, imagining the horn as an extension of his body just as Wess had told him to. *Think of the circle, the circuit, you're creating,* Wess had said. *Body to mouth to horn to hands to body. It's unbroken.* In flashfloods of romantic majesty, Latif sometimes scripted creation fables for his horn, cribbing from mythologies he'd pored over as a kid because the truth—that his mom had bought the tenor for him at Alphonso's Discount Music in Dorchester—seemed unworthy of his axe. Latif preferred to recall divine mandate: the Arthurian Lady of the Lake chucking the horn at him, a staff of lightning flashing on the water as God boomed *Swing, o chosen blower, swing.* Or some Homeric hero-test *Whosoever can draw forth sound from this, Apollo's saxophone, shall have it as his weapon.*

The boardinghouse room also took on epic grandeur, became Latif's woodshed. The shed was both a place and an idea; it could be a downhome Alabama backhouse or a pearl-gray studio with cracked plaster nestled in the ventricles of Harlem. Anyplace you could seal yourself inside, stone or wood or thatch no matter, just so long as your thin stringy sound would bounce back off it pure and let you know how wack you sounded, how far from total tonal fullness you were. The woodshed was where loneliness was never lonely, where solitude was total yet attended by the omnipresent imperative to whittle away deadness, rub off flaking flesh, to chisel life down to just the burning habanero nowstep agitation parts.

The shed, Wess told Latif *is where you hole up til you whole up,* sprinting til your horn is within shouting distance of your heart. You crouched in the woodshed-as-sauna, rocksteady over fire, fat cells sliding off your brain, tongue tingling with sweat-as-nourishment. Perhaps inside a spare splitsec you relished the offhand wondering you knew was lazyfloating in the air, mingling with cigarette smoke, in the spots you used to hold down as your turf: *Where so and so been at? Dunno, man, haven't seen him for a minute,* spoken languid with a hidden tinge of jealousy because whenever a cat cuts out unexpected, motherfuckers know he might be shedding and thus fear a triumphant return-slash-asswhipping. And feel lame for sitting, smoking, and bullshitting while the next man is off invisible somewhere getting his game tight.

But more than game was being tightened. The shed was a couples' retreat, one of those *learn how to listen and become one* joints for a musician and the mouthpiece through which he pulled thick sweetness from that big center-of-the-earth guarded-by-a-many-legged-goddess one love honeypot. A cat might stay in there a day or a year: however long it took to formulate what he'd been fumbling with or teach his fingers what his brain was playing. To catch up with himself or the motherfucker that cut his head last time he hit the afterhours session full of pith and vinegar. *The shed ain't no quick fix,* Wess cautioned. *You gotta get your mail in there. Come back from the gig, hatrack your brim, inhale the mildewed necessity of constant struggle and then get the fuck to work.*

There weren't too many woodshed stories to be told. No witnesses and not a lot to say, really. What could you say? *I went in there looking for something and I found it.* Or *I didn't, and here I am drunk at the bar.* A cat who did have shed stories to tell was suspect, Wess said; more than likely he was in the deep end of the pool, treading water with his brethren in the biggest jazz fraternity of all, the Bullshit Motherfucker House. Certain stuff you were supposed to do in private—fast, pray, woodshed—because to have cats know about it might sully the ritual's purity, shade your motivations with self-consciousness. All of a moment you might find yourself looking left then right before helping a blind man across the street, not to check for traffic but in hopes of being seen.

Alone in the shed, Latif pictured himself as the young Zorro in exile, hand over the smarting sticky wetness of his swordswipe fleshwound, fingers scarlet on his cheek and blade in hand, practicing parry after parry, sidestep combo shuffle stab en garde, brain squeezed tighter than the black spot pirate murder sign and dreaming lucid of revenge. Or as a banished kung-fu student deep in some bamboo sanctuary, slurping rainwater from leaves and mastering his body until every sinew screamed with hardness and a single arched-foot kick was deadly, crumbling the wispy ghosts of as-yet-unfaced foes like faded charcoal.

He played every day until his shadowed form against the wall grew long and slender and the sun slid underneath his window. Latif's shadow looked the way he felt; pure, solid, undernourished, and flowing perfectly into his horn. He barely ate, had neither the desire nor the money. Enough of each to fill his stomach once a day, and that was plenty. The give and take of man woman and child ascended lazy from the street and Latif paid it no nevermind. He needed nothing but the sharp, crisp, weighty feelings of the woodshed. The ritual of his days pleased him; he gloried in his lack of wasted motion, in the drama of his mind and mouth and fingers banding together like lone gunmen in a Western to face down the enemy. Ideas were floating in the air and packed into his horn and somehow, effortlessly, he was snatching them and pulling them out, picking them apart and rolling them together.

Sometimes Latif spent all day on one song, running it through an ever-evolving battery of tests to find a way to make it his. He'd play it through slow first, warming up and feeling it out: where were the curves, the dips and tricks, the hotspots? He and the song tradeoff-psychoanalyzed each other: What emotions was the composition made of? How did he respond to that palette? What complementary tinctures or ideas could he funnel back into the song, and how would it receive them? What had others heard in it; what might they? Latif tried to play the song the way Albert Van Horn would—the young Albert full of passion and power and then the older Albert he knew now, the master craftsman of sensibility who grappled with the nuances of intimacy, delicacy, rage, and love on equal terms, for whom passion and power were not totality but tools.

He put Albert aside, elated if so much as one phrase matched, and tried to play the tune with Sonny Rollins' sense of humor, keen angled phrasing, and dexterity. He swigged some sink water, came back and hit it with as much Thelonious Monk verve as he could, trying to translate that rambunctious piano style onto horn. Latif dug Monk even before he knew what jazz was: That motherfucker bled pure hip hop thirtysomething years before its birth. Monk attacked the keys with percussive b-boy dementia, uncontainable illmatic violent-playful genius, and you could tell from listening to him that he didn't give a damn about no niceties, would no more pause to tune his shit before he started banging than take off his porkpie on command. Or, as Latif's boy Shane had said when Latif hipped him to the *Straight, No Chaser* album,

That's a crazy ghetto nigga if I ever heard one. Soon Shane was bumping Monk back to back with Wu-Tang.

It couldn't go on forever, or even for another month, but until Latif's savings expired and he had to cop a job he'd savor the asceticism of his days: waking up just shy of noon and falling to the floor for several sets of push-ups, sit-ups, and knee bends, wrapping himself in a towel and jaunting down the hall to shower. Then came breathing exercises, warm-ups, three or four hours of shedding.

All the while, Latif teased himself by ignoring the hunger twisting his belly. It vanished, chased off by the concentration with which he practiced, and returned vengeful in the late afternoon. Only then, when it weakened him, did Latif take a break and go to the store for something to sate it. Rice and beans, beans and franks, canned soup, mac and cheese, bags of potatoes he would slice and fry in the always-empty communal kitchen, sandwiches. He ate voraciously while looking out onto the street, serene in the separation he felt from the aimlessness with which so many people seemed to walk or loiter on the block. He realized the snobbery of such thoughts, but Latif indulged himself; anything which might increase his sense of the mission was worth cultivating.

The music settled somewhat during lunch, worked itself out under the supervision of his subconscious. When Latif got back to business, turning his attention to the task of playing the same tune as much like himself as he could, he felt fresh and studied and surprisingly coherent. The exposition and excavation of the morning gave him a buffet of ideas to dismiss, build on, and synthesize. Latif documented his work on a little miked Walkman, and once or twice a week cupped cushy foam headphones to his ears and walked downtown along the westside water, memorizing and wincing as appropriate. Although he'd been archiving himself since fourteen, Latif never went back to any tape more than a month old.

Around eight-thirty he showered again, dressed, and made his nightly trek downtown. Vine-wise, he couldn't afford to be dipped, but Latif was inventive. Four-button suits were the baddest shit going, so Latif bought two new buttons and some sewing scissors and transformed his only jacket, ironing the lapels until his black church suit was jazz world hip. He spent the downtown trainride itemizing what he planned to focus on that night: Would he hover in the wings, beneath the exit sign, and concentrate on Van Horn's fingering, breathing, and stance, the precise progression of his every solo? Or would he sit at the bar and take in the band holistically, as he did most nights, shifting his attention when he felt like it?

Perhaps he would allow himself the luxury of room-roaming, people-watching, indulge his growing habit of jazz club voyeurism. Latif was beginning to recognize a cast of regulars, and he found himself wondering about them as he rode the train back up to Harlem every night. The musician-looking brother with the brown sueded fedora who always tapped his straw against his Scotch and soda. The cute young waitresses who bustled through the room during uptempo tunes and glided delicately, lifting their trays above their heads, during the ballads. The chintzy, overdressed women who flashed large glinting teeth at the bartenders on their way to the bathroom and then returned to their husbands or boyfriends and slid their hands together. The cleansuited whiteboys who nodded studiously at back tables in threes and fours, as if afraid to venture closer. The constant human backdrop of middleaged whitefolks and Japanese tourists—so many that Van Horn ended his opening remarks with *Nihonjin tomodachi, kitte kurete arigatou* and got big applause. The population breakdown brought to mind a joke Wessel had told him:

Whatchu call a black man in a jazz club?
A musician.

Latif exchanged headnods with a handful of familiars, but he never gave them any opening to chat. He didn't want to add anything, even an errant word, to the sauce lidded on his stove, simmering whether he was in or out, awake or asleep, and growing richer every time he took a taste. The most Latif said some days was two sentences: *Take it easy*, to the supermarket clerk and *Lemme get a vodka tonic, thanks*, to the bartender at Dutchman's. Latif saved language for his horn, as if there was only so much of it. He allowed himself to sink into superstitious silence, verbal reclusion, with delight. It was a game Latif was playing with himself, and he won every time he picked up his horn and found himself stronger, his fingers pinpointing ideas as fast as his brain generated them, the process of translation smoothing itself almost flat. His courtship of himself engulfed him.

The thought of ruining it with a job was repugnant, but there was no choice. What could he do? What kind of gig wouldn't throw open the woodshed doors or infringe on his study time at Dutchman's? In his eagerness to play, Latif was only sleeping six hours a night as it was. He was on the verge of answering a help wanted sign posted in the window of a diner down the block when a better solution, or what seemed like one, jumped up on the jam session bandstand and called out a blues.

The middle set concluded with a piece like an unclenching fist, a flower opening. Bookended by bowed bass intros and outros, Amir Abdul's "A-tension" was a study in how hard you could play softness. Amir anchored the tune with a low Early Music drone sound, dragging the bow slow across the strings so that it hummed in a way that was half mournful yet unsentimental. The constancy was life and death at once, slow growth and slow decay. In it was an awareness that the world is made of cycles that are longer than our lifespans, or so it seemed to Latif as the soloists made their statements one by one and faded, leaving only the ageless drone. Even Murray Higgins was displaced from his stewardship of time on this one; Amir's bow slid with hourglass-sand steadiness and Murray worked around it.

The drone lingered long after Amir had eased off into silence, and Latif reflected that it was a good thing that another set was coming; send folks home on a vibe that deep and there's no telling what they'd do. Van Horn picked up his soprano sax in one hand, cradling the bell of the tenor hanging from his neck in the other. Wess had told Latif that early on *Let it dangle from your neck and you're asking for back trouble.* Seeing what he'd been taught confirmed, knowing facts beholden only to musicians, made Latif feel locked into apprenticeship. He felt like sending Wess a postcard from the Holy Land.

Tonight, he'd laughed with The Quartet and The Quartet alone at a joke Sonny Burma had made onstage—a reference to something Latif had hovered close enough to Burma to observe. Just before the hit Sonny had been talking to a woman, smiling intimately, standing close to her with his hands in the pockets of his suitpants and his jacket open and drawn back behind his arms, a pose Latif had already cribbed and practiced in his room because Sonny looked so goddamn slick when he did it. Out of nowhere, just as he was leaning close and making her laugh, some overenthusiastic clown had clapped Sonny on the back, offered him his meaty hand, introduced himself, and begun asking music questions.

Sonny'd had no choice but to shake the cat's hand, smile, introduce him to the woman, and spend his last five pre-set minutes chatting with this cavalier, oblivious dude. When Burma took the stage, the cat offered Sonny's chick a seat at his table and she took it. *Cockblocking motherfucker*, Sonny muttered to Amir as he sat down. When it was time for Sonny's first solo, his new best buddy in the audience shouted out *Yeah Sonny!* giddy with camaraderie. Burma responded by playing a long series of block chords. Amir broke into a smile and leaned low to tell Higgins, whose laughter boomed out over his bass drum. Latif cracked up with them and noticed the people to his left and right staring at him with respect, wondering what he knew that they didn't.

You can dig a record, Latif thought as the band played on, but you can't get it all unless you're there and in the know. If you don't see the chick who dissed the trumpet player walk into the light, you won't understand when he weaves "Get Out My Life Woman" into his solo. And unless you know the piano player remembers her for giving his bandmate some head once in a cab, you're outside the joke and busy analyzing the harmonics when he responds with just one bar of Bob James's "Theme from *Taxi*."

The band filed offstage after Van Horn and Latif followed them down the winding back corridor that led to the dressing room, hoping to overhear something of interest. He was hovering closer to the band lately, still staying unnoticed but unable to resist eavesdropping on the intimate details, the backstory behind each performance. Sonny and Amir often stopped to smoke a cigarette in the corridor before going inside, but tonight they weren't there and the locked red door of the lounge cut short Latif's pilgrimage. Bereft of other options yet unwilling to reassimilate into the audience he'd left behind, he idled dumbly. The graceful clack of heels on parquet floor dissolved his contemplation of limbo and Latif turned to face a dapper pinstriped cat and inhale a blast of noxious cheap tobacco.

Say, brother, you looking to cop?

The words squeezed together past and present, Boston and New York, so familiar was the tone of the refrain. It matched the automated greeting of every cornerman in Latif's neighborhood; it was a mysterious solicitation he had overheard a thousand times growing up and never dared investigate further. By the time he was tall enough for such entrepreneurs to address him as he walked the block, most of them knew Latif well enough to know better than to bother. In response to the inquiry of any street pharmacist who didn't, Latif would slow his pace slightly, shake his head once across the right shoulder, and mouth a jowled *Naah, naah* while walking on, as if declining a discount shopping flyer.

Say Brother had none of the nonchalance of Boston's cornermen. Against Latif's *Naah man, I'm good thanks* he drew again on his cigar and leaned forward confidentially, polishing upper teeth with tongue behind closed lips and raising bushy eyebrows. *Say, brother, this shit is goood*, he drawled, basso profundo. Latif smiled, iterating his refusal with a headshake, and slid past the man to return to the barroom. *Suit yourself*, replied the dealer, head cocked like *These kids today!* and rapped solid on the red lounge door. Latif froze flat against the wall as the entrance swung open and was filled with Murray Higgins, an unlit cigarette like a matchstick in his leather hand. The dealer disappeared into the room, dwarfed by Higgins' arm around his shoulders, and the door clicked shut behind them. Latif gangled slowly to the bar and got a beer.

He was still sipping it, drawing out the last drink he was budgeted for, when Say Brother cleaved a course through the thinning mingle of bodies and found the bar. He tossed Latif a wink and shouldered in beside him. A two-fingered tap on the bartop yielded a pair of whiskey shots; Say Brother raised one delicately between thumb and middle finger and beckoned Latif toward the other with his open hand. *It's on me.* Say Brother smiled, lifting the spirit to his lips and knocking back the drink without a shiver.

Thank you, said Latif, and extended his hand.

Say Brother clasped it between his own two and slid down off the barstool with a winking *Don't mention it*, snaked smoothly through the parting crowd and put his hand on the doorhandle. He stopped and turned, knowing Latif's eyes were still on him; *It's on me*, he mouthed again, tapping his chest, and pulled out his pantspocket with a stagey armsweep. Latif reached instinctively inside his own pocket and started when he felt a small tinfoil square. He looked up in puzzlement for explanation, but Say Brother was already in the wind.

It's on me looped echo circles in his mind as Latif strolled to the men's room to flush what he assumed was now in his possession. The dealer's scam was textbook corny—the freebie turn-on guaranteed to make a believer out of you—and Latif resented the distraction. Still, it was titillating to know he had a dimebag of jazz history in his pocket; whole lotta cats' lives had been tied off at the elbow and he'd always wondered why. But shit, this wasn't nineteen motherfucking fifty. Nobody thought some skag was gonna make them play like Bird. Latif wondered if anybody even fucked around with this stuff anymore. *He wouldn't be up in here if they didn't*, he answered himself, then wondered about Higgins. The ocean god himself?

The toilet stall was locked, so Latif stood at a urinal to guardedly unwrap the parcel Say Brother had passed off on him. Latif opened the tinfoil slowly at waist height and watched the fine white powder intently, as if it might burst into flame. This shit was supposed to make you fly. It was the magic carpet ride that kept heads nodding in sloppy no-music rhythm out front of Giant Liquor Mart in Roxbury around the corner from his mother's house—kept fullgrown men pissy high, limpid, and fragile, wispy tendrils of human flesh buck-and-shuffle scavenging for change.

And it made Say Brother fly, fly enough to bypass the line and stroll the players' lounge with lavish confidence. Yellow tube-lights hummed like drunken bumblebees as Latif played absent-minded games with the portion of skag, letting it conjure back Say Brother as he slipped into the red room, to and fro through the crowd, on and off the barstool. When he finally became conscious of being watched, Latif didn't know whether he had stood in seance for ten seconds or ten minutes. He merely felt hard eyes cornerchecking him and turned his head to answer their over-curiosity.

The man piping glances Latif's way stood at the adjacent urinal, sizing him up as he waited to be acknowledged. He zipped his fly and smoothed imaginary wrinkles from his suit with non-chalance, granting Latif an equal chance to take his stock. Openness glinted in his mellow eyes, the hint of satisfaction that hangs on a man when he stands yards away from recognition in any direction he might choose to turn. Before the echoes of his first gestures had dissipated, Sonny Burma saw a flashbulb-pop of recognition in Latif's eyes, and he turned and came quickly to his point of interest.

You look like maybe you don't want that, Burma said politely, pointing to the foil. *I happen to have just missed my connection.* Only minutes before, Latif had watched the same graceful hands coax and conjure rain from Dutchman's old piano, warm spring aromatic drops that tinkled daintily at first, then swelled and crackled into floods and thunderstorms, pounding at the earth with syncopated Old Testament calamity. Sweat had beaded on

Burma's brow and he had funneled small blasts of coolbreath up from his lower lip to dry it, playing on. Burma, Higgins, and Abdul connected in a pyramid of studious intersubjectivity, bulging and collapsing as Van Horn transversed the stage. They rummaged ancient catacombs, brought pharaohs back to life.

Sonny Burma, who flipped sarcophagi like seersucker mattresses, stood at the next urinal down adjusting his dick and waiting on Latif: *You look like maybe you don't want that.* The red lounge door swung open in Latif's mind as he handed the foil to the pianist. Making friends is making friends, he thought, torn between exhilaration at talking to Sonny and embarrassment that after a month of undetected observation he should meet Van Horn's pianist in the men's room over a dime of smack.

Here. You can have it.

Good lookin out, Burma tossed off, taking the foil and jowling his cheeks in quick product appraisal. He slid it in his wool pantspocket and the same hand reemerged, scissoring a tenspot in the first and middle fingers toward Latif, who shook his head.

No, really, it's on me; I moved to the city just to hear you cats play. It's an honor to meet you, Mr. Burma.

Burma chuckled friendly from the gut, a rumbled three notes of amusement, and gave Latif his hand with vigor.

Call me Sonny, bruh, shaking Latif's hand, *and you are?*

Latif James-Pearson, from Roxbury.

Latif James-Pearson from Roxbury. Good to meet you. I got some family in Mattapan myself, cousin and her kids. I used to play at Ramshackles—piano bar down there before it got closed down. Latif nodded that he knew it though he didn't. *Now listen here, Latif, you take this money. You're new in town. A man's gotta make a living somehow. Gotta be a businessman about it, am I right?* Sonny cocked his head rhetorically, palms upturned at his shoulders in expectation of agreement.

Latif smiled. *You got a point there, Sonny.* He plucked the folded bill and placed it in his shirtpocket.

There you go, said Burma, with an intonation flavor that was Wess Gates all the way. The kinetic mantra was the teacher's clearest signal of approval, surprise, royal badness, and the phrase set Latif at ease when Sonny said it, wrapped him warmly in the coils of tradition.

You play, Teef?

Latif felt that Sonny Burma knew he did, *Yessir tenor,* as if the force of his long consciousness of them had somehow rumbled tremors in their own. As if they'd watched him watching them.

Well, bring your horn down here sometime. We been talkin about opening the last set up. Meantime, maybe I'll catch you for a drink between these hits.

I'd like that, said Latif. Sonny saluted him, spun on his heel with mock-military crispness, and was out.

When the next set crashed to an end Latif staked out a place on the receiving line, watching Burma handshake and flirt expertly as he made his way from the piano to the lounge. Latif's words, devised and revised during the set, were planted firmly in his mind. They were friendly but casual: *As a businessman, I'm gonna have to hold you to that drink you mentioned, Sonny.* But when Burma took his hand he leaned in close before Latif could speak: *Hey partner, can you help me with another you-know-what?*

Latif opened his mouth in silent mute surprise and Sonny read the answer from his face and just like that Latif was gone, wiped from Sonny's good graces; he watched it as it happened. Sonny pressed together his lips, nodded in disappointment and moved on, face blanking for a moment before he reanimated to greet the next person in line. Latif could not accept the setback; he felt that he would do whatever he could to please Sonny again, and so he jostled himself into position further down the line and when Sonny reached him Latif whispered *Give me forty-five minutes.*

My man! Sonny grinned and slapped him five. *That's what I'm talking about.* And Latif was right back in it. He jogged the stairs and hailed a cab, a firecracker of nervousness exploding in his chest as he lifted his arm like a New Yorker. He told the driver his boardinghouse's address and hoped the cornermen who'd hawked their wares as he'd walked past them to the train earlier that evening were still there, leaning up against the payphones next to Kennedy Chicken 'N' Biscuits. They were: two cats posted nonchalant in kicks straight out the box, white Jordans and black Paytons, rocking fitted Yankee caps on top of doo rags and eyesurfing the block like wary lion cubs. Latif told the cab to wait, hopped out wondering what the hell he was doing, and threw a quick chin-up headbob at the brother who caught his eye. The cat head-beckoned Teef to follow him and they walked halfway up the block, into the shadows where Latif was spending so much time lately.

You the musician from 2B, right? Latif shook off shock at this easy peeling of his anonymity veneer: It was their job to know who folks were. He nodded reluctantly, feeling suddenly that everybody knew more about something than he did about anything.

We can hear you on the street. Sound pretty good. You was killin' a few days ago. Played some shit the Darkside Crooks used.

Teef nodded. *It's called "St. Thomas." Bad tune, right?*

No doubt. The cat smiled and Teef noticed his babyface. They were probably the same age, although Latif had passed for older since he'd hit six-one at sixteen. He started to scat the head and the dealer joined him on the tune's four note tag.

Yeah. The dude nodded. *I could rip shit off a beat like that. So whatchu need, yo—Redman, Clapton, or Cobain? Dimes up to Susan B's.*

From the Holy Land to Babylon in ten minutes, Latif thought, glancing to make sure the cab was still idling cornerside and noticing his own dark window longingly. The neighborhood had never seemed so menacing, and Latif realized he'd hardly been here between evening and dawn. Before Latif could stop it, his mind churned out a ghetto Halloween menagerie of crack babies, welfare queens, and Staggerlee street pimps, all lurching toward him with blank eyes and outstretched zombie arms. He shook clear his head, embarrassed.

A dime of Kurt, Latif said, and absorbed the powdered-over look of shock on the kid's grill. Hardly appropriate for a hustler. *It's for a friend*, he added lamely.

The kid was busy whistling to his junior partner, who disappeared around the opposite corner of the block, then sauntered back into view and over to them, made the handoff to his man, and jogged back into first position by the payphones.

Anything you need, my name is Spliff, the kid said, giving Teef a product-exchange soulshake. He glanced up at the 2B window. *I'ma listen at you*. Spliff walked back toward Kennedy and Latif jumped in the cab, worrying that he now represented a source of future income in this brother's mind.

Let's make it a round trip, Latif directed, and the taxi shot downtown. He handed Sonny the package and accepted a shoulder-bang embrace and a second tenspot with three seconds left in the allotted time frame.

Latif picked up a redrimmed shaving mirror at a cornerstore between Dutchman's and the train that night, doublesided with standard and distorted magnifying panes. His room had no looking glass, and the windows were too grimecaked to hold his image right. He could not trust his reflection to the plateglass shopwindows he passed nor be satisfied in catching transitory optics on the fly while swifting by. Without a way to meet his own eyes in judgment and privacy, Latif thought as he paced the sedate subway station on dead legs, he might forget himself. The mathematics of hustling demanded a rigid and cross-referenced knowledge of self; before he could calculate the prism angles of the game, Latif had to understand his own trajectory, know what he was capable of doing.

The iron horse dropped him uptown and Teef walked slowly home, improvising an unconscious transformation ceremony on the empty street. He flexed his hands and cracked his knuckles, repeating his rationale like push-ups until his mind was swollen with belief: *I gotta make some money without sacrificing any of my time*, he told himself. *I gotta work while I study and this is how to do that.* Already he felt some of the gentler rainbow arcs of his persona stiffening and straightening, shaving themselves into taut wires. Or he imagined that he did.

Spliff was still hugging the block at this late hour, alone now, a twenty-four-hour walk-up convenience mart for crack monsters, boom fiends, and junkies. Latif picked out his shape against the streetlight and wondered what that lifestyle took and if he had it in him. Almost reflexively, he told himself he did: He could be hard and quick, unflinching. He knew how to talk and think and improvise.

Still working? Latif smiled when he was close enough.

Spliff's head snapped fast and body tensed, but he relaxed

when he saw who it was. He's probably got a gun, Latif mused. He'd be a fool not to.

Not really. A crackhead who hasn't scraped together five bucks yet ain't gonna find it at this hour. Spliff balanced his heels on the curb's edge. *I should crash so I can get up and serve the weedhead moms who wanna wake-and-bake before they take they kids to school, but I dig this time of night. Only time the block is peaceful. Where you coming from? Some jazz club?*

Yeah.

Must be hard being a jazz nigga in a hip hop world. Latif laughed, digging how the night carried the sound. *Y'all cats don't make no money, do you?* asked Spliff.

Not unless you're Kenny G. Or Wynton. And that ain't Puffy money either. Far from it.

Apparently jazz cats still using smack.

Apparently, said Teef. He paused, wondering whether to iterate that his purchase had been an errand for a friend, a onetime thing, and gave a mental shrug. It didn't seem necessary anymore.

Spliff rubbed his cheek with a palm. *Rap niggas just smoke weed.*

You feelin rap these days? asked Teef, curious whether his own boredom with the music of his youth was epidemic.

Spliff's head rolled listless from one shoulder to the other. *Few niggas is flipping some new flavor, but mostly it's the same old tired bullshit.*

Same with jazz, Latif admitted. *Cats been playing the same tunes for thirty, forty, fifty years. And playin em the same way, too.*

Seems to me like jazz is fooling itself, said Spliff.

How you mean?

You know, cats up on TV acting like jazz some noble refined shit and everything else just dirty nigger music. I'm like, come on. I'm pretty sure some of these cats step off the bandstand, suited down clean, dignified, and playing some beautiful and complex shit no doubt, then snort some shit and smack they bitch up. At least hip hop admits it. Jazz keeps that shit off the books.

Well, said Latif, *we all got some lover and some pimp in us. Jazz might deny the pimp, but hip hop denies the lover. To me, that's a much heavier omission.*

I'ma have to marinate on that, said Spliff, *but I do know I'd rather hang with cats frontin like they worse off than they are than mufuckers frontin like they better.*

Fair enough. To be continued. Guhnight.

Easy.

Latif went upstairs, strangely comforted by Spliff's sentrylike presence on the block, and hung his new handmirror from a nail in the cracked plaster wall at perfect eyelevel. The thin sneering upper lip of Alexander Hamilton, pierced by the same nail, jutted disapprovingly from Sonny Burma's crucified tenspot toward the sax resting in the corner. Latif fell asleep wondering what was more chauvinist: the stylized, sanitized pimpery of telegenic rappers or the women of Albert Murray's jazz fiction—starlets and European socialites who dug jazz without a hint of patronization, validated by black musicians as sisters of Sarah Vaughn: women who were accommodating, beautiful, and cosmopolitan, who expected nothing but some good black dick and the occasional pithy statement about music, art, or life.

Latif woke up exhausted, and for the first time since moving to New York he passed the day without playing. Instead, he sat in bed and stared out at the block with a new sense of kinship. Brothers down there didn't seem as mundane as they had the week before, squatting on the stoops and propped casually against the brickwalls with one leg cocked parallel to Earth. With quick reflexes they eyechecked everyone who passed by: squinted with understated menace at strangers, greeted friends and neighbors with benign style, scanned the landscape for police.

By the time the sun waned and Latif stood outside Dutch-man's, buttoning and unbuttoning his jacket in the night breeze, his calisthenics and calculations were complete and his curves ironed hastily into sharp crooked creases. He waited for Say Brother to arrive, resisting the last-second urge to rehearse what he would say as he had done with Sonny Burma. It was better not to have a gameplan; listen and react, let form follow simply from boom stimuli.

I had a feeling I'd be seeing you again, Say Brother laughed, stepping deliberate from the airconditioned cushioned comfort of a gypsy cab and smoothgliding to Latif's side with a tobacco-breathed exhale. Here in the objectivity of outdoors, he cut an eccentric figure: nimbletoed and keg-shaped in a bowler hat and doublebreasted suit, smoothing his mustache with the same hand that clutched his cigar. Latif wondered how he'd gotten away with smoking one of those things in a cab.

You were waiting for me out here, weren't you brother?

Yeah. Teef nodded groundward. *I was.*

Ha ha! I told you that shit was good, Say Brother crowed, merryfaced and drawing out *told* like a jackleg preacher.

Yeah, it was good, mumbled Latif into his beltbuckle. He counted off a tiny grace note pause then swung up face to face, eyes hard, and deadpan smacked the next words flat at Say Bro's florid mug: *It put ten bucks in my pocket when I sold it.*

The dealer paused to shift brain gears and Teef played on, breath coming easy, loose and cool. Say Bro, as rhythm section, had dropped out just like Teef hoped he would, and the silence was Latif's to soar on. Say Brother was a pro and he would come back playing time, so the key was not to turn the tune around. Get your shit off, but don't mess with the tempo.

I want to work for you, said Teef. *I know this place and I can work it every night, hard. I'll double your money. I learn fast. I'm smart and motivated.*

Say Brother said nothing, stared level and ignored the intro cue. The silence fucked Teef up; he'd only thought to play a quick volley in fear of getting cut off, and now instead he looked lost and ridiculous, floating in dead air. He'd thrown a wild salespitch. Say Brother let a vaporous silence swirl up thick around their shoulders, holding Latif's eyes steady tensed, and when he finally spoke his tone was bloodless, stripped of music. *What, if anything, do you know about this game, son?*

Don't get high on your own supply.

Don't get high on your own supply. Probably heard it on some rap song, but you got that right. He stroked his chin with thumb and finger, waving the cigar at Teef as he did so. *How many winters you got under your belt, anyway?* Say Brother's eyes flickered up and down Latif's length and he filled the air between them with a slow billow of smoke. *You tall as all hell, but you look like you ain't been out your mama's house more than a couple years. You got that neophyte shine to you. You nineteen or twenty, maybe blackjack twentyone, and you sure ain from New York, are you?*

Latif glossed the intimidation he felt. *From Boston, man, Roxbury. I'm nineteen*, he said, declining to claim an extra year. Say Brother seemed like the type of cat who'd be happier to be right than impressed to be fooled. *But I been paying dues since way back when. Latif*, he said, extending his hand and hoping Say Bro wouldn't press him on his nonexistent resume. *You nail everyone like that or am I just a sore thumb up in here?*

I nail everyone like that, Say Brother assured, shaking it. His hand was small but his grip tight. *I'm an excellent judge of character, horses, and most especially women, but let me not get into all of that. I tell you what, neophyte, you got a nice vibe going on. Shit, you might be a natural—I hit you with a freebie and you turn right around and flip it. We'll see if you take a shine to the game. Not here, though. I'll put you on deliveries; that way you'll get to see the city.*

I'm sorry, Latif interrupted. *I appreciate that, sir, but I gotta be at Dutchman's. I'll do deliveries too and whatever else, but this is the spot for me. I'm a musician.*

Say Brother snorted and rocked back on his heels. Ash jumped from his cigar to the ground. *A musician. I'm not looking to hire no musicians, phyte. I'm hiring a runner. If you a musician then go play some shit, go ask The Horn for a goddamn gig. Matterfact, wait here.* He brushed past Latif and shuffled down the steps, raising the back of his hand. *I'll go ask him for you.* He disappeared into the darkness of the not-yet-open club, door slamming behind him. Latif suppressed the young fool urge to run away; the only thing that stopped him was uncertainty over whether he had been dismissed. It would be his worst misstep yet to leave if Say Bro wasn't done with him, so Latif stood and listened to his belly gurgle apprehension. He felt like a soldier on night watch, left with only his own lonesome thoughts and the imagined rustlings of enemies. Although he'd never smoked, Latif felt the acute desire for a cigarette. He was still decoding the sensation when Say Brother and Sonny Burma popped out of the building.

This the cat, Sonny, Say Bro rasped, one hand draped over the pianist's shoulder and the other one outstretched and pointing. *This the new musician I got for you. I couldn't find The Horn so I brought my man Sonny up here to judge your musicianship potential. Well, whadda you think, Sonny, you gon give his ass a job?* Say Brother laughed and his whole body shook. He toyed with motherfuckers any time he had the power to: as a prelude to acceptance, a cruel elongation of dismissal, or simply for sport. Say was a cool cat if he respected you, scrupulous and funny as fuck. Thick veins of compassion marbled his professional ruthlessness, but if Say Bro judged you a punk, too weak to navigate a man's world, you'd never get a chance to prove him wrong. He'd break on you any time you crossed paths, hoping you'd give him an excuse to beat that ass.

Do you believe the nerve of this cat? he asked Sonny. *I'm offering his outtatown behind a job and he tells me no, he'll only work for me here cause he's a musician! I told him I'm not hiring no musicians!*

Sonny Burma turned to face Say Brother, sliding from underneath his arm until Say's palm rested on Burma's shoulder. *Oh, I think you are,* said Burma. *This here's my man Teef from Roxbury, Massachusetts, and I want him well looked after. This brother is one hell of a horn player and I want him hanging here where I can chart his progress. You dig?*

Say Brother looked from Burma's raised eyebrow to Latif's slowly unfurling forehead. *Is that right?* he said, wide smile spreading. *You telling me this skinny-ass nigga got game?* He chomped down on his cigar, hip enough to dig the unexpected and savvy enough to relish the opportunity to do Sonny a solid.

Game like all get out, said Sonny. He winked at Latif, then turned to Say Brother before Latif could wink back. *Flipped yours around on you, ain he?* Say Bro flicked his head in an acknowledging sidenod. *This here's the man you need taking some weight,* Sonny went on, businesslike. *You got a lotta longtime customers in here who ain't been so well taken care of since you started expanding your clientele. I was looking for you just last night and couldn't find you. Had to go elsewhere. Ain't that right, Teef?* Burma reached up to shake his hand.

There you go, Latif responded, grinning.

Say Bro looked from one to the other, did the math, and laughed. *Well well well. Ain't that some shit?*

Ain't it? said Sonny.

Sure is, said Teef. *When do I start?*

Teef hardly had to do a thing. He made no leering solicitations; there was no garish hustling. To approach a cat out of the blue was dangerous and inefficient. Say Brother himself did it only on such sparse occasions as his impeccable instincts recommended brashness. *I shouldn't do it, but what can I say. Sometimes I get a sense about these things*, he told Latif.

You were wrong about me, Teef said, wanting to tease him.

Wrong is you're a cop. I wasn't wrong. I could tell you were from out of town, and it's always good to talk to outtatowners. Not tourists, mind you, I don't give a good goddamn bout tourists: outtatowners. But don't you worry about that. Just keep cool and don't do shit; the word will get around just fine.

It seemed to Latif that what got around just fine was Sonny Burma, and that the word moved mostly where and when he did. The shrewdness of hitching your business to the social butterfly with the biggest wingspan in the room dawned quickly on Latif; Say Brother didn't miss much. *I got you this gig*, Sonny told Latif, smirking, *and if you fuck it up I'll have to hear about it for the next ten years, so listen close.* Sonny expected a little hook-up now and then, a product royalty on sales made, but that was no big deal. Say Brother knew Burma well enough to build in the expense. A small arrangement among friends.

With the bond of benefaction between them, Sonny was a different cat; Latif looked back on what he'd taken as a snub that first night between sets and wondered if he had imagined it. Perhaps that second favor had etched him into Burma's good graces, or perhaps Sonny was simply hungry to mentor someone, somehow; whatever the reason, Latif found himself snug under Burma's wing, nestled closer than dictated by duty.

Sonny made all the introductions the first night and even

seemed to get a kick out of showing off how many people he knew. Burma strolled from the tables to the corner Teef had claimed, chatting and laughing back across his shoulder as he led one cat after another over to Latif. *Latif, this is my man Larry Calvin; L.C., Latif James-Pearson. I think y'all tenor players might have some business to discuss*, and Sonny smiled, clapped his home-boy on the shoulder, and was gone, only to return minutes later with another client. Latif's web of associations spun out from Sonny, and by the fourth night he knew everyone he had to. They came to him. They brought their friends.

A week earlier Latif would never have imagined how much business went down in here. Cats flowed in and out around the static oblivious tourists, chatting and copping and checking out a tune, then bouncing. He was the quiet nucleus of all of this activity, and despite his professional detachment, his low profile, the way he stayed serious and studious and made clear that his ears were on the band even while making moves, cats chattered at Latif on the regular. They didn't seem to notice his reticence, the way he slipped away within seconds to listen to Van Horn. *Every customer wants to be friends with his dealer*, Say Brother had warned him. It was true. The handful of musicians who were clients treated Latif with so much familial camaraderie that everybody else in Dutchman's wide circle of insiders did too. It felt a little bit good, Latif had to admit; if nothing else it eased him into comfort with what he was doing.

The first few transactions had revulsed Latif, made him shudder with small loathing as he placed the product in the eager palm and slid the payment in his pocket, but soon he made himself forget what he was selling. It was easy to forget. These were well-dressed men who laughed hearty prizefighter laughs, whose powerful hands gripped his firmly when they met, whose girl-friends were fly and flirty. He never saw a single needle, never heard the drug discussed. These cats had too much class for that. These were musicians, not degenerates. They held snifters and highball glasses with casual assurity, bought him drinks now and again, invited him to come and check out their upcoming gigs. They discussed macrobiotic diets, new age books and saxophone reeds, told tour stories and asked after friends.

At their treatment of him and his easy slide into the life, Latif felt the embrace of a secret relief familiar from his youth. It was the relief of ducking a trial, and it was mingled, as always, with a splash of letdown: disappointment that he had once again made the team without being forced to try out. As he fraternized with the musicians like a colleague, cool but graceful in accepting their fellowship, Latif was again aware of his own strangeness, the lack of a résumé he'd been afraid Say Brother would intuit, his unspoken exemption from certain rituals of passage.

It was a privilege Latif had carried since childhood. The other kids had read between the lines on his forehead, glimpsed something in the taut way he held his hands even before he played any music, something that marked him as different. He was still their neighbor, playmate, homeboy, but with the wisdom of children they made small acknowledgements that his destiny was different.

A jazz nigga in a hip hop world. Latif could never decide if they treated him more like a younger brother, not ready for the grit of things, or like an older one, above such foolishness as they engaged in. He was accorded slightly more respect and less inclusion, and he was never expected to fight. When the crew began smoking herb in seventh grade they assumed he would abstain, and Latif's first step into the smokers' cipher a year later was a gala event. Anytime he jumped feet first into the mix was celebrated, whether a brew-and-weedsmoke latenight with the crew or the six straight rainbow jumpers he once drained to win a pickup game at Marshall Courts. There weren't as many stories about Latif as there were about Shane or Rook or White Boy Mike, but the ones there were they told more often. At least when Latif was around.

It was a role, this part-time membership, that had bothered him before he understood it, when he was young and just wanted to come in off the outskirts and be down like other guys. He could never make himself do it, though—take the steps he knew were necessary to feel real inclusion, to meet the crew's definition of true manhood. He couldn't sacrifice the hangout time or force himself to drink enough to act a fool. He skated on the margins of acceptance because being fully down meant committing to too many things he couldn't, too many ideas and activities better kept at arm's length.

A little later on Latif was grateful to his crew for understanding him so well, for not trying to make him something he was not, and the anxieties of his younger years faded but never washed away. Sometimes, although he tried to banish the thought from his mind as both self-aggrandizing and depressing, Latif felt that they saw him as the only one of them who had a chance to make it in the world. First Shane and then others had started calling him T.T., for Talented Tenth. It was a name he tried to hate, but couldn't.

By high school, most of the stories about Latif involved the girls he'd been with. Sex trumped drinking and fighting in importance and Latif gained by the shift, not the first cat on the block to bag a chick but the one who most consistently had action going on. The crew didn't pretend to understand what pleasure Latif derived from female company besides the obvious; the party line was that women were only good for one thing. But Latif found he could rap to girls about his music and they would listen as he seldom felt he had the right to ask his crew to. The crew said only *What's up with the horn?* or *How's the music going, bruh?*, questions asked not out of interest but respect. Latif, unwilling to take up space, answered *It's cool, it's cool, I'm tryna do my thing*, and talk flowed on.

Not so with his girls. The knowledge that passion and talent were attractive dawned gradually on Latif, but it was not something upon which he chose to trade. It was gratifying just to talk about the music, to unpack his struggles and ideas. He could do it with Wessel, but Wessel offered answers and advice, posed questions. With Wessel he was self-conscious in the presence of an expert; with some of the girls he knew Latif could simply speak until he caught himself saying something useful, and feel the heat of admiration warm him as he spoke. There were seduction techniques embedded in Latif's discourse; he noted and cataloged them, but he felt somehow that he would sully the music if he used his status as a player to get drawers.

There was more to the strangeness of himself, beyond status and women and the early curfews that kept Latif in his bedroom playing, listening, or reading when other cats were out of doors finding opportunity and trouble. Latif had a sense of timing that eluded sensible explanation; music's elastic relationship with the clock seemed to carry over into his life. He managed not to be in the wrong place at the wrong time with such frequency that Shane, the namesmith, and then others, began calling him Lucky T.T. and Rabbitsfoot and asking him to wave his hand over their heads in blessing before they went to cop some weed or shoplift beers from the bodega.

Even now, when he ebbed into sleep, Latif often thought back on the day five years ago when he and two of his boys had gone to Cambridge to hang out and go shopping. He had lingered in a clothing store, trying on some pants, while Shane and Jay Fox walked back out and down the block. When he emerged from the shop ten minutes later, new light-green khakis folded crisply in a drawstring plastic bag, the cats were gone. He waited outside the store, searched the block and didn't find them, and finally went to the train station and saw the aftermath of what had happened: the blood and the medics and the clump of mumbling bundled onlookers, arms crossed and breath visible as they whispered, shook their heads, and stared.

A gang of older Cambridge whiteboys laying up near the trainstop had jumped Shane and Jay Fox, trying to rob them, and Shane had been stabbed in the chest and side with a butterfly knife. He spent a full month in the hospital getting better and then got arrested his first week back outside for carrying a blade. Jay Fox broke loose from the fight and ran into the street, where a yellowcab hit him going thirty-five miles an hour. He flew over the hood and died when his head hit the tarmac. The body was gone by the time Latif arrived, but the cab was still there, beached coldly in the middle of the street atop a bed of glass, with doors jacked open and its windshield shattered jagged. Latif imagined Jay Fox flying up into the air, twisting like an Olympic highboard diver against the backdrop of the rich blue sky. He never imagined Jay hitting the ground, just gliding through the air above the taxi cab like that, over and over. Latif wore the khakis underneath his suitpants at the Fox's funeral.

There were other times too; a weed run Latif had skipped which ended with cats getting stopped, frisked, and fucked up by Irish police, even surprise quizzes he had missed by staying late with other teachers. His nascent good fortune in running into Say Brother at the bar and Sonny Burma in need of product crowned the list of serendipities. Before long Burma treated him like family, although when he first met Sonny's brother the last thing in the world Latif thought he'd ever want to be was Sonny's kin.

Anyone who knew Sonny knew better than to ask after Marlon, even though many of them had watched the cat grow up. Marlon was fifteen years younger than Sonny and their father had died when he was four; Sonny became the man of the house and raised Marlon practically himself while their mother worked sixteen-hour days at white folks' homes. He took Marlon to most of his gigs rather than leave him by himself, and Marlon would sit at a table next to the piano with his crayons and draw pictures of his big brother, the band, people in the club.

He was a beautiful little boy, quiet and well behaved, and every cocktail waitress and bartender in the city loved to look after him whenever Sonny brought him by, slip him pretzels and sodas and lose to him at cards. Marlon had been a wonderful artist even then, and his drawings were still scotchtaped to the mirrored walls behind the bars of many of the city's clubs. When he was a little older Marlon switched from crayons to watercolors, and Sonny would pass around the paintings and say *Check out my little brother's artwork, man. Only twelve years old and already a motherfucker.*

When Marlon was sixteen, Sonny got the opportunity to travel throughout Europe on a State Department concert tour, and he took it. It was his first chance to see the world; Sonny was a Brooklynite who'd hardly been west of the Holland Tunnel. Other cats migrated to the city to play, Higgins from Oakland and Amir Abdul from Chapel Hill, North Carolina; Burma simply hopped the uptown number three. But Sonny took to travel right away, learned to live with, then to love, the fastpace of check-ins and check-outs and soundchecks, trains and planes and en-route naps. He flourished on a diet built of free meals: complimentary hotel breakfasts and post-show dinners at the club or the promoter's favorite restaurant. He knew how to accept and reciprocate the constant hospitality and enjoy the changing company of the people he met at gigs. And the women; in the year and a half he was over in Europe, Sonny told Latif, he'd slept less than a month of nights alone. Made love in thirteen different languages.

Burma came back to Fort Greene eager to see his brother, who was eighteen now and going off to art school, amped to hang out some and get a milkshake and tell Marlon all about the things he'd done and the places he'd been, all the funny and wild-out shit that had happened in Europe, show him some pictures and maybe flash a few quicktongued phrases in French or Italian. He had been planning to tell Marlon that he would try to get him a job carrying equipment the next time something like this came up, so that Marlon too could get out of New York and see the world, swim on the nude beaches of the French Riviera and browse dozens of museums all over the continent. Every time Sonny navigated his way through a roomful of art, strolling arm in arm with whatever lady had offered to be his local tourguide, he thought of Marlon and his paintings, of how much his brother deserved an opportunity like this.

But when Sonny came home Marlon was a faggot and Sonny blamed himself. He wouldn't listen to anyone who told him it had nothing to do with him, that his presence or his absence didn't figure in, or to anyone who told him that it didn't matter anyway; if Marlon wanted to sleep with men that was his business and he was still the same sweet kid who painted beautifully and thought his older brother hung the night moon in the sky. Nor would Sonny suffer those who told him, out the sides of their mouths and with an eyebrow raised, that they had always kind of known that Marlon was that way and they thought everybody else did too, Sonny included.

Sonny hadn't thought he hated faggots, although he'd never given it much serious consideration. When he saw them on the street it never bothered him, didn't turn his guts or make him want to throw a punch the way it did some cats. He peeped faggots with curiosity and slight bemusement; theirs was a world he knew little and cared less about, and he was cool with peaceful coexistence. But when Sonny walked into the airport and gave Marlon a bearhug and held him at arm's length to look him over, he saw trepidation looming in his little brother's eyes. They darted left and Marlon said *Sonny, there's someone I want you to meet.* Sonny turned his head and only then noticed a slim white boy a few years older than Marlon with his hair cut short and pasted neatly to his skull. *This is Theo.* Sonny smiled, nodded hello and extended his hand. *He's my . . . boyfriend.*

Marlon took Theo's hand timidly, as if to demonstrate what boyfriend meant. Sonny stood still for a few ticks. Heat rose in his face and he imagined things he didn't want to: Marlon and Theo kissing, his brother prancing down the street limpwristed and bitchlike, a stereotype faggot. Sonny's stomach bottomed out, but it wasn't until he pictured Marlon and Theo in bed and wondered who was fucking who, whether the black boy or the white boy was the one taking it up the ass, that he picked up his luggage and walked away fast as he could. Marlon said *Shit* and dropped Theo's hand. He followed Sonny toward the cabstand and caught up with his brother as Sonny lifted his suitcase to the trunk.

Sonny! Where are you going?

Where am I going? I'm getting the fuck out of here, that's where I'm going. He slammed the trunk shut. *I can't believe this shit. Now you're a faggot, Marlon?*

I always was, Sonny. I haven't changed. I'm still your brother.

Sonny closed his eyes and tilted his face to the sky. *I knew I shouldn't have gone away.*

I'm still your brother, Sonny.

Don't do this to me, man.

Do what to you, Sonny? I'm not doing anything to you. Look what you're doing to me.

Jesus Christ, Marlon, said Sonny, getting in the cab. *You better get the fuck away from me before I really lose it.*

He pulled the door shut and the cabbie shifted into drive. Sonny knew Marlon was staring at him through the window but he forced himself not to meet his brother's eyes.

Latif knew nothing of this or of what else had gone down between the brothers in the years since then. He knew only that during the second week of his tenure at Dutchman's, as he and Burma walked through Times Square one latenight, he heard a voice shout *Sonny!* and turned to see a tall young man crossing the block diagonally in a walk that was almost a run. His arms pumped back and forth faster than his legs as he moved, as if his body was in conflict over how fast to go. *Sonny!* the man shouted again.

Just keep walking, Burma told Latif. *I don't wanna see that cat.* Sonny sped his pace but it was too late. Marlon broke into a run as the crosswalk came alive with traffic, and intercepted Sonny at the corner.

Are you just going to ignore me, Sonny? You gonna keep on acting like I don't exist?

Nothing moved in Sonny's face but his eyes burned. He looked straight ahead, as if entranced by the rhythm of his stride, and spoke one loud firm word.

Yup. Latif ground his teeth and looked at Marlon. He seemed gentle and Latif felt a quiver of unwanted sympathy—two words which the drug game, benign as it had so far been, had linked in his mind.

Marlon bobbed his head, sucking the insides of his cheeks between his teeth and puckering his lips. *Fine. Fine. I don't know why I give a fuck.* He paused, still walking with them, easily matching Sonny's getaway quickstep with his long legs. Marlon was a good six inches taller than his brother. With sudden, artificial animation, he smiled sweetly and offered his hand to Latif.

Marlon Burma. Nice to meet you. My brother's not too good with introductions. You a musician too?

Before Latif could shake it, Sonny reached across and slapped his brother's palm away.

Latif pointed his already-extended hand at each of them in turn. *Y'all are*—he began, curious, then censored himself when Sonny's hard face opened to speak.

Alright, alright, enough of your shit, Marlon. Just get outta here.

He pushed Marlon hard with both arms, stepping into it, locking his elbows. Marlon was off-balance and the push knocked him back a few stumbling feet. It was all the space Sonny needed; he filled the distance with his outstretched arm, pointing a finger at his openmouthed brother like a pistol.

You know how I feel, Marlon. Stop pulling this shit. Just do your thing and I'll do mine. Sonny turned the corner without looking back. Latif scurried after him. Marlon stood in place, hands on his hips, and called after his brother.

I'll say hello to Mom for you!

You just saw the worst of me, Burma apologized to Latif as he trickled liquor over ice cubes twenty minutes later, leaning back against the kitchen counter in Amir Abdul's apartment, spicy with the smell of cedar from a walk-in closet for bass storage. Amir was in there now with two guests, running down the history of each instrument: One had belonged to Jimmy Blanton and was featured on some Ellington recordings, passing through the hands of George Morrow before landing in a music shop in London. Another was on loan from Richard Davis. A complete tour of the eight-square-foot area took fifteen minutes.

It's a messy situation between me and my brother, and it's probly gonna stay that way, said Sonny. *I don't want to get into it right now, but you gotta understand. I raised that cat like I was his daddy, so everything he does hits me right here,* pounding his chest, *and it hits me twice as hard, as a brother and a father.* He shook his head and squinted at his scotch. *Sometimes shit is just too much, ain't it?*

Latif smiled, the loathing he had felt for Sonny dissipating at the first sign of remorse. His own brother, Latif thought, shaking his head, but now he pushed it from his mind and granted Sonny the doubt's benefit. To hate his closest New York friend was impractical anyway. *Fuck it,* Sonny said, putting his glass down. *Let's have some fun. Come on. We hiding in the kitchen like a couple of old drunks while all kinds of pussies on parade right in the living room. Tell you what, Teef: I'ma put you next to something flavorful out here.*

Oh, so now I need an assist to score some ass? Latif grinned with a flippant confidence he hardly felt. New York women moved with a daunting playgirl slickness wild different from the tender undeveloped game of chicks he'd messed with back in Boston. Thus far he had satisfied himself in distant flirtation, stares and glances from across the room at Dutchman's, all the while promising himself that as soon as he was slightly more settled into the life he would stop bullshitting and kick it to the baddest chick he could find, prove to himself that girls were girls and he was not out of his league here there or anywhere.

He took his drink in hand and followed Sonny down the hall into the living room, and there she was. He gulped down first a draught of air and then a swish of vodka, looked at her and thought about the three nights last week when she had been the woman whose image hovered naked in his mind as he lay on his back in bed at four A.M. eyes closed and jerked himself off, a spattered facetowel draped over his stomach.

Latif wondered how she'd feel knowing that alone in his bedroom some strange man had used her, made her do the things he had. He looked at her as if she'd really done them, as if she was the woman he had made her in his mind. There was no one else for her to be. He had seen her only twice, both times at Dutchman's; she wasn't a regular, but she moved like one. The first night they'd traded glances, made eye contact and tried not to be caught looking after that. He'd watched her flit from table to table, smoking cigarettes with different friends. Some were musicians, but he didn't want to ask them who she was, or to be introduced. Lurking in shadows was habit forming and Latif found himself not wanting her to know him yet, wanting to study her like she was Albert or some shit before he kicked hello.

Last night they'd progressed to smiles and to ignoring each other, alternately. When she left—hours before he could go, he thought, annoyed—she turned and found him with her eyes and he waved goodbye and she returned his wave goodbye and smiled. He went home feeling happy and childish, wondering why he was playing these signal games instead of handling his business as he always had: walking over, introducing himself, buying her a drink. He told himself that work and study were crippling his game. He didn't want to think that the reason he was bullshitting was that this woman was white.

I was hoping I might see you here. She approached him while Latif was still playing the doorway, and his brain delighted him by switching over quickfast into mack mode. The extensive catalog of vibes, eyes, smiles, and movements appropriate to first-encounter convo propeller-whirred itself up from the depths and snapped into forebrain position with a rusty click. Somewhere else in him an adding machine turned on; numbers scrolled like slot machine symbols with every word and gesture.

Some cats played their instruments like this, he thought: depended on empiric grasps of math and possibility, eyecorner checked themselves nonstop to see how they were doing. They tended to sound nervous, soulless, overly intentioned. He didn't play like that and knew he shouldn't think like this. A stimulating conversation, like a hot rhythm section, could push you right into the moment; Latif hoped she'd give him that push, but he knew he was smooth enough to overthink and still swing if she didn't.

I was hoping the same thing, he smiled, interlocking his fingers around his drink and shifting the glass over to the left so he could offer her his right. Hands were important; women had told him they watched hands and he'd begun to do so too. *I was hoping the same thing* was garbage, technically, but it was the kind of line that could come off with the right smile and right eyes behind it, a smirk and a sparkle that conveyed elements of both sincerity and silliness.

Her fingers were long, slim, and her hand fit well in his. He took it lightly, held but didn't shake. *My name's Latif James-Pearson.* The prolonged body contact introduction was a power play, and she knew it and liked it.

Latif, she repeated, digging—what? The sound? The juju power? *It's a pleasure to meet you, Latif. I'm Mona.*

Mona's eyes were shimmering oceans and sharks swam in them, zagging left and right in search of prey. *Oh shit*, Latif thought when she gave him a second to really check them out *this chick is nuts. Something happened to her.* The delighted terrified excitement he'd felt as a kid at the aquarium, watching those monsters swish through the water and feeling that there was no way glass could really hold them, wriggled through Latif and out the soles of his feet.

Nothing else in Mona radiated volatility. Her hair was cherry black, stylishly cut to frame a face surprisingly comfortable with itself, no longer mesmerized by its own grace of composition. Her mouth perked when she spoke and matched her small elegant nose and small round unadorned earlobes, just visible beneath the forward sweep of hair. Against the flawless creaminess of Mona's skin, her maroon lips gleamed. They were soft and slightly thinner than Latif liked: a relief. He tried to find flaw with a beautiful woman immediately, to deflate any intimidation blooming in his chest.

Just Mona, huh? No last name. Like Madonna. He studied her. *No, more like Michelangelo.*

Her straight teeth opened when she laughed and Latif saw the pink flash of her tongue.

Something like that.

Latif smiled. *Mona's plenty. I like that* moan *in there. So what's your thing, Mona?* He leaned left against the doorway, crossing his ankles, getting comfortable.

You mean what do I do? My job?

Only if your job is your thing, and not a lot of people are that lucky. He gave her a complicated smile, a blend of flirtation, amusement, playful condescension, expectation. It was a lot to mix into a smile and it came out slightly muddled but charming. *I know you got a thing. I can tell.*

Oh can you. And what makes you so sure? asked Mona, wondering why men wanted to tell her who she was all the time.

I can just tell. You look like a serious person, somebody very devoted to something.

Well, it's nice that you think so. Once a guy at a bar had had the nerve to tell Mona, after a one-drink conversation, that he knew her better than she knew herself. She sloshed her drink in his face, a cliché she'd always admired but never thought she'd have use for, said *Well then you should have seen that coming*, and stalked away regretting it. Maybe he'd follow her outside, drunk, violent. Or push her into the bathroom and rape her.

She looked at Latif, this sweetfaced gangle of limbs she'd traded sexlooks with at Dutchman's. He was trying too hard, but she liked the cavern of absence beneath his eagerness. On the downlow he wasn't really here, just like he hadn't been at Dutchman's; he was somewhere more important, somewhere private and intense. Mona could relate to that, and she could wonder about it. Men were so unmysterious that Mona rarely flirted anymore. But Latif didn't know that, so he wasn't flattered.

We're back to Michelangelo, she said. *I paint.*

You don't sound too confident about it, he observed. Latif was pulling pleasure from language again, loving the challenge of kicking game with perfect timing and coming on just strong enough to make a woman squirm and pulling back with debonair preemption. He watched Mona's eyes jump, happy with the normalness of the reaction: She was surprised at his perception or presumption, maybe both.

Well, it's hard, she said, tone chilling. Why did men have to be so intrusive, and why did women let them? A dude could walk up to a woman in a bar and ask her where her parents were from, or if she'd ever kissed another girl, and get an answer every time.

Still, Mona had to admit, what Latif had said was true. She

was far from confident about her work; maybe he'd picked up on that, which wasn't so hard to believe, and he was trying to swing the conversation into something real. Sometimes Mona's asshole-meter was too sensitive. She was trying to recalibrate it.

I love to paint, she said, voice warming to room temperature *but it's not usually something I discuss.* Her eyes darted up from underneath thick lashes and thin eyebrows and pinned him to the wall *So if you wanna talk to me about it, you gotta be nicer than that.*

Latif held his hands up to his chest, palms out in mock surrender. *Point taken. I understand completely. I'm the same way.* A seamless segue into the music, he thought, but Mona said nothing. It was a subtle, intelligent move, and Latif appreciated it. She knew she was being cued, that he had pointed her toward *Oh, really, what do you do?* and she withheld it, let him know where he could stick his conversational agenda. Latif decided not to give Mona the satisfaction of stumbling heavyhanded into what he'd meant; he was looking wack enough already and she was probably as sick of hearing motherfuckers talk about themselves as she appeared to be with fielding their brokenbat questions.

She beamed a level take-no-shit stare, and surprise that Mona was still talking to him mingled in Latif with odd confidence; she was digging something enough to forgive him his trespasses. Latif ditched his plan, riffed briefly on his words, and banged a rubberburning left into more casual territory. You could get away with anything from speeding to reckless driving to illegal parking if the eye convo stayed hot.

Same exact way. No doubt. So how do you know Amir?

Oh, his girlfriend Ada is a friend of mine. We live in the same building.

You live on 135th Street?

Does that surprise you? A white girl living on her own in Harlem? Mona put a finger to her lip and curled her drink into her hand.

It was a cranberry-and-something and it matched her nails. Mentioning her address had rejuvenated her; it was a badge of independence, raciness, and she wanted him to prove that he could handle all that. She smoothed her black dress around the waist and gave a subtle slight tugdown, so that her breasts rose a bit.

The only thing worse than white people who avoided talking about race, Latif thought, were white people who couldn't wait to bring the subject up. *I don't know*, he said. *I don't know too many white folks.*

Mona laughed. Did he really have the gall to hit a separatist pose while trying to scoop her? *I've seen you talking with a lot of white cats down at Dutchman's.*

Maybe, but I don't know them. She was getting too feisty. He wanted to back her off, scare her, fuck her on his terms. *They're business associates of mine. I got nothing to do with them other than that*, he said, satisfied with the ominous vagueness of the statement and hoping Mona was too cool to ask him just what business he was in.

If Latif needed to distance himself from whiteness to feel okay about getting with her, that was fine with Mona. She wasn't overly fond of her race either, and though she didn't want to be one of those corny race-apologetic white people, she found herself wanting Latif to know it. In some fuzzy channel of her mind the fact that he didn't like white folks made him more attractive.

Green is the only color that counts, right? Mona said. *Though not to some people, I guess. My family owns my building, but nobody except me will live there. The rest of them moved downtown in the twenties; you know the routine.*

Latif nodded, stirred his drink. *I do. Course, a bunch of white people came uptown then, too. Show me a wellspring of black creativity and I'll show you a line of white folks ready to dive in and hold their breath until they prune up.*

Mona smiled. *Some of us breathe better under water.*

Yeah, but y'all tend to piss in the pool. They laughed.

So do you have lungs or gills? Latif asked.

I'm amphibious. A frog.

I happen to remember a thing or two about biology, said Teef, hardly understating the case, *and I don't think you are. You know how frogs catch flies?* She shook her head. *Their brains detect motion and their tongues react. Dangle a batch of dead flies on strings in front of a frog and the poor sucker will starve to death. You strike me as a little more perceptive.*

But maybe there's dead flies all around us and we just can't see them. Maybe we're starving to death and don't know it.

I was until I saw you. Cuz baby, you fly as hell. He said it in a highpitched leering pimpdrawl and Mona rolled her eyes and gave him a new smile, closemouthed with lowslung eyelids and heavy cheek action. They locked eyes.

So if I kiss you, Latif said *will you turn into Princess Charming?*

It's no fun if I tell you. She stepped a little closer. *The question is, how many frogs have you slobbed down looking for her?*

He slid his hands into his pockets. *I haven't even been looking. I'm just tryna catch enough flies to survive.*

Mona warmed. She wanted to need, and be needed by, someone like herself: Someone who didn't need anybody. *Well*, she said *you catch more flies with honey . . .*

Teef edged closer. They were standing near enough for him to drop words right into her ear now. *I think we've taken the frog thing about as far as it'll go*, he said.

What's the matter? Got a frog in your throat?

Latif bent his chin to his chest and smiled with delight at Mona's jazz-level riff chops. *Mmm. I stand corrected. Come to think of it*—he flicked his eyes down her body—*I'm experiencing my first craving for frog's legs.*

Is that right? Mona breathed into his chest.

His nose and mouth were to her hair and he inhaled Japanese musk. *That's right.*

And how do I know you're not a scorpion who wants a ride across the pond?

He reached his hand around and rubbed her back, up down and up, kept his palm between her shoulder blades and pulled away so she could see his face: *I won't sting you*, he said. *I ain't tryna drown.*

They finished their drinks and left the party in a cab.

Where are we going? Mona whispered in the taxi backseat, curled into Latif. The driver had some rhythm in him; he hit every green light as they moved uptown, toward both their cribs.

Latif's right hand cupped Mona's left thigh. Disinterest was spreading over him already, now that he knew she was down. It was the pimp in him, rising like steam from a streetgrate, the legacy of all the growing up he'd done on blocks where romance was wargames and the necessity of being in control and the fallacy of trusting women comprised the main rules of engagement. He tore his eyes from the windshield and said, *How bout my place?*

I'm more fun at my place.

Your place it is. He wondered what Mona knew about him; she could have found out plenty at the club. *Stay on the low*, Say Bro had cautioned. *All kinds of fools want something you got now, and want it bad. Fine junkie bitches will fuck you for dope, Phyte. Cats will shake you down or scam you seven ways from Sunday if you let em. It's pretty civilized in here*, sweeping a cigar around the club, *but don't sleep. The minute you clock Zs motherfuckers will jack you for the entire alphabet.* Maybe Mona hadn't asked him what he did because she knew.

He turned to her. *Can I ask you a question? Why did you pay me any mind those nights at Dutchman's?*

Mona let him hook a compliment to cast away suspicion. *Be-*

cause you're beautiful, she said, squeezing his arm. *And because you had this energy. I watched you and I said to myself, this dude is working.* She declined to add that he reminded her of herself in some younger incarnation, fierce and guarded, a deep well of feelings gurgling inside high stonewalls. She'd watched him and twinged with gut desire to climb to the top and plumb his depths, let him plumb hers.

Latif jerked up and pulled far enough away to scrutinize her: *Working? Whadda you mean, working?*

Mona pretended not to notice his agitation, looped her arm through his and played it off. She knew what he thought she'd meant but she wasn't even going to get into that: Let him know it was a false alarm and keep flowing. *You know, like you were thinking something serious. Working something out. What's wrong?*

Latif resettled. *I'm sorry. Lately I've had a lot of reason not to trust people.*

Mona turned to whisper in his ear. *You can trust me*, she intoned, grazing his earlobe with her lips. *I promise.* It was the kind of thing Mona never would have said or believed a few years back, before she'd noticed how her internal rhythm had come to match New York's, how both she and it were struggling to keep past sadnesses in check by acting ruthless, heedless, needless. She knew Latif wouldn't believe the statement now. Fine. Her job was just to say it.

Mona's breasts rubbed Latif's side as she whispered and he pulled her to him tight, pimp nonchalance banished by a new-sprung Bonnie and Clyde fantasy of us-against-the-world gangster couple solidarity, some ol' *my girl strapped with a gat, always got a nigga back* shit.

He turned to lay the kiss down, and she tucked her hair behind her ear in expectation, and the fantasy dissolved. Something about Mona's gesture was too eager and all of a moment he was back on a pimp vibe, disdaining her for wanting him and peeved at her presumption: *Girl, who you think you is?* He was so preoccupied with the power of dispassion that he almost didn't kiss her, but Latif checked himself, knocked the pimp back to the netherlands of noir and got his mind right. A second later Mona's hand was soft and cool on the back of Latif's neck and her tongue wild in his mouth. Too wild. He touched her chin lightly and Mona eased into his tempo with responsive smoothness; she'd let him lead until Latif forgot about such things. He rubbed his hand between her legs, against her dress, and Mona gasped, then murmured: Her sound was high deep and immediate and Latif loved it, wanted more, imagined concerts built of future notes. The taxi stopped in front of Mona's building and they went inside.

She led him to the bedroom in the dark and he saw only stacks of canvases against the walls, clothes striped with jags of streetlight, dark outlines of furniture. They undressed on the bed, piece by piece between kisses, and Latif entered her as quickly as he could, after a few wild exploratory handslides down her body; they'd both been ready since the cab. He felt himself engorge inside her and a feeling of control flooded his mind as Mona closedmouth groaned. She writhed beneath him, wrapped her arms around Latif's back, reached her hands under his arms and cupped his shoulders from behind; pulled him up inside her, chest to hers, and waited for Latif to call the tune.

They began to move together, first in long sweeping strokes, slow tidal back and forths, then fast arpeggios cresting in echoing suspended-animation notes, Latif suddenly wholebody pausing deep inside her. The sweet erratic fast-and-stillness gave Mona body-memories of freezedancing in a club: rhythm cacophony and strobelight madness and then suddenly the DJ lifts the needle from the groove and hits the lights and everybody's gotta hold still, panting and sweatdrenched, exposed just long enough to contemplate the moment, and then zigga–zigga and the music cuts back in on time.

Latif unfroze, pushed himself up off of her and locked his arms to see her face; Mona's eyes were tightclosed and damp hair stuck against her neck and forehead. She was exhaling in whimpers and he wanted her to scream. He threw his hips harder and she arched her back, opened her eyes; her mouth became an *o*. He thought about putting his dick in that mouth as he'd imagined in his room and grunted pleasure, past blowjobs swifting through his mind, then bent onto his elbows with his ear next to her mouth. The sounds of sex were what excited him the most. Mona got louder and they moved faster and harder, and he held onto the bedsides for leverage and drove himself into her harder. Mona lifted her legs and color spread over her face, cheeks lips inflamed, mouth splayed. Her low moans rose to loud long ones and Mona screamed shuddered and came, totalbody tension spliced with show-offish ragdoll thrash abandon. Latif watched, pushing back hard, flushed with refracted pleasure and relief, then rode the ebbtide of her body, slowing with her as she poured herself thin and became shallow water. They rocked slow and meditative, Indian raga rhythm, until Latif felt himself tingle and swell. Mona squeezed and undulated doubletime in re-excitement wetness and Latif tensed tightened and exploded quietly, unincredibly, and they rocked slower and slowed down to a standstill and were silent, breathing.

Latif slid the rubber off his dick and lowered it onto the nightstand like a gold bracelet, then hunted down a cigarette. He tried to feel relaxed. Mona was mellow on the bed beside him and Latif didn't want to sour the vibe with politics but he did it nonetheless, put the truth out there because he needed to and because sex had freed and obligated him. He didn't do it to test Mona, but he knew it was a test of sorts as well. Mona watched his grill open to speak and knew some ugliness was coming. The connectedness of sex either jittered men so much that they had to do more than pull out to reclaim themselves, or it made them feel entitled to say anything. Part of her wished she could tell him how easy it was to make her come. That she could do it with all her clothes on.

I want you to know I don't usually go for white women, Mona. I'm not one of those cats. He paused. *I only bring this up because I like you.*

Mona stiffened, felt old impulses rising. There was a time when she would have said *I don't give a shit, cowboy. I'm not white women, I'm Mona, and if you think I'm gonna listen to wet-dick politics from some kid who thinks I'm opening my life not just my legs you can go fuck yourself.* Now she crawled playful up the bed and took the cigarette from him. *Well, then*, she deadpanned *I guess I'm flattered.* He noticed how delicately she held the filter in between the tips of her first and middle fingers, how crisply the cigarette snapped when she flicked the ash off with her thumb. She was a better smoker than he was. Latif's bowels still quivered if he pulled within a half inch of the filter.

I don't usually go for black men, either, Mona said, and Latif wanted to palm her face like a basketball and push it far away. He stared at her as hard as he knew how, unsure what angered him more: the idea that Mona didn't usually go for black men or the idea that she did.

And why is that?

I don't know. She renestled herself in Latif's armpit and blew a smoke ring.

Let me guess, Latif said. *You never really thought about it much.*

Mona had ignored the hostility in his voice as long as she could, and now she looked up sharply. Dumb bitch, Latif thought. Bout fuckin time you noticed.

I've thought a lot about it, Mona said. She sat up across from him against the wall, Indian-style with a pillow on her lap, and Latif looked at her eyes and blanched: just when you thought it was safe to go back in the water. *You know what motherfuckers on this block call me?* Latif waited. *Miss Crazy White Girl. I get called Miss and Crazy now cause after a year of listening to them pop the most disgusting shit I stopped and screamed on them for half an hour. Now they act right.*

He scowled. *So what?*

So I've had this fuckin conversation before, that's what. If I don't like black men I'm a racist, but if I do I'm some nasty freak, right? This is exactly why I don't get into it. Her hands fluttered, frustrated, and landed in her lap. *Am I supposed to be happy I'm your first white woman?*

That's not what I said, and you're not. His voice was a guillotine blade, cold and even. Now Latif was lying in defense of what was true.

Well, you're not my first, either, Mona retorted, going sullen. She crossed her arms over her chest and Latif reflected that a lot of women would have covered themselves with a sheet. Mona didn't mind arguing naked. He liked that. *And the last one was an asshole,* she added, staring off ahead of her.

Well, I'm sorry, Latif said quietly, one part reconciliation over four ice cubes. Mona twitched her lip in receipt. Latif moved closer on the bed, sat side by side with her so that their upper arms touched. A minute ticked by and Latif said, *I guess I meant that I like you in spite of your race, not because of it.*

She turned to eyeball him. *And I'm supposed to like you not because of or in spite of it, right?*

Latif saw that she wanted to battle this one out, and suddenly he lost the will to do so. He wished the two of them were lying still, twisted in bedding and each other's legs, talking about nothing or not talking. He didn't feel like trying to make her understand: for what? She wouldn't get it and he'd wind up questioning himself because he couldn't make it come out right.

Mona saw him drifting between angry and pensive and took his hand. *Don't get mad,* she said. *I don't mean to sound aggressive. This is just the way I am. I like to go right after things and I don't take offense and I don't expect anybody else to either. So explain to me how you saying you don't usually go for people like me is different than me saying I don't usually go for people like you. Please.*

Latif looked at her for a long moment and saw she was in earnest. He took a deep breath. *It's different because every time you and I get into a fight I'm gonna wonder when you'll get mad enough to call me nigger. I'll be wondering how many times you've thought it. It's different because when we make love I'll be wondering whether you're pretending it's the slave days and you're the master's daughter sneaking her favorite darkie into the gazebo to see if what they say about niggers is true. It's different because I'm going to twitch every time you ask me could I please bring you back a glass of water when I get up from bed to take a midnight piss. It's different because when I look at you and think you're beautiful I've gotta wonder to myself if I've bought into some white notion of beauty, I've gotta twist my head around until I find a beautiful black woman just to even out the score. It's different because maybe you fucked me because you like me, or maybe because you hate yourself or you want to get back at your parents or you want to say fuck you to society or you want to be hip or maybe even because you hate being white. It's different for a lot of reasons.*

Mona waited until she was sure Latif was done before she spoke. *Let me ask you this,* she said. *Were you thinking that slave-master's daughter shit just now when we made love?*

No.

Would you tell me if you were?

No. Maybe.

Mmm. Latif watched Mona think, her eyes downcast and fingers rubbing at a daub of gray paint on the inside of her wrist. He hadn't noticed it before, but now he saw another, turquoise, just below her knee. *I feel everything you're saying,* she allowed, finally, the spot gone. *Those are some of my reasons too. It's hard to cut through all of that, and I'm not dumb enough to think that just because I live in Harlem I know anything. But there's a flipside, Latif. I want you to understand that. I've got to wonder if you think I'm really thinking all those things.*

Oh, come on, he said. *That's not the same. Feeling like a slave is not the same as feeling like the master.*

Of course it's not, she said *but they're both pretty horrible. They're both pretty debilitating.*

Maybe so, Latif said with a patronizing smile. *But one's a lot worse than the other, wouldn't you agree?*

Of course I would. But they're all twisted up together. Maybe you want a white chick on your arm like all those stuck-in-the-fifties musicians at Dutchman's. Maybe you think white bitches are stupid and naive and you can game me. Maybe you want to hurt me for what my people did in the past. Or in the present.

Right, said Latif. *And maybe you'd like that.*

Mona heaved a giant sigh and flopped face and pillow first onto his lap. She flipped around, circled her arms around Latif's waist, and looked upside-down into his eyes, suddenly playful, cute as hell. It bugged him out that Mona could backflip off a desert impasse and land in a waterfall like that; still in race mode, Latif reflected that only white people could switch vibes so quickly and wished he knew how to pull off such carefreedom. Even with his horn in hand, he never felt he had the luxury.

Well, she said *if anybody can survive a night in the haunted house of race it should be some young, sexy, unhorrified folks like ourselves. Right?*

You'd think so, Latif said flatly. He tucked her hair behind her ear. *You'd think so.* He continued playing with her hair and was not surprised when Mona fell asleep.

Do you still like me? Mona asked by way of good morning, sliding a leg against Latif's as he blinked into waking. Her hair fell pretty, wavy, and her chin was hidden in a pillow, and Latif nodded a true yes, drifting pleasantly through the kind of half-rejuvenated body haze that follows a latenight of megawatt intensity. He generally experienced it after jam sessions: the feeling that he'd sacrificed today for yesterday and it had been well worth it. They'd gotten into some shit last night and Latif felt good about it, honest and invigorated. He rolled over onto his back and they lay flat and grinned with morning goofiness.

After a small breakfast of tomato, cheese, and sourdough bread, Mona showed Latif her studio: a corner of the sunsplashed living room with cardboard duct-taped to the hardwood floor to catch paintsplatters; long looping strands of flesh and plasma, sprinkles of magenta, orange drips. An empty easel stood solo in the middle, surrounded by paint tubes, turpentine, brushes in metal coffee cans. Low jetties of finished canvases jutted from either wall, almost meeting to enclose the space. Latif asked what she painted and Mona buried her hands in her bathrobe pockets and looked out the window at the Harlem skyscape of decaying jack-o-lantern buildings, window caverns glaring like empty eye sockets. The tentacles of gentrification hadn't wound around this neighborhood and revitalized it by forcing folks to move out yet. Shit was straight ghetto. Latif was glad that he lived further west.

You'll think I'm crazy when I tell you.

Mona painted her mother. She said it with her eyes still on the view. *She died when I was ten. She hated pictures. So I work from memory.*

Her gaze nosedived from the window to a portrait at the jetty's end. She moved to pick it up, then seemed to change her mind. She fingered a canvas edge, flossing her nail with a loose thread as she spoke. *I remember her so clearly. The way she looked standing at the stove, chatting with me while I sat at the kitchen table doing homework.*

Mona looked up and Latif tried for a sensitive expression, something to show how closely he was listening. He *was* listening, but sometimes you had to dress the truth up or it didn't look right. Lotta tenormen threw in a little extra shoulder, a little legshake or backward bend or forward bow, at crucial moments. It started out as showmanship, a way to clue the audience in to how hard you were working, and soon it became habit. Latif clamped his teeth so his jaw flared. Mona dropped her eyes. *Everyone says she was beautiful. But she liked to remember things her own way, and she said pictures ruined that. It took me three years to get her mouth right, but I did it. Now I'm working on her eyes.*

It must be frustrating, Latif said absently.

No, not really. I'm in no rush.

He pictured Mona standing there, paintbrush in hand, frowning at the slanted canvas night by night, and a quick gust of the tradition lifted him: Latif looked out the window and imagined New York and the world as nothing but a billion little woodsheds full of heads bent to the task, honing their craft and blazing midnight oil. Beautiful. But something about Mona's discipline seemed so methodical and lonely: all those solitary hours and no payoff, no interaction. You could lurk in the gallery and watch people scope your work, but come on.

We're not so different, I think, Mona mused. *We both change thoughts and emotions into something else, something abstract.*

Latif remembered the times he and Wessel had discussed such things, tipping backward side by side in folding chairs before a music stand in Teef's room, horns forgotten on their laps for as long as it took them to uncover whatever they were digging at.

He loved this kind of contemplation and was glad to be doing it with Mona, excited to hear what she'd say and to drop some bad shit on her if he could. *My sax teacher used to say that music and painting are first cousins*, he said *and writing is a cousin once removed. It's all translation, like you said, but colors and sounds exist in nature. Words don't; it's an artificial palette.* It sounded vaguely like an insult, but Wess read more than anyone he knew.

Yeah, but writing and painting are both solitary. I'm always amazed a whole band can communicate. It's hard to be close to even one person. It takes a lot of work.

Well, you're really by yourself out there. Latif crossed the room, crouched on one knee, flipped through a stack of canvases and waited for Mona to ask him to stop. She didn't, but Latif heard the crack of her knuckles and knew he was making her uncomfortable. He smiled to himself and stood up. Her discomfort with her work pleased him, made him feel like the more serious artist.

Do you ever worry about being understood? asked Mona.

Latif shrugged. *If you worry about that, you'll go nuts. Cats spent half Coltrane's career telling him how angry his music was, and this was the most gentle man since Jesus.* He paced toward the window with hands pocketed, hoping to catch his reflection in the glass. He wondered if he looked as good as he felt, sharp and casual, wearing last night's jacket in his new lover's apartment, talking about art while coffee brewed.

Not your music. I mean you. Do you feel like people understand you?

Well, if they understand my music, they understand me. So I guess I concentrate on that.

But you're more than your music. And you just said yourself that never happens.

Well, not everybody understands. But some will. Those are the ones who matter.

What about real life, though? The people around you?

Latif crouched again, pretending to look at the back of a canvas. *There are no people around me.* He glanced up at her. *I've always been kind of a loner.*

Me too. Mona sat on the floor; parallelism was important to her. *Although not by choice.* She was suddenly self-conscious. *Maybe this is more than you want to get into right now.*

Latif lowered himself the final inches to the ground and spun a few degrees to face her. He pulled his knees up to his chest, clasped his hands around them, looked her in the eye and tried to raise an eyebrow. He couldn't quite do it; his whole brow lifted instead. *I don't think either one of us is much for bullshit conversation.*

Mona nodded, looking at the slats beneath her. *This is the first place I've lived that's felt like home since I was ten*, she said. She placed both palms and both feet flat on the wood floor. *Can you play your horn in a way that feels like you're crying?*

I can make it sound like crying.

That's not what I mean.

Latif teetered. *I don't know. I've never really tried.*

I cry a lot when I'm alone, said Mona. *I wish I had somebody I could cry around.*

I don't remember the last time I cried, Latif said. *It used to feel good, though.*

Don't you have anything to cry about?

Latif raised and opened his left hand in vague confirmation. *Who doesn't? I guess I'm no good at being sad.*

Do you ever feel like you're not in control, Latif?

Of myself? He puzzled at the thought. *Who else would be? Do you?*

All the time. Mona sized him up. *Musicians sort of control the way their stuff's consumed, don't they? Not like staring at a painting or reading a book.*

Yeah, he said, relieved to return to a topic less—what? personal? How could music be less personal than anything? *But time's controlling us, too. Somebody like Albert seems to have all the time in the world—even makes you feel like one note says it all, explains the whole song—but really he's working within a tight form. And the shit's not democratic. Good notes can't cover for bad ones. Not for long.*

I was wondering when we were gonna get around to Mr. Albert Van Horn, Mona said. Then, teasingly *Is he your hero?*

Nah, said Latif, sliding backward on his ass. *My hero is Blade. Nigga kill two hundred vampires in three minutes and ain't afraid to walk around Manhattan rocking body armor.* She looked at him like he was twelve years old, which was exactly what he wanted. He liked women he could be a kid around; Latif hadn't been twelve since he was eight.

Alright, he amended, growing up. *Yes. Van Horn is the reason I came to New York, on some old corny forties hear-Bird-on-the-radio-and-pack-your-bags shit. Great man, Van Horn.*

Mona walked over and leaned against the back of the couch, legs crossed.

Great man or great musician?

You gotta be the first to be the second, Latif answered. *You're drawing on love, on the whole range of what it means to be human.* He spoke without considering the truth of his words, curious whether he believed the statement as he made it. He wondered what Wess would say. Or Spliff.

So you've got to be emotionally in tune, Mona surmised.

Well, on the bandstand anyway.

And yet you never cry.

Do I have to cry to make you cry?

Mona shrugged and let it go. *Is Van Horn very spiritual?* she asked.

I don't know. I've never met him.

Mona looked surprised. *Sonny's never introduced you?*

I won't let him. I'm not ready to know Albert yet.

So until you are you're just going to play by yourself?

I'll play by myself, said Latif *until I play in a class by myself.*

Mona laughed, stood up, and flopped backward over the couch. She crossed and uncrossed her legs in the air. *Okay*, she said. *So you're a musician and I'm a painter. Now suppose we tell each other what we do to make a living.*

Latif smiled. *Fair enough,* he said. *You first.*

Former temp turned office manager. The hideous truth. Your turn.

Drug dealer. Temp drug dealer. By now Latif was confident she wouldn't mind, that it would appeal to Mona's sense of the exotic. For better or worse.

I thought so, Mona said, *but I wasn't sure until you flipped out in the cab when I said "working." You like it?*

He looked at her with grudging, smirky respect. *It's alright. Good hours, good location. I won't be doing it forever.* He spoke to convince himself, and he knew Mona knew it. How could he explain to her that he was beginning to dig the glamour of exchanging fraternal money-product handshakes with musicians, and that the fact shamed and disgusted him? How could he lay bare the part of him that was relieved to have been yanked out of the silence of the woodshed, grateful to be distracted from his own regimented intensity, the part foolish enough to be unafraid? He could stay out here, he found himself thinking sometimes, out in this world. Develop a taste for veneration and the trappings of the life. Learn how to tell good wine from rotgut and where to find the baddest split-toes. Play his horn just well enough to work.

He tracked such feelings like a hunter, trying to catch himself in the act of bullshitting so he could squeeze the trigger, but they flitted past his scope too fast. They were small game, nothing to really sweat. He still practiced for hours every day; so what if he no longer picked up his horn as soon as he awoke but sat in bed and smoked a cigarette and replayed the highlights of the previous night first? So what if instead of immediate vigilance against a lover's potential to distract him from his music what was flaring up in Latif at this moment was big anticipation of the raised eyebrow Sonny would shoot him when he strolled into Dutchman's tonight with Mona on his arm?

Mona laced her hands behind her head, still upside down, and Latif wondered how much of his inner conflict she could read from his face, how much she felt it was even her business to see. She didn't seem to miss much. *Well*, said Mona *far be it from me to levy moral judgments. I just hope you're careful.*

Latif smiled, pleased at her concern and the fact that this was one fear he could comfortably assuage. *All I do is man the store and ring up sales.* He walked around the couch and knelt beside her. *I've still got plenty of time to buy a certain someone drinks.* They kissed.

Sonny Burma wheezed on smoke and passed his bass player the herb. *This is too stressful. I feel like I'm fifteen again.*

Amir doublechecked the towel underneath the red lounge door and blew his hit up toward the narrow window crowning the unfinished cement wall. *Really though. Smoking on the low, afraid somebody's mama gonna bust in on you, start whylin'.*

Wife, corrected Sonny. *Someone's wife.*

Amir shook his head and handed Latif the joint. *Wife, manager, judge, jury, and executioner. Damn, Marisol be trippin. I don't know how you cats put up with that shit.*

You'll learn. It's part of the gig. Wanna play with Albert, you gotta deal with Marisol. Sonny laughed. *Besides, since your big country ass been in the band she's laid off me.*

Shit, I'm just glad we're in New York and she don't be around too much. On the road that woman gets all up in a motherfucker's ass. Bother you on the plane! Walk from first class back to coach and wake you up to tell you for the third time you gotta take your bass to the club before you go to the hotel. Talking that half-Portuguese half-English nonsense like somebody sposed to understand her.

Well, said Sonny pensively *she's kept Albert clean for thirty years. Until she starts calling set lists, I'm cool. Plus, that little Brazilian woman cooks the killingest soul food you ever tasted in your life. The killingest. Albert claims he didn't teach her. Who knows where she learned?*

Dutchman's had two dressing rooms, and if any smoke leaked from the rhythm section's down the hall to Van Horn's, Marisol would flip—pound the door and scream about professionalism, young musicians' ignorant, selfish, funky ways, the fact that Dutchman's would lose their license and fire the band if anybody in the club smelled weedsmoke. Which was bullshit, according to Sonny. He'd smoked hash with the owners in their office once.

The first time Sonny brought him through that red door,

Latif had feared he'd find himself grill to grill with Albert. But it didn't work like that; if Van Horn wasn't in the audience between sets, sipping a lightmixed Campari-and-soda and visiting with fans, he was behind closed doors with Marisol. She seldom left the dressing room even during sets, convinced somebody would break in and steal from Albert. *It's still nineteen seventy-four to her,* Sonny explained. *She doesn't look at me and see Sonny Burma, honorable motherfucker. She sees Pete Crocker or Anderson Hainey or some other dirtbag musician who'd steal out her purse in a second to cop dope. Shit, Albert himself was nothing nice back in the day, and he and Murray and those guys dogged Marisol hard when she first started managing. They'd have her bring the drums down on the subway—make three trips for Murray's drums—and then go back up to the Bronx and bring Trey Valenzuela's bass down. She did it cause she loved Albert; same reason she does everything. I can't hate on her, though; she saved his life.*

And now she ran the show. Albert would drop by the band's dressing room ten minutes before the hit with a bottle of Merlot to run down set lists and bullshit briefly with the fellas, but for the most part if you wanted to hang with the man you had to come to him—and go through her. Murray Higgins, Albert's old friend and contemporary, moved freely between dressing rooms. Sonny and Amir and everybody else had to endure petty ungrammatical assaults on their manhood and musicianship from a woman who'd never played a note in her life. It was a roadblock cats lost patience with. They settled instead for Albert's company during designated hang times: airports, rehearsals, nights when Marisol stayed home and Albert was a font of jokes, wisdom, and stories, not caring who partook of what and even threatening to one day dig out, spark up and pass around an heirloom joint Dizzy Gillespie had given him.

Tonight, though, the leader and the elder statesman of the rhythm section were both down the hall, entertaining each other by cannonballing over and over into the river of history which rushed beneath the stone bridge of their friendship. Marisol listened, laughed, played amen corner. She loved Murray because he was the only drummer on the planet who could do what Albert needed; she felt, watching them together in the dressing room, the way the world felt watching them together on the stage.

Trey Valenzuela, the Albert Van Horn Quartet's original bass player, had died twenty-three years ago today, and that was why Sonny dared smoke reefer in the dressing room. He knew from past experience that Albert and Higgins would keep to themselves tonight, toasting their bandmate. Albert would take Trey's portrait from Dutchman's wall and hold it while he commemorated his friend to the audience. They'd play Trey's tunes, all four of them, and that would be the first set. A long burning Latin suite Albert had composed for Valenzuela, *Desayuno Domingo*, would fill the second. Albert and Higgins would play their asses off in tribute, and Amir would do some of Trey's trademark things and have the old men glowing with appreciation.

There were thirty minutes to showtime and the weed was almost gone. Amir unzipped his bass bag, started warming up. *I went to college on an art scholarship*, he told Latif, high and suddenly loquacious *so when I started playing bass, I memorized the hand positions, watched myself play and said* Okay, if I make this kind of triangle with my fingers on the strings, I get this kind of sound. If I spread the triangle like this, I get this kind of sound. *I don't watch my hands anymore, but I'm still thinking geometrically.*

Sonny Burma plucked the jointbutt from his lips fast, dropped it to the floor, and called a new tune. He'd heard this all before. *Ah, you are jazz musician?* he asked Amir in an Eastern European accent, cuing him to a routine they'd honed in the two years since Amir had joined the band. *I love American jazz musi-*

cian. You like Lee Konitz? Here, I show you picture. Is me with friend of me and Lee Konitz, nineteen sixty-three.

Where you are playing? Amir responded in the same accent. *Ah, yes, is my town. Very good for jazz. I maybe will come. If I don't go fishing, I come. Here is picture! This me with halibut, nineteen forty-one. You know halibut? Is important fish of my country.*

You know Gregor Zileski? asked Sonny. *Is best schlugenhorn player in all of Blutdendorf. I have picture. Here is Gregor Zileski with important halibut, nineteen seventy-one.*

On airplane, I teach you traditional song of my homeland, for play on schlugenhorn and soosenfracht. You know Benny Goodman?

Where you are from? New York? I have friend there. Jim. You know Jim? I never been New York. I always say I like to go. Maybe now that I know you, I come. You, me, Jim, we go for drink. And halibut.

I have daughter! Maybe you like meet. Here is picture. Ignore rash on mouth. She very good cook halibut with smurgenfrugen sauce. You have this sauce? No? You must try. Is best sauce of my country.

How long you stay here? Only one day? Why you not stay longer?

Amir collapsed in laughter. *Because, motherfucker, if I stay longer I'll kill you.* He turned to Latif. *I swear, man, every airport.*

Shoot, said Sonny *half the time the club's no better. I swear, if we ever play to a welldressed, mostly black room it'll be such a fucking shock I'll lose my mind.*

Well, you're safe tonight, Latif said. *The white guy at the first table's wearing a V-neck sweater backwards.*

Any chicks out there? asked Sonny.

Latif leaned back and laced his hands behind his head. *Just the one I brought,* he smirked.

Amir shook his head. *Mona, Mona, Mona. Robbing the goddamn cradle. Shit, I was in Baghdad when you was in your dad's bag. Whatchu got for her, youngster?*

Hey, said Latif. *I might have been born yesterday, but I stayed up all night.*

With her? I bet you did, said Sonny. *I just bet you did.*

I know I did, Amir said.

Me too, Sonny agreed.

Fuck y'all. Y'all can't even lie.

Who's lying? asked Sonny. *Welcome to the Mona Club. She's fucked damn near every nigger in here.*

Yeah, right, Latif said, snatching a cigarette from the pack inside Sonny's suitjacket pocket with fake angry flair. *Matter fact, she did mention something. She said outta everybody she's fucked, y'all two were the worst.*

I know I wasn't worse than Larry Calvin, said Amir.

Damn, Larry Lo-Cal tapped it? I feel gross now. Better see a doctor, Teef.

Nah, on the real though, said Amir. *She did date a trombone player who used to hang in here. Cat named Smiley. Real bloody knuckles type of motherfucker.*

As in he hit her?

As in knuckles dragging on the floor, kid. Dude was like the missing link.

Sonny put a foot up on his chair and leaned an elbow on his knee. *He was talking mad shit when they broke up. Told everybody who'd listen how crazy Mona was.*

Amir cackled. *You wanna know why? She threw that fool the fuck out her apartment half-naked, yo. He came down to Ada's holding his pants in one hand and half his trombone in the other. I bout laughed my ass off. Then we hear this crash, and the other half of Smiley's bone is lying in the street. He never did tell me what happened, just made me promise not to let it get out. So you see what my word's worth.*

Whoo. Sonny shook his head. *Better watch yourself, Teef.*

How long ago was this? Latif asked.

Amir squinted at the ceiling. *Bout two years ago. You think she's changed?*

She seems to think so.

Ada does too, Amir agreed. Giving *is the word she used. Mona's gotten more giving.*

Shoot, said Sonny *if she's giving, I'm taking.*

Alright, alright, groaned Latif. *I'm going to go buy my girl a drink. Have a good set. I hope y'all both break every string.*

He swung the door shut on their laughter and walked back to the bar. Mona sat with Ada at a back table and as Teef strode toward them lightfooted none other than Larry Calvin, erstwhile tenorman, addict, and pimp, bent over their table candlepiece to light his cigarette. Lo-Cal lingered, one jeweled hand on the back of each chair, leaned in between them and cracked some joke that made Mona and Ada laugh and slide each other sideways eyes.

Every cat in here had probably tried to rap to Mona, Latif thought, watching. Motherfuckers posted up on the musicians' wall were nothing if not slick, nothing if not pussyhounds who zoned in on the scent and chased it at a charming trot which accelerated to an ugly galloping insistence as the night wore down. He'd seen dudes cajole and intimidate their ways into some skins, seen women pull their coats on looking like they'd lost debates and were thus resigned to forfeiting their bodies. If you were persistent enough to never give up and smooth enough to make your interests seem gentle and complimentary until the cloudy point of no return—that moment when a woman might begin to feel she'd justified your expectations by drinking with you so long, absorbing all your come-ons—then you could take one of these stranger-to-the-game-or-were-they white women home a lot of nights.

Latif slid into an extra chair and kissed Mona and Ada hello. Mona was rocking a green silk shirt and her eyes looked practically fluorescent in contrast. He watched them flash and had no problem seeing Mona, wronged, whyle out and wreck a mother-fucker's livelihood and prized possession. She ever fucks with my horn, he thought mildly, I'll kill her. For perhaps the fifth time in the minute since Amir had told the story, Latif wondered what Smiley and his trombone had done to her.

Latif waved a raised finger and the waitress turned to fetch a vodka tonic.

How's business? Mona asked.

Steady, he replied. As if to prove it, the pager Say Brother had given him buzzed against Latif's hip, flashing an address. *Shit.* He read the message. *Listen*, he said, feeling smarmy *I've got to take a little walk.* Mona nodded placidly into her drink. *Wanna come?*

She looked up. *Is it okay?*

Sure. It's not far. We'll only miss one tune.

Alright then. She grabbed her purse.

Afternoon rain made the night air crisp. They walked in silence for a few blocks, until they'd left the loud bright center of the West Village, dotted with yellow and red pizzeria awnings. Latif acted out the music they stepped through when they passed by the open doors of bars: Belted two lines of "Break On Through" and did his best sultry-sloshed Jim Morrison impression, then became himself again as the song faded. It turned into a game; he and Mona whipped imaginary tresses back and forth, thwanging air guitars with rockstar abandon to some eighties crap metal blaring in some seamy dive, nodded tortured screwfaces in time to the gutbucket blues filling Chicago Joe's Tavern, and shimmied like teenyboppers to some unidentified generic pop whining from mounted speakers high on the walls of a cafe.

On Ninth Street they turned west and strolled a quiet brownstone block sheathed by a canopy of trees. *This is so pretty*, Mona said, hushtoned. *I'd love to live down here.* She took his hand.

There's a block like this near my office. I eat lunch there every day it's warm. I sit on a stoop, and you know what I do? I smile and say hello to everyone who passes. Everyone. And I get at least a smile back from almost everybody.

Latif smiled. *Probably makes people's day.* He wondered why she chose to perform her random acts of kindness down here instead of in her neighborhood. *A few weeks ago,* he said, *I was going to the music store to buy new reeds. I get off the train and it starts pouring. I stop at the ATM and the guard, this older black lady, asks me how to spell* umbrella. *She's making a sign. I tell her, and then I say,* As in I forgot my umbrella, I'm gonna get soaked without my umbrella, *just joking around. She says to me* where are you going? *I tell her a few blocks south to the music shop, and she says* Here, take mine. Just bring it back. *Not so spectacular, right, but it was. I said* Thank you, *and I took it. And I was just happy. Brought her back a hot chocolate, made her happy.*

Mona's smile sparkled through the dark. *That's so nice.*

They turned the corner, found the building, and walked into a white marble lobby. A doorman announced Latif over the phone and they took the elevator up to 9D. A full-figured lady in a cafe-con-leche-colored dress just lighter than her skin was waiting for them with the door open. *You must be Latif.* She smiled, grandmotherly, with beautiful white teeth. She put a hand on Mona's forearm. *You I wasn't expecting. But I love your blouse.* Her voice was rich, melodious, a large ripe blackberry. She ushered them in gracefully, light on her feet: She was a singer, Latif thought. No question.

I hear you play tenor. She winked, sweeping ahead of them into a spacious livingroom of beige leather couches and mocha carpeting. She cast hazel eyes at Mona, winked again. *Is he gooood?*

I hope to find out myself, Mona smiled back, charmed.

Latif stood with his hands clasped behind him, looking

around on best behavior. A framed advertisement poster caught his eye. *Is this you?* he inquired, pointing.

Years ago, dear. She gazed lovingly at it.

Odessa Childs with the Lester Young Big Band. Latif turned to her, excitement in his eyes. *This was one of my teacher's favorite records. It's gorgeous. You sound like, like . . .*

She waved her hand at him, pleased. *You're a sweetheart to say so. If you can, come up to Smoke next week.* A bashful downcast smile: *I don't sound like I did then, but . . .* Odessa looked up and spun lightly, abruptly, toward the kitchen, separated from the living room by a formica bar. *Well, I don't want to hold you beautiful young people up. Let me pay you and send you on your way.*

She opened a drawer and handed Latif a hundred dollar bill. He gave her a bag of dope. She looked at it grimly, then smiled at him. *Give Say Brother my best.*

Will do.

Hope to see you all again.

Good night.

He stole another glance at the poster. The strange feeling that Wess had somehow failed him rushed through Latif's body and vanished. He smiled back at her.

Good night.

Latif scooped up a flat chunk of packed sand and started to bore a slow hole through it with his thumb and middle finger. The key was to keep the motion gradual and circular, so the brittle chunk did not collapse. The beach was cool between his wiggling toes now; the sun had disappeared beneath the water in a swirl of pink and orange gauze. The air's contaminants added texture to the sunset, Mona claimed, actually made it more beautiful. Latif smiled when she said it, at the New York attitude embodied in the statement, civic pride even in pollution. He asked her if the smog was what made her beautiful too, and she laughed and stuck out her tongue at him.

Mona had two laughs. The one she used at parties trilled light from her palate; her eyes lit momentarily on whoever was funny and then she glided down and landed in a tightlipped smile. The other laugh was real, unguarded, Mona at her goofiest, a raucous belt-out that sometimes crested in a little snort. The first time he had heard it, in his bedroom as they sat up smoking and joking one night, Latif felt retroactively cheated for every time he'd heard the first one, became this new laugh's jealous suitor. He sought any reassurance that he wasn't alone in watching his defenses fall. Not fall; the walls still stood, but Mona was walking through them like a cartoon bully, leaving Mona-shaped holes in her wake. Latif's mind miosed into two camps as her footsteps rumbled closer; exhilaration and fear eyed each other, wary. Pimpery turned its back on both of them and mumbled into its fur coat, angry that Latif had not yet understood and mastered Mona.

He wished it wasn't whispering so close to his ear, but Latif couldn't find the strength to shoo it. In life's other realms he surrounded himself only with people who knew more, who were badder than he was, people from whom he could learn. Why then wouldn't this impulse to dominate shut the fuck up and leave him alone? Perhaps it was some mechanism of defense Latif's psyche had generated, a rope to tie him to the ground and prevent him from soaring off in weightless adoration. But Latif didn't want to be protected from himself, from Mona. Part of him, at least, wanted the two of them to protect each other from the world. In the past few weeks he'd begun thinking of himself and Mona as a unit in quick fantastic flashes, warm moments of holistic satisfaction when all doubt seemed to vanish like the sun behind the dirty glimmering Atlantic.

He was caught up in such a flash now as he and Mona sat on Reese Beach, capping a laidback day of playing hooky from work and the woodshed with a twilight picnic of white wine and boardwalk vendor hot dogs. Latif crossed his legs, leaned back onto his elbows, slid his hand beneath Mona's shirt and brushed away the sand specks sticking to her back. He loved the privilege of touching her casually and found excuses to do so in public if they were in a white or wellmixed neighborhood. In Harlem USA, Latif kept his hands mostly to himself. Mona hadn't brought it up yet.

I think you're supposed to have a red wine with hot dogs, he said.

That depends on what they're made of, Mona replied *which is something I'd rather not think about*. She arched her back and Latif took the cue, lifted his hand to her shoulders and pushed his thumb against a pressure point. Mona said *Ow*, which Latif knew didn't mean stop. Tradeoff massage—back, neck, shoulders, and especially hands and feet—was a cornerstone of their relationship.

Mona looked around and sighed contentment through her nose. *Sometimes I think the best thing about living in the city is getting out of it*, she said, and stood. *I'm going to test the water. Wanna come?*

So soon after eating? My mother would be scandalized. He raised his arms to her and Mona pulled him to his feet. *I'll watch you*, he said. Mona kissed him quick and ran with arms down and wrists up, taking small skipsteps and disappearing down the steep side of a sand dune only to reemerge a second later at the ocean's edge and spin and wave, holding her hair back in a ponytail. The gesture melted him, and for an instant everything seemed easy and eternal and Latif pictured them old together. Where this sudden warmth came from he didn't know, couldn't predict. He wondered if Mona felt it too, and winced imagining she didn't.

Too cold, said Mona, flopping back onto their blanket. They sipped the wine from paper cups and Latif faded reluctantly back into reality. *What's wrong?* Mona asked, turning on her side to look at him. *You seem a little dazed.*

Do I? He caught her eyes and held them tight, reflecting on the countless times he'd faked a look like this. He actually felt, now, the laserbeam intensity the look had been designed to mimic—or did he, if he had enough spare brain to think so? Latif wondered if this was a case of growing into what you long pretend to be, an example of how honesty can creep into that which starts as showmanship.

Perhaps he was wrong not to abandon old vocabulary in describing new phenomena, Latif thought, and then remembered something Wess had told him about the importance of standards to the music: *We keep on coming back to them because when we play them we transform them, and at the same time they keep us rooted in the past. Every art has them; painting's got the still life and the nude, and we've got "Caravan" and "Satin Doll."*

Absolutely nothing is wrong, Latif told Mona. *Not a single solitary thing.* They stared long at each other and slowly they began to smile. Those aren't sharks in her eyes, Latif thought, delighted. Those are dolphins. The smiles grew to grins, and they stared and grinned in the waning twilight until it was too dark to see, but still they didn't move. Latif began to wonder what could possibly break it up, enjoying the game but halfway wishing for an errant tennis ball to splash into the sand between them and give both an excuse to dart their eyes. But Mona ended it: *Come on, I got work in the morning.* They rose and scooped their stuff into her beachbag.

When he stepped off the sand onto the weatherbeaten wood, Latif was back in his own skin. They were one of perhaps a hundred couples walking arm in arm or hand in hand along the boardwalk, and Latif found himself staring at each pair they passed, trying to determine from their gaits and faces whether they were happy, what they talked about, who came first when they made love. People walking by themselves and in groups were outnumbered here; they tramped apologetically around the couples, awkward in their numbers.

A gaggle of white adolescents murmured together just ahead of them. They snickered quietly and the girls giggled as a white guy and his black girlfriend passed by holding hands. Latif watched the couple. Each stared straight ahead. The man's mouth curled with angry knowing and he looked as if he might turn around and lunge for the closest of the boys and rip his throat out. He's said what they're saying, thought Latif. The woman's face was placid, revealed nothing.

Did you see that? Latif asked Mona softly. She nodded and tightened the loop of their arms. *I thought he was gonna go back.* He twisted to glance at the receding couple.

She would never let him, said Mona quietly, as if she knew what the woman was thinking, and they walked on. She was right, Latif thought.

I don't want them staring like that at us, he said.

Let them stare. She moved her fingernails against his arm. *I don't give a shit.*

I do.

Everybody else is staring at us anyway, said Mona. *Hadn't you noticed?*

Latif frowned. He'd been enjoying himself so much with Mona that he had forgotten what they were.

You know what else I noticed? Mona asked. *I do it too. I don't mean anything by it but I do. We're just more interesting to look at than other couples.*

She eyecorner checked him, wondering if she'd spoken something wrong. They were partway through construction of a hothouse in which the relationship could grow strong enough to weather storms, and thus views were teased out cautiously, with a perfect eye toward understanding and agreement.

Latif said *Maybe so.* Mona seemed not to mind the stares. Perhaps she liked people to see him with her, or maybe she was simply used to the attention; eyes followed a beautiful woman everywhere. Eyes pretended not to see her and watched her on the sly, the same way eyes followed him, yet altogether different. Maybe knowing what men were thinking was like knowing what white people were thinking: a survival skill that made you want to kill yourself.

The day had tuned them to the same pitch, and that night Latif and Mona lay in bed and traded snippets of their pasts: Latif's father for Mona's mother, fire-escape spiderwebs for worn security blanket edges, half-forgotten dreams for misbegotten eavesdroppings. They trickled slowly into each other, word by word and story for story, and Latif found himself remembering things which fit he knew not where into the jigsaw puzzle of his mind but which came back when he spoke of them and asserted the importance of their having happened. He didn't know why he thought of them or what made him tell Mona. The memories were raw and grainy; they were not the kind that became glossy and took on storyform from constant recollection.

He remembered the first fight he'd seen in full, from taunts to blood. He and Shane had watched together from his window, hours after Leda had told them go to bed. It was summer and the older crew was barbecuing on the corner, lounging in their fathers' lawnchairs with a cooler full of brew. A dude in a black jeep pumping EPMD's "You Gots to Chill" pulled up across the street to pick up Vanessa, the sixteen-year-old neighborhood heartbreaker, and from the minute the cat parked his ride the whole block watched his every move. They didn't like the idea of Vanessa dating a stranger and they especially didn't like to see some punk disappearing with the princess of the block as they sat helpless on the corner like their fathers. Vanessa and the dude drove off to catcalls and wide-armed threats, and when they returned after some hours it was late enough for everybody to be drunk and bored and sick of fucking with each other.

Shane woke Latif and they hunched by the window and watched the crew surround the car and try to coax the cat onto the street. Vanessa sat in the frontseat, crying and pleading with her man not to get out; Latif could read her lips across the block. She grabbed his rigid arm, his fist still wrapped around the steering wheel, and Latif silently hoped that he would do what was intelligent and drive away. *Stay in the car*, Latif whispered, sweating for this cat now, but part of him thirsted to watch what would happen if he didn't. Shane, sitting beside Latif, was philosophical: *Man, if this nigga dumb enough to get out he deserves to get his ass beat.*

I always wondered what made him do it, Latif told Mona as she kneaded his palm, pinching the skin between his fingers so hard that he twitched. Mona gave, liked, and expected harder massages than he. *Eight cats, drunk, holding bottles, won't let him leave, on some* We just wanna talk *shit. And he's on their block, with their girl, pushing a whip no one in the neighborhood can pay even the insurance on.* Latif paused self-consciously, until the curiosity in Mona's fingers pushed him on. *After it was over, I snuck out and helped Vanessa get the guy inside. He was a mess. They stomped the shit out of him, ripped the soft top off his Jeep. Shane tried to stop me, said if anybody saw me helping this guy I was gonna have all sorts of problems. But I didn't feel right just sitting in my window, watching Vanessa try to get him up.*

So we haul him in, and as I'm walking back home, Vanessa says Wait! *runs outside and grabs a paper bag out of the Jeep and gives it to me.* Latif chuckled. *I went home and opened it. Half a cheeseburger. Her doggie bag. Me and Shane looked at each other like,* What?

There was a patch of thinking silence. Latif inhaled the warm, intimate quiet and thought of what Wess said about white space and the haze around a candle's flame: *Whatever you don't play, you play around.* Mona turned and lay on her stomach and Latif traced a hand lightly along the naked curve of her back. She smelled of lavender; he smelled of her. Latif watched the dance of his dark fingertips on Mona's skin, entranced, and Mona shut her eyes and pulled up artifacts heavy with sadness—artifacts which although huge seemed buried shallow. Latif listened intently, feeling guilty that she was sharing more with him than he was with her. He should at least, he thought, try to absorb her life as hungrily as she did his.

My father was so sad when Mom died that he barely left bed for a month, said Mona, distant with memory. *We didn't know what to do. Finally, my older sister Anna put on one of Mom's dresses, stood next to his bed and said* Bill, get up. The girls need you. *And he got up.* Latif kept quiet, rubbing Mona's back with slow open-palmed circles, wondering if she wanted him to speak and hoping he didn't have to because all he could think to say was *Damn, that's some weird shit.*

But Mona continued on her own. *I guess the simplest way to say it is that Anna started acting more and more like Mom—like a mother to me and a wife to Dad. I don't mean they started fucking, but they might as well have. It was sick. I felt totally abandoned, confused and embarrassed and fucked up. When I was twelve I started planning to get out of there, and the older I got, the worse they treated me. It made them feel more normal, I think. I just went into my shell: barely spoke, did my own thing. Cried. Moved out when I was seventeen, got a job and went to night school.* She craned her neck to look back at Latif. *Anna's thirty-four now. She still lives with him.*

Dig it, Latif said idiotically. It was one of those super-hip old school musician things Murray Higgins said, and he'd been making a concerted effort to draft it into his vocabulary. He had no idea why it popped out now. Mona looked at him oddly and Latif felt he had to reciprocate the story best he could. He seldom talked about his father, and when he did he always said the same things, told anecdotes he'd repeated enough to be unmoved by, became one of those lames who played the same solo every time instead of trusting themselves to the moment.

When my father left, all I remember is that we started going to church all the time, he said. *Every night. My mother said* Lord help your father, son. *But I was like* Fuck that. *I knew he'd hurt her too much to be praying for his ass. I'd sit there and think of ways to torture him instead— stuff from movies and my book of Greek myths, like Prometheus getting his liver torn out by eagles every day—until I was sure Jesus was gonna come down off that cross and smoke my ass. Eventually, though, I decided God would look the other way if I ever ran into the cat.*

Latif reached across Mona and took the last cigarette from the nightstand. He lay on his back and crossed his hands behind his head. Mona threw her leg over his leg and wrapped her arm around his waist. Latif held the cigarette to her lips, then to his own. He didn't feel a thing but he hoped he looked pensive.

I didn't miss him at all, Latif said. *There was barely anything to miss.* His father was a ghost: a scratchy face hunched over the breakfast table silent, a bathrobed figure who made occasional pancakes and was seldom seen even before he left. A pair of arms that retucked Latif into his bedding late at night, after his mother had put him properly to sleep. The whiskey and sandalwood smell of a raincoat in the closet. All Latif really remembered of his father was the sense of tension he brought with him, the staccato nervousness with which Leda moved when her husband was around. When he disappeared so did all reminders of him; there were no old pictures, no wristwatch left behind.

The only thing Leda kept was his name, or so Latif had thought until two years ago. Cleaning out the hall closet for his mother, he'd unearthed a cardboard box of LPs: Coltrane, Pharoah Sanders, Archie Shepp, Don Cherry, Van Horn, Sun Ra, Herbie Hancock's Mwandishi Band, Black Heat, Gil Scott-Heron, Cymande, The Last Poets, Freddie Hubbard, Eric Dolphy. He carted the collection, sixty-five albums in all, to his room and never told Leda. The song titles underlined in ballpoint were always the baddest tunes, and Latif listened and imagined his pops digging these records right as they came out, he and his boys passing a joint and picking their Afros and saying shit like *Man don't Trane just blow your mind?*

It was only a week later that an old neighbor, meeting Latif in the hallway, told him *Boy, you your daddy's spitting image.* Leda shook her head no when Latif risked upsetting her to ask if it was true, but he didn't believe her: started to wonder what his mother saw when she looked at her son.

Mona stubbed the cigarette and blew a final smoke ring. Latif reached up and poked his finger through it. *You don't like to talk about him, do you?*

What's there to say? That nigga left. I'm still here.

You could say how you feel.

He shrugged. *I could.* Latif sat up and Mona tumbled off him, annoyed that he never told her he was getting up, just displaced her like she was a cat. He walked across the room naked and picked up his horn. *You wanna hear something?*

Her eyes darted to the ceiling. *Isn't it a little late?*

Nah. He slid the strap over his head and clipped the horn to it, then wet and attached the reed. He'd never played naked before, and the bottom of the horn rubbed cold against his dick, exciting him a little. He decided to blow a little "Volunteer Slavery" for her. Rashaan Roland Kirk's moody soulful meditation was the underlined selection on the first album Latif had pulled from his inheritance. He'd taught himself to play it right away, entranced by the way Kirk wove a modern worksong out of baleful chants and horn lines, evoking generations of oppression physical and mental, enforced and self-inflicted.

Latif could imagine it sung in the cottonfields or the Cotton Club, and he had closed his eyes and mourned and marched and danced next to Rashaan, and just when he was zoning hard that brother flipped the script and "Volunteer Slavery" turned into "Hey, Jude" without you even noticing at first. Latif opened his eyes confused, wondering what had happened and what Kirk was trying to do: Indict pop culture or shake hands with the Fab Four. Rashaan was as proto-b-boy as Monk, dropping that Beatles shit in there and challenging you to figure out the meaning of the sample, whether homage, dis, or joke. Everything the blind three-simultaneous-horn-playing motherfucker did was crazy hip hop, from writing new lyrics to dead men's songs to pioneering unheard-of instruments, blowing notes on the manzello and the strich.

Latif unpressed the sax from his body and played the opening notes true to the record: *Oh vol-un-teer slaa-vry, has go-ot me on the run, has go-ot me on the run,* flicked eyes at Mona and turned the phrase around, chopping and switching intonations: *run on me, oh me run on run on.* The milky way starswirl of edginess blinked away and Latif's brain was a starless night, dark with confidence. He heard his own first sounds and knew that he was showing

Mona who he really was. Latif's skin twitched with sensitivity and he bounced sonar notes around the room, responding to everything without tearing the fine parchment of the tune: A fluttering wall shadow became a butterfly of sound which rose and shed its form and disappeared into a floating scarlet cloud. Latif felt both honest and bad as hell, close to himself and Mona, and the cloud grew full and heavy and Latif stood under it and closed his eyes and felt the raindrops on his scalp, hands, shoulders, soaking him in freedom. He played *slaa-vry* backward, *vry-slaa*, a chopped note then a long sweet one, all the time in the world, played it again sounding like *oh-yeaaah, oh-yeaaah*, which reminded him in turn of the bridge to a Joe Henderson tune.

He's not playing for me anymore, thought Mona when his eyes closed. Sometimes the same realization hit her midfuck: He's by himself; I'm just here too, and she felt lonely with him, abandoned in a sad familiar way, and hoped he would return and quickly lost patience with hope and yanked him back where he belonged—touched him, moved, or spoke.

She had no right to do any of those things now, Mona knew, nor did she want to. Watching him was beautiful even from the outside, made her feel many things at once: pride in him and in herself for knowing from jumpstreet that he was no bullshit motherfucker but a real musician, sheer joy at the fun he was having, pleasure at his sounds. A touch of melancholy, even minute jealousy, because she knew deep down that there was nothing she did so well or with so much passion.

Latif was wide open, breeze against his body cooling him as he swayed to what was jerking out his horn bell. With every note the path before him branched in five and six directions, and Latif walked with chessmaster precognition, making choices that would pay off ten moves down the line. Outside a fire truck went by, siren whining, and Latif reached out and stabbed the sound like a spearfisherman, threw it wriggling on the table, chopped it up—internalized the interruption by breaking his own phrases with the sharp wail every few notes. Mona clapped her hands, delighted, and laughter rose up from the street.

A handcupped shout from down there: *"St. Thomas"!* Teef smiled around his reed and banged out the tune's head fast. *Aight!* came the response. *Encore!*

Come on, Latif grinned, *let's go down there.* He found a pair of pants, shrugged on a shirt and tossed Mona another. She buttoned it while shuffling down the stairs behind him.

Spliff was standing on the stoop with two of his boys. *Ahh*, he said, dapping Latif with a wideswinging hand *the man, the man.* He introduced Latif and Mona to his boys Donald and Equality, and everybody traded handshakes and greetings, Latif acknowledging the compliments on his playing with a headnodding *Good lookin out.*

So whassup man? He sidled up to Spliff. *I still ain heard you rhyme.*

Some cats took twenty minutes to prod into performing, but Spliff wasn't one of them. He grinned and dipped a shoulder at the ground. *Well, if I can get a beat from my man here*, tapping Donald's shoulder, *and a little suhmn suhmn from my other man here on the sax, I might be able to kick a lil bit.*

Donald raised his eyebrows at Latif, who readied his horn and told him *Set it off.* The cat amplified himself, both hands arched to form a tunnel between his mouth and the world, and started to beatbox. His cheeks emptied of air as he pushed sharp kickdrums out from his throat, and he refilled them with percussive inhalations, the in-breath marking time like a hi-hat. He clicked his tongue against one side of his mouth like a snare drum, and filled the rest of the measure with tone-drops, verbal cutting, whitespace, occasional double kicks or snares. Hip hop drumbeats had a dynamics all their own, Latif thought. Every hip hopper who'd ever banged a beat onto a lunchroom table or walked down the street making music with his mouth understood them; it was just the overstudied so-called musicians coming at hip hop from outside who couldn't make it swing, played too fast or too thick, left the rapper no space.

Mona, Latif, Spliff, Donald, and Equality tightened instinctually into a cipher circle, heads bobbing synchronized. Latif knew his job was to get in where he fit in, so he played low and rhythmic: fit the underwhelming head to Coltrane's "Syeeda's Song Flute," a line that was almost metronomical, over Donald's crackling mouthsnare.

Donald threw down an old-school scratch pattern, an obvious cue, and Spliff came in on time, voice clear and strident. Latif could tell the verse was written, not freestyled, by both its complexity and the way Spliff looked while spitting it, catching Latif's eyes like a showman rather than a seeker. Latif had been hoping to hear some freestyle shit, always enjoyed comparing rappers' improvisational techniques with his own, but no big deal. A lotta cats wanted to kick written shit first to impress you, and hell, it was working. Latif had expected some generic serve-fiends-to-survive rhymes, considering Spliff's occupation, but instead his neighbor hit him with

Manchild in the promised land/I'm sitting in with the hottest band/my name known, plus I got it sewn like a monogram/in this modern land, I search the world's womb like a sonogram—Donald, listening, suspended the beat and kicked a medical *beep beep* behind the line—*hold a torch for an honest man/til it makes me wanna holla man*—Latif played the melody of the Marvin Gaye song Spliff was referencing, a little late but still nice—*but like Solomon, a scholar can/take a solemn stand, like a column and/I'm modellin', myself on Assata and/Bambaattaa, Flannery O'Connor and my grandfather/*—Damn, thought Mona, did he just say Flannery O'Connor?—*a rare honor, cats who dare bother/on my bookshelf martyrs find rare harbor/I tune out the world and at they words stare harder . . .*

His verse was over but Spliff was getting heated, so he kept going. *Uh, yeah, on some freestyle shit/my name is Spliff, got my man Donald on the beatbox/I'm too hot, rhyme even when the beat drops*—Donald and Latif, obedient, cut out, and Spliff dropped money lines in the clipped silence, as the rules of dopeness dictated he had to—*I'm hip hop like Willie Shak, with the milli mac/peelin Phillies back/battle any cat for they skelly cap/if they belly fat slash bellies/adventure with steel like Flash and Melle*—Donald kicked two bars of the Furious Five song Spliff was referencing, and Equality broke into laughing applause; Latif responded with the chorus of the group's megahit "The Message" and the cat nearly lost his mind—*get open like young minds before they lock shut/hip hop makes Dom from rotgut/gourmet from potluck/peace to all my peoples locked up/and all the rappers who got bucked/leavin legacies of young seeds and hot cuts*—Spliff's whole vibe was different when he freestyled: face taut, hands chopping and molding the air, fingers splayed—*in due time, police state gon turn rap to moonshine/replace these one-ninety-proof rhymes with weak theses/when the prohibition hits, sip my words in speakeasies/and drink up, everything the kid think up*—

Spliff inhaled wrong, gasped and coughed it out his system and came back in—*yo, I cough but I play it off/motherfuckers lost, who the boss? they shit is soft/I paid the cost like B.B. King, my shit swing/like Ellington/I stay* Suite in the Far East/*rockin* Black, Brown, and Beige/*when I step on the stage*—Latif was struggling to keep up with the tunes Spliff was dropping, both of them grinning as he did so, and Spliff flowed on, ripped for a good five minutes before calling it quits and giving his man on the verbal percussion a much-needed break.

That was great, Latif told Mona, flopping onto his bed when they finally came back upstairs, many rhymes and several solo saxophone spotlights later. *I haven't had that much fun in months.*

Gets a little claustrophobic in the woodshed, huh?

Only with the door open.

They were quiet and so was the block; minutes passed and soon Mona was lightdozing, but Latif couldn't come down so fast from the session and so he lay thinking.

I had this dream once that I still think about a lot, he confided in the stillness, and Mona jarred alert. *Anytime I'm somewhere with a free minute and a pen and pad I try to doodle it, which is how I learned that I'm a shitty artist.* Mona turned onto her side and listened to Latif describe a saxophone player composed entirely of bubbles, as if made of water. Snakes slithered from his horn, hissing, frozen in midair, and the musician's leg was chained to a stake in the ground. Atop the stake rested a sign, an advertisement reading *Jazz Tonite* in fancy menu–style writing. *I don't think the sign was in the dream, though. I think I added that myself.*

Mona sat up. She could go from half-conscious to intrigued in four seconds. *So what is he chained to, do you think?*

Maybe to what he thinks he has to play, the limits he imposes on himself.

What about a slave to the music, like that old saying goes?

I hate that saying. That's some old black-musician-as-juju-priest shit.

Mona nodded solemnly. *I heard Amir say once that Albert's horn was like a conduit for the spirits of his elders*, she recalled, jiggling her index finger. *Which is a perfectly beautiful statement, but in the hands of some ofay reporter I can see it becoming something very different indeed.*

Hold on. Did you just say ofay?

Mona grinned. *Yeah, ofay. What?*

Latif threw back his head and laughed.

By the time they went to sleep the sun was creeping up over the bottom ridge of Latif's window, squeezing in around the loose slats of his broken paper shades. The light crawled as far as his feet, hanging over the edge of the bed. Usually Latif slept only on his stomach, arms by his sides, lest his gangled limbs freeze on him and he awake to find them uncontrollable, asleep, empty of blood. Sometimes he had to pick up one arm with the other like some sewn-together horror movie monster and move it back down below his head, feeling the strange weight of the limb like it wasn't his own.

But Mona spooned against him, curled inside his outstretched bicep, and Latif forced himself to drift to sleep without adjusting. He wanted Mona to oversleep; she was supposed to be at work downtown at nine and he hoped to spend the day with her instead. He'd been glancing furtively at his watch all night, thinking as the small hand crept past three and four that Mona might be exhausted enough to call in sick and stay in bed and let him take her to a long, late breakfast, mushroom omelettes and lots of coffee. It would be the second day in a row she would be missing work, and the second day he'd miss his time to practice. That's not good, Latif thought, dozing off. I gotta watch that shit.

It was getting harder for Latif to find a comfortable spot at Dutchman's; anywhere he stood, he was paces from where he wanted to be and yet a universe away. He rose from the corner barseat wedged against the wall and cut precisely to his next designated spot, a landing midway down the staircase where he stood halfsmiling at the waitresses as they rushed down to the kitchen and back up. Five minutes later, restless, Latif loped over to the wall across from the bandstand, the musicians' haven. Then back to the bar, the other end now. He bounced his weight from one foot to the other, wishing the hip leathersoled Italian shoes Sonny had taken him to cop at a warehouse on Thirty-sixth Street—a wholesale spot plenty of cats would have killed to know about, run by a cool-ass Italian Jew who sold beautiful Ungaro and Valentino suits with mysterious pasts by appointment only for three bills apiece—weren't so uncomfortable.

I should be practicing right now, he thought, and raised a finger to request another drink. Say Bro had a tab, but Teef never had to use it. The bartenders comped him like a musician. It was an irony that slapped him in the face, but it was better than having to settle up with Say Bro at month's end. After sliding seventy percent of his gross to the bossman, Latif took home a bit more than the busboys and a lot less than the waitresses.

This gig was fucking with him like everything else, he thought: draining his energy and sloshing his entire life the same flat housepaint grey. Even his joy in listening to Albert was jealousy-stained and distracted; if one more fool approached him in the middle of a tenor solo like Latif didn't have shit else to do but turn around and serve, if one more palsy hey-buddy musician tried to game him for a little friendship cut-rate on his dope, shit was gonna get ugly.

The set was starting with a ballad, and Latif leaned back on the mahogany bartop and nodded a greeting at Larry Lo-Cal, wedged in next to him. Latif felt like he'd whiffed something nasty every time he saw the cat now, thinking of Amir and Sonny's riff about him fucking Mona, but he shook Larry's hand and then both focused on the stage. If there was anything redeeming about Lo-Cal, that was it. He copped between sets.

The entire band was shuteyed, as if lost in some communal dream. Sonny bent in reverence over the piano, Murray rocked tranquil as he brushed the drums, and Amir swayed at the hips, caressing plushtones from the warm brown bass. Albert stood with rigid marchingband posture and held his soprano sax gingerly between his fingertips. His eyes flitted open once or twice, as if checking whether he was still standing where he had been when he closed them—and as if he was surprised and slightly disappointed to discover that he was.

The song was called "Forlorn," and Latif had played his recording of it until the grooves were worn and filled with static, memorized the cracks and hisses until they were integral to the composition. The song began with a four note bassline mantra: *for-lorn for you, for-lorn for you.* Then Albert's soprano crept in, soft as air escaping a balloon. He was mournful, quivering, and introspective, trying to resign himself to living with the pain of heartbreak. Murray's gentle brushwork rippled through the song like wind stirring a placid lake; his current was crossed only by Sonny's raindrops plinking on the water's surface. The record was a gift from Wessel, his example of how a ballad should be played. *Remember that playing is like dancing or talking*, he said. *The faster you do it, the easier it is to bullshit. Nothing's as pretty or as pure as playing slow and true. That's how you force yourself to deal with real emotion.*

Latif hadn't dealt with shit today except his own frustration. When he'd stirred this morning at ten-thirty, squinting and sliding an arm up underneath the pillow, Mona was still asleep beside him and Latif was instantly annoyed that she was there. All he wanted to do was play his horn, refuel with the residue of last night's session, and force himself to get to work. The less he played, the less he played—and Latif was picking up his tenor later every morning.

He'd stared at her, distant from six inches away, and wondered why he couldn't bring himself to massage Mona awake and tell her that he needed this morning to practice. He knew what he would do instead: say nothing and wait for Mona to read his sourness, then fume when she didn't see it or wouldn't address it. Translating his thoughts into a language she could understand compromised Latif's integrity; instead, he flashed his artistic license and endured in sullen silence. He nurtured hidden antagonisms as if they were precious—as if grinding his teeth in secret anger at Mona's presence or Van Horn's freedom would energize him somehow. As if this was like the time in high school when the sheer desire to bust his hated English teacher's ass had turned Latif into a voracious, careful reader.

Mona folded her arm up underneath her chest and nuzzled the pillow to her cheek. Latif brushed a strand of hair behind her ear and thought about the fact that having breakfast with Mona would shave another hour off his day. He'd have to go to the store for real food, not just eat a few spoonfuls of chunky peanut butter out the jar and grab his horn. Perhaps Mona was just an excuse—maybe he was being a punk playground kid, the kind who talks shit when his boys are holding him back but doesn't swing a fist when they release him to do battle. Was Latif afraid to be alone with his horn? Angry at himself for even thinking it, he threw the covers back and walked across the room to his turntable. As the first notes of "Better Get Hit in Yo Soul" hit the air, Mona stirred. He watched her stretch, blink, rub her eyes, sit up. He said *Good morning, sunshine.*

She smiled sleepily and raised her arms above her head to crack her back. *What's this?* she asked.

Charles Mingus, he replied, and watched her listen. He'd done this before when he was feeling ornery: played a piece about which he felt passionately and examined Mona's face for signs of understanding, unsure what response would not annoy him.

Mona smiled at him and nodded with the music. *I've got to borrow this sometime,* she said.

You always say that. Latif laughed.

Well, it's all great.

What's your favorite?

Mona saw sharpness darting beneath the placid surface of the question and knew she was being tested. It was a game she refused to play; she flunked them all deliberately and watched him stew. She wished she didn't understand Latif so well; it made his behavior too easy to forgive.

I don't know enough to say. That was his point anyway, whether he knew it or not: that she wasn't fit to hold opinions on his music, only to celebrate it uncritically, the same way he wanted her to celebrate him. He wouldn't let her plead ignorance, though, Mona thought. He'd take it as a sign of feminine self-effacement, out-of-character as that might be, and try to build her up.

Sure you do. You hear me play, you go to Dutchman's all the time. You know more than most folks, that's no question.

What's your favorite? Mona parried, sure that Latif kept a personal top-forty chart in his head. She reflected briefly that men were obsessed with ranking things, list making, hierarchy, then stood up and walked past him as he began enumerating albums. *I'm making coffee,* she announced. *Want some?*

No thanks.

What should we do for breakfast? Mona asked with her back to him, pouring water in the coffeemaker. She knew he wanted to be alone; she just wanted him to say so. *Or do you have plans?*

I'm gonna be practicing all day, he said. *So yeah, I guess I do.*

See? she thought. How hard was that? *I'm glad you're working*, Mona said, returning from the kitchen alcove. Her naked breasts swayed as she walked. *You know I worry I'll distract you.*

He didn't believe her when she said such things. They were disclaimers. They shifted the burden of keeping space between them onto him and let Mona feel good when Latif didn't shoulder it and push her away.

Don't worry, he said. *Nothing can distract me from my horn.* He tried to imagine Albert saying something so ridiculous and couldn't.

Not even this? asked Mona, sitting on his lap. She kissed his neck and whispered *You should be practicing right now*.

It was a joke that turned serious as the heat of her body against his melted Latif's animosity and his resolve; he watched them drip into a puddle with a smirk of resignation, said *I might resent you for this down the line*, and bent to circle Mona's nipple with his tongue. He wondered what was more pathetic, that he couldn't resist her, or that Mona knew it and used sex to end arguments and rebalance their relationship when he was caustic.

It was another three hours before Mona left: sex, downtime, showers, hunger, shopping, breakfast. Latif took out his horn at two in the afternoon, stared at it until three-thirty, played like shit until five and retreated to his bed pissed that he had wasted the day, that the energy and inspiration he'd awakened with were gone, that the walls of his room had lost their resilience and instead of bouncing back at him, his tones slid sickly to the floor and lay there panting. And in a few hours he had to be at Dutchman's, watching other musicians work while he paced, watched, and hustled.

"Forlorn" was still swaying when Mona walked into the club and spotted Latif leaning limply with a shotglass in his hand, looking as morose as when she'd left him. He didn't move to greet her, only smiled and dumped the brown liquor into his mouth between his thumb and finger like an oyster. When Mona approached and asked him how his day had been, he crossed his finger to his lips, shushed her, and pointed calmly to the stage.

Perhaps he didn't mean it as such, but to Mona the gesture was one of total disrespect. It was the same thing her father had done any time she tried to talk to him while he was watching baseball on TV, and Mona hated it. *Daddy!* she would bound into the living room, *guess what*—only to be silenced for the sake of something more important. A baseball game, one of a hundred he watched every summer. A ballad, one of a hundred Latif heard The Quartet play every night and every week and every month. And Larry Calvin swigged his beer and smirked at her and looked at Latif out of the corner of his eye, and Mona knew exactly what that asshole was thinking: *He's got his bitch locked down.* With one gesture, Mona thought, Latif had managed to display his sanctimonious reverence for the music and make her feel completely fucking worthless.

They stood in silence, looking at the stage, and then Latif peeled Mona's sterncrossed arm off of her chest and took her hand. She did nothing, let him brush her fingers with his own and rub the curves of his nails along her palm. When she felt him look at her, Mona withdrew her hand and refolded her arms. The song ended and she turned to face Latif. *Don't you ever shush me again*, she said, and stalked off toward the bathrooms. She knew Larry Calvin was back there shaking his head, chuckling *Whoo boy*, and Latif was playing it off cool, deliberately staying where he was. Probably ordering another drink to make his point. He would apologize later, at the set break, after she'd had time to cool down, doubt her anger, wonder if she'd overreacted and become the old lone gunman Mona. He would work music into his apology as a disclaimer, say he'd been wrapped up in what was happening on-stage, shake his head and make some small sad reference to his own horn problems and say *The only time I'm not thinking about playing is when I'm with you.*

Don't bullshit me, Mona responded. *The only time you're not thinking about playing is when we're making love. If you just want to meet and fuck, then I can do that.* She scrutinized him, ready to jet if Teef's eyes lit up. *But I want to know you, Latif, and I want you to know me.*

Could there be room for her? Latif stretched and recoiled wildly, toward Mona and away. He wondered if she could make him stronger, if his feelings for her could amplify and clarify his feelings for the music, if they could multiply each other. Perhaps all his self-discipline had been misguided and his devotion to the music was preventing him from loving someone else, from feel-ing fully human.

I want to be known, he whispered.

Mona looked at him with soft eyes. *Yeah?*

And then Albert tapped Teef on the shoulder.

Dutchman's was half empty, the first set not scheduled to start until nine-thirty and the candlepieces on the tables still unlit. The trickledown of hustlers from uptown's shining faucets never accelerated to a steady flow before midnight, when the second set was swinging. Even The Quartet seldom made the scene much in advance of showtime except Murray Higgins, whose custom it was to hold down the bar from six o'clock on, sipping whiskey sours with the waiters and pettycash betting on whatever game came on the set, anything from tennis or basketball to hockey. Sometimes Amir Abdul drank with him, and drank faster than the drummer when he did, but more often the other players were nowhere to be seen until Van Horn's official backstage call at five to nine. Sonny usually woke up at four or five and had dinner-slash-breakfast in Brooklyn before heading to the club to undertake a stretch of work and play that seldom ended before daylight.

But not today. Burma had barely caught an hour's rest since standing up from Dutchman's old piano bench the night before, or had a chance to visit any of his favorite afterhours spots or lady friends. He'd been sitting in counsel with Latif, drinking first martinis, then beer, and finally, by midmorning, grapefruit juice with pancakes and home-fried potatoes at a diner down the block from Burma's brownstone, Latif marking off each overtired hour and returning to the same unanswerable question chorus all the while: *How long has he been watching me? How does he know if I'm frustrated? Is he gonna cut my head?*

Sonny was under strict orders not to tip Van Horn's hand, and he said nothing. What would Teef have gained anyway by knowing that the incognito softstep he'd developed to avoid attracting Albert's attention had been a complete failure, that although it was sleekly suited to his business and a welcome change after the splash and flash of The Say Brother Show, it hadn't worked a week?

Six days after Teef started work, Albert had summoned Sonny to his empty dressing room and closed the door, walked slowly to the low leather couch and eased himself down. Sonny stood, like a kid before the principal's desk, and watched Albert change from his street shoes into the shining pair he kept in drawstring felt bags and wore only on the bandstand. He wondered whether he was in trouble until Albert crossed his legs and offered the pianist a couch seat and poured him a glass of wine.

We used to go through New Orleans twice a year when I was with The Emperor's big band, Albert recounted, and Sonny was glad to be sitting. When Albert felt like talking you wanted to be comfortable and open-eared and emptybladdered, with some time in front of you. *Once*, Van Horn went on *Milford Montague, our trombonist from the Big Easy, took me with him to see Madame Dujeous, this old local fortuneteller he'd been knowing since the days of way back, growing up. They exchanged their greetings and Milford introduced me, and we all sat down over some sweet tea and she looked at me and said* Well? *and I said* Well? *and she said* Well, aren't you going to tell me my future? *I laughed and asked her wasn't that her job. And she looked at me and then at Milford and said* It may be my job but he can take it if he wants it. This boy has got an aura I wish you could see, Milly. It's like a suit of fire licking and sizzling and buzzing. You can hear a pin dropping on Saturn, can't you, Albert?

Everything for me is heightened up on stage, Sonny. You know what I mean. Burma nodded, wishing he did. *It's like I'm in a rocketship, blasting away from earth into the blackness, riding my instrument like it was that rocketship and holding on for life. But there's a powerful telescope on board too, and any time I want to I can look through it and see what's happening on earth, and focus on the smallest kind of detail and the littlest particular: what style of shirt the bartender is wearing or whether the Germans at the back table have had too many drinks.* Albert refilled Sonny's wineglass, from which the pianist had taken only a sip. *Usually I notice that kind of stuff by accident, if my concentration is failing, because like I tell you all, you should never play for anyone but us. I don't care what kind of fine-ass chick is throwing fuck faces at you from the front table or which old Harlem stridepiano legend just walked in the joint; the only people you can depend on to understand shit are your bandmates.*

But sometimes another energy comes into the picture anyway, like a wind blowing against the side of my rocketship, and that's somebody in the audience who's up inside my thing. Albert lifted his clasped hands off of his lap, uncrossed his legs and refolded them the other way. *I used to try and block that out, play past it, but that approach is wrong. That energy will still be there, and instead of converting it to usable fuel you wind up killing yourself to pretend you don't feel what you do. Better to acknowledge that energy and probe it, run your hands around it til you find a pressure point or pleasure spot.*

Albert smiled. *Now, having said all that, what can you tell me about your tall young friend out there? Because he's thumping up against this old hull of a rocketship quite fierce. And I dig it, Jack.*

What Sonny told him impressed Albert even more; that Teef was here to study in silence, that he didn't want his name spoken in Van Horn's direction, that he was deep in the shed. *That's a mark of maturity and what's more it's a mark of respect for the music, for himself and the music,* nodded Albert, and left it alone except for occasional inquiries about Latif, the kind you'd make after somebody's unknown family.

But things changed. It wasn't that Teef's energy had simply waned, Albert explained in agitation, that he'd numbed to the music as cats often did who got into the hustles even if the music and the music alone was what brought them downstairs to begin with. Once these new-jack movemakers realized that they were indeed playing for keeps, the band faded gradually like bed linens until they heard only a background ambience of sound, merging with the crowdnoise. That was fine with Albert; politicking hustlers and the player miscellany enriched the flavor of the vibe, souped up the room. They hung tough and made musicians' habitats their own in a symbiosis of mutual celebrity, celerity, and enterprise, and that was better than an audience of cats stroking their beards and concentrating on chord changes.

Occasionally I'll feel a hustler break through into the music, Albert had told Sonny just tonight, in another dressing room conference *see him look up in the middle of his business and feel us burning and stop, mouth the word* goddamn! *and catch a headnod something furious that might last til the solo ends, or maybe the song or even til the set break. And by the same nickel there are folks who come in simply to check out some tunes and then they start to look around and realize* something's going on in here, *and soon the foci of their fascination have become the interactions of a cast of welldressed characters whose smoothness and flamboyance, private language and eloquence of movement, make them almost musical in their own right. It's not very much music going on with most of them really, just rhythm, but rhythm will fool a lot of people who don't know.*

But none of that is our boy Teef, Sonny, Van Horn said firmly. *Most cats would catch an ego from a gig like his, but for him it's joyless. He's not becoming something. He's drifting away from what he needs to be and he knows it.*

And the only way he knows to drop anchor is to drop it right on me, make me his secret enemy. Your boy is poisoning the room just when I've gotten used to looking his way for nourishment. Burma was on his feet this time. The wineglass and the cigarette in his hands notwithstanding, he felt like an infantryman awaiting orders. Albert clearly had a battle plan in mind. *This is a dude I've never met,* Albert allowed *but I consider him a friend. And I'll be damned if I'm gonna dodge an unrequited goddamn laser beam of illness every night.*

If Teef hadn't been bothering him so much, Albert told Sonny afterward—laughing himself at Higgins' jokes about the old vaudevillian ringmaster spirit guiding him—Albert never would have done what he had. And even so it was nothing he had ever done before. He walked off the bandstand and stepped up to Latif out of the clear blue without introduction: *You got some stuff you need to work out, brother, and we gonna help you work it out cause I can't have you staring at me like that anymore. I want you down here tomorrow night at nine o'clock sharp all tuned up, and we're gonna deal with these frustrations you feeling right now, alright?*

I can only imagine what this cat thought, Albert chuckled, tipping the last of the Merlot into Sonny's glass as he recounted the exchange to his band between sets. *The way I phrased it was so smooth, too: not friendly and not hostile, just calm and businesslike, so he wouldn't know if this was my way of issuing a challenge or offering to heal his troubled spirit. Truth be told, I'm not quite sure myself, although I suspect it was some of both.*

I also suspect your man would still be staring at me, wondering what he was supposed to say, if I hadn't let him off the hook some after that shit. Albert twinkled. *I hit him with a little smile and said,* Do you accept my invitation? *and he snapped out of it with a* Yes Sir *and I said* Good, I'll see you then, *and walked away clean.*

But Latif wasn't supposed to know the prologue to the invitation and so Sonny said he didn't know the whys or how longs of Van Horn's countersurveillance. Instead he leaned back into the familiar if undesired role of mere steady accompanist, house piano player and groundwork layer. He spoke only the necessary words just as he played only the necessary chords, letting Latif not listen to his heart's sweet hot content. All they could do was show up and see what the bossman had in store, Sonny said, and all Latif could do was get some goddamn sleep beforehand. Latif nodded but he couldn't stop graphing what few facts he had, and he was one moment euphoric at the prospect of playing with Van Horn, and the next tightfisted and terrified, ready to prove himself by swinging blindly at the heavyweight champ the moment he heard the first bell echo through the mostly empty club.

But when it rang, it whispered. Latif walked alone into the club to find them all onstage, as if they'd lain in wait since last night. He climbed awkwardly from the pit onto the bandstand, highstepping the two-foot embankment instead of walking around. Mistake number one. He watched them enter and exit every night and they did it from the side, so what the fuck was he doing? Get it together, he told himself. Be a musician.

Albert shook Teef's hand and that was it; they took their places wordlessly and Latif squared his shoulders and took a few deep breaths to open his throat. Sonny began quietly and eased Latif into the music, splashing him with playful incandescent droplets like a child who has already jumped into the ocean and returns to shore to rush his rabbithearted friend's progress. Murray Higgins made a slight tightwristed brushstroke against the ride cymbal, smiling at Latif and steady-nodding him the rhythm until Latif noticed and nodded back, fingering his horn pedals in practice. His hands moved fluidly over the instrument's controls: He'd burned away the hours of the day by taking his sax to Hanson's Horn House and having every cork and felt pad replaced, every spring checked so the instrument performed at its peak. The new-shined horn gleamed bright beneath the stagelights just like Albert's, and Latif felt muscular and sleek, nervous but alert, alive. He looked down from the stage and saw the room from a completely new perspective, saw how visible he'd been even from the spots he'd always thought were hidden. He breathed and tried to focus on the moment rather than the fact that the last quarter of his life had been spent in preparation for it. He was glad he had asked Mona to stay home.

The tune, "The Omen," was something The Quartet did at Dutchman's only once in a great while because, as Sonny had explained when Teef had asked after his sentimental favorite *It's a high holidays type of thing.* The Horn himself was said to have blacked out on stage for a moment once while playing it at a festival in Nice, his solo a forty-minute soliloquy of chaos that eradicated the critical sensibilities of even the most judgmental listener at once, scraped away the intellect and left raw the emotions underneath.

You couldn't stand ankle-deep for long on this one. "The Omen" was structured to accelerate exponentially, from Murray's tender brushwork to a pounding fullness of percussion and from there into staccato bursts of drums and piano stab clusters behind unbroken loping horn lines. Latif had often mused that if he knew what Albert was thinking when he played such songs as this, what slideshow flashed across his brain, he would understand the man himself; there could be no truer way. Did Van Horn see unborn children, lost loves, burned churches, iron shackles, untouched snow? Was he celebrating the unspeakable or lamenting the horrific?

It was all at once, and so thinking Latif shook his head and bowed it toward Albert, declining the opening solo and insisting that Van Horn be the first saxophone to speak. Sonny watched, astonished, and ruminated. To claim the privilege of going last was rude and practically against the rules; if this had been a regular session instead of what it was, Latif would have instantly been branded a punk, perhaps shouted offstage. Tactically, it was a cagey gamble; Latif was on one hand accepting the task of following the leader wherever he might roam, of replying to what in all likelihood would be a flamethrowing nerve twister of a sermon. On the other hand, he gained the opportunity to find his themes in Van Horn's discourse, the chance to extrapolate, rebut or confirm, to prove he was not merely a talker but a listener and a conversationalist. Besides which, Burma reflected as the bandleader began to blow, anyone together enough to play coherently after The Horn got loose was no joke.

Murray had already switched from brushes to his drumsticks, turning up the gas beneath Van Horn quicker than usual. Or perhaps Van Horn, conscious that his time was theoretically halved by the presence of a guest, had been the one to initiate the upswing; from where Latif stood inside the music, cause and effect blurred. He strained to hear Van Horn with the ears of a technician, to footnote phrases and ideas for his own response, but soon such an approach lost viability. Van Horn was all over the register, scaling castle walls and nosediving from the highest precipices into the grungy moat below. The logic of his solo was suspended in its own fluids, self-contained and conforming to a physics as emotional as musical. The colors changed so quickly—esoteric hues Latif would never have thought of but which became primary in Albert's hands, magentas melting into mellow greens and deepest browns, shining sliding and changing before Latif could rightly catalog them to begin with. *This is all for me,* he remembered, and forced himself to listen with emotional ears, to recognize the vital question not as *What is he playing?* but *What is he saying?*

There was not a hint of animosity to be found in Van Horn's solo, Latif realized. There was a feeling which sometimes accompanied such, a certain aggression, a challenge with a pointed tip, but it was an invitation most of all, *Come into this with me, come explore these stellar regions if you can. Take a deep breath because there's only what oxygen you bring with you out here, there's only the cord of the tradition to breathe through. We might float past God or your dead kinfolk; we might get lost in the infinitesimal wrinkled pathways around your grandma's aged eyes or beat our heads against the smell of sweet un-worldly pussy.*

Van Horn kept it quick or so it seemed. He didn't ease himself back down onto the ground by lateral degrees the way most soloists would do, swaying his way to a landing like a feather in a breeze. He did most of the time but not tonight; tonight he hit a peak and that was it, he vanished in midair without a warning. It reminded Sonny of charades, that old parlor game of folks guessing a phrase from mimed and acted cues. A cat would be up there doing all he could, acting his ass off while people tossed forth a cacophony of wrong answers, and it all stopped on a dime at the exact moment that someone in the audience shouted the word. All of it led up to that, the sudden fingersnapped *I got it*, and once the word was said, the actor merely pointed to the answer and sat down. Van Horn was playing charades with himself tonight, Sonny thought, and once he got where he was going, guessed what he was miming, he knew it and cut out with the quickness.

Just where that left Teef, Sonny didn't know; Van Horn had purposely released the baton in deep space and it was on Latif to grab it up before it plummeted to earth or floated weightless toward the sun. Murray Higgins bought him some ascension time with a long cymbal-crashing drumfill, and when it ended Latif wrapped his lips around his reed and reared his head back, jumping into the music with a long clear shrieking exclamation, train whistle and train at once, fast but earthbound, straight ahead. Even as he started he could feel defeat glistening on his skin, and he struggled to ignore it, to dismiss the very concepts of winning and losing, of beating Van Horn—what did that mean? He played a quick volley of question marks, looping curves punctuated by fat round weighty dots, and as Latif's mind unclenched and began automatically dissecting the groove, mapping what went where, the footnotes he'd made on Van Horn's solo bobbed up to the surface of his mind.

He remembered the first phrase Van Horn had toyed with, the way he'd rearranged its sounds every which way like scrabble letters, and Latif replayed a few permutations, bending the notes his own way, looking for an intonation The Horn hadn't voiced, a pun Latif could wring from source material. He found one and made it twice, afraid to spare a look over at Sonny but sure the pianist was smiling with him; Burma plunked down a bass clef amen and adrenal confidence surged through Latif just long enough to power him through a few fast triples, shaving closer and closer to the front of Murray's beat before he calmed down. He had scored a point but it was bullshit, mere linguistic wrangling. To address Van Horn on the level of meaning, not vocabulary, was the real challenge, and Latif turned to it now.

His careful study of Higgins' drumming had paid off; Latif was able to intuit enough of the drummer's math to hold up his end of the intricate game of addition and subtraction, multiplication and division. He filled the spaces Murray was leaving open for him with a spiraling truncated pattern based on Albert's phrase while hanging weightless in the very middle of the beat. Between the push and pull of rhythm instruments—drums pushing the tempo and bass dragging behind it, piano darting quick and slowing slow—there was a magic spot where gravity didn't exist. If you found that balance point you floated, supported in every direction: That was the secret physics of the game. In there, you could do anything: backflips, whatever. You never had to answer to the ground.

Thanks to Higgins' sympathetic understanding, Latif had a few ungravitized moments to scroll through his palette, searching for some way to express his thanks, to comment on the profundity of exploration as he understood it. He hunted furiously, aware of time collapsing all around him, trying to work what he had up into a theme.

Latif thought back to Boston, to his days of listening to Van Horn with Wessel Gates, to the first real draughts of music he had breathed, how they had filled his lungs and changed the shape of things to come. He tried to blow that feeling, the ecstasy of discovery, to let Van Horn know what he had been to him and still was now. Murray Higgins fed him electricity and Sonny comped behind him and Latif played on, grasping for the sounds to run it down. He couldn't quite wrap himself around his thoughts; they vaporized a quartersecond before he could squeeze them and screamed away like firecrackers in wisps and whining tendrils. Latif found himself playing counterpoint to his own mistakes, chasing them down and wrestling meanings from them before they sailed too far away.

It felt overly academic, as if he were talking about music instead of playing it, and Latif shut his eyes and refocused on Burma and Higgins, on meshing with them instead of trying to make the ceiling cave in with the rogue intensity of his contribution. Coherence was a lost cause now; Latif had abandoned every concept he'd introduced, and the only thing to do was latch onto an idea so compelling that the multiple personality disorder of his solo so far would be forgotten. He opened his ears as wide as he could and Amir's quick, serpentine bassline nudged its way into the forefront of the mix.

The bass player was outside his line of vision, but Latif could imagine him bent over the thing, his top hand strong and rigid, gold rings flashing as he thumped thick rich bottom from the hollow mahogany. Latif rode the brawny simplicity of the bassline, taking cues from Murray's accents, and the four of them came together abruptly and synched into a groove. Latif lassoed long bright lines around the rhythm section, roping them in like he was hugging them, and found that he knew just how to interlock his phrases so they rose like stairsteps. He surged toward the peak, saw where he was going and sprinted two steps at a time. It came into sight and Murray let everybody know the moment was Latif's; he applauded with bass drops and crash cymbals as Latif stood at the summit and blew down toward the abyss, disappearing and letting the exhilaration he felt speak for itself.

When he remembered himself, the effect was jarring; Latif forgot everything he knew about descending and began to stumble, clubfooted. He clutched wildly at the dangling safety line of his opening riff, somewhat histrionic since it hadn't been heard for so long. Latif knew he had lost the moment and he wanted to close with a modicum of grace; he toyed briefly with the phrase, chopped it, bent it, played it straight, slowed it to halfspeed, and cut out, exhausted. He had blown for seven minutes and though frustrated, Latif ended his solo knowing he had held his own and also something else.

My name is Tristan.

Latif started, opened his eyes and took the whitehaired white man's hand.

Tristan, he repeated, disoriented. They stood alone inside the guts of the city, waiting in an empty station for the uptown train. I must have dozed off, Latif thought. I didn't even hear footsteps.

That was some solo you played tonight, said Tristan. His eyes bounced with something Latif couldn't identify. *I bet you waited a long time for that.* An upturned eyebrow matched his mouth.

You were at Dutchman's? Latif asked. He was sure he'd never seen this cat before. He would have remembered such a face.

I was indeed. And for the first time in years. Tristan stared at him and smiled. *I wish you luck. May you succeed where others fail.* He shifted his weight slightly, left foot to the right, and something in the way he did it told Latif that he was drunk. Just then the train snaked into sight. Latif walked further down the tunnel, wanting to board a different car than Tristan. The doors parted, and he entered and sat down, leaning back and wrapping his legs around his horn case like a barbershop pole. He shut his eyes in a long blink.

Like for instance me, Latif heard at his ear, and there again stood Tristan, eschewing the empty seats of the unpopulated train to hold onto the metal overhead handrail. *I wrote novels,* he went on, oblivious to Latif's deliberate glaze-eyed stare. Tristan's body sagged, swayed as they moved over turbulence. *You've got to be careful, boy—*

I'm not a boy, Latif snapped.

Tristan gave him a withering look and waved his free hand: a slurred unapology. *I don't mean it like that. I call my grandson boy.* When Latif said nothing he resumed. *You've got to understand the responsibility you have. Coltrane, rest his soul, he understood it. Albert understands it.*

The heavy door to the next car opened and the mechanized scraping of metal wheels on metal tracks poisoned the air. Tristan and Latif both turned to watch a homeless couple shuffle through the car, the man hugging the woman to him, neither looking up. The man swung one leg in a half circle as he walked, as though he couldn't bend his knee.

Tristan sat down. *I understand it, but it doesn't matter*, he explained. Latif stifled the impulse to recoil from the liquor-wizened breath. *There are no words for what makes my body shudder strangely after pissing and jerks me upright like a marionette in my bed in the chill in the night, and I want them. To scrawl them on the doors of my house and puke them out over the world.* Tristan paused and Latif swallowed painfully. The old man's hand burrowed into his raincoat and reappeared with a halfpint of gin, empty save a swallow. *I mix my own drinks*, he disclosed. *Damned if I'll pay seven dollars for a glass of tonic with a splash of gin.* The slender bottle punctuated his speech.

We don't know what we think, my friend, because we don't know what we mean when we say what we say. Falling in love. We say falling in love and what in hell do we mean? Crude symbolism. A filthy agreement to pretend we understand each other. Latif nodded his head, oddly captivated. He had the sense that he was watching someone dangerous but that he himself was safe, that he was watching someone crazy who was making perfect sense.

War, Tristan whispered, fixing opaque, liquidy eyes on Latif and refusing to move them. *What is your war? How goes the war? I believe this war must end. You believe the war is justified. I have seen a man in the war who has fallen in love and now is dying, melting into a soupy puddle of his own self with open casket eyes. We say love and war and think we know what we mean and we don't. And I will die soon, and smoke my cigars in purgatory. In the smoking section.*

He shook the bottle by its top and liquid sloshed inside. He looked at it curiously, shrugged his lips, and drank it open-throated. Latif watched, waited. Tristan wiped his mouth on his sleeve and offered the empty bottle to Latif. Without thinking, Latif took it.

The artist, said Tristan, a wicked smile touching the corners of his mouth. Latif's heart played doubletime for a moment. Who is this cat? he wondered. *If his goal of expression, flowing truth, comes to its impossible climax of synergetic clarity, then he has created heaven, and who needs art in heaven? Heaven casts out or castrates the artist, my friend. We are by nature self-destructive. Why then is the world surprised to see us kill ourselves and drink ourselves to death?*

He snatched the bottle back and squinted through it, optimistic. Finding nothing, he cast it to the floor. Latif cringed and picked up his feet, but the old man hadn't thrown it hard enough to break. He turned back to Latif as if he had been interrupted, pulling his sleeve back and pointing a long well-manicured forefinger at the ceiling. *Perhaps God is bored with man as we are bored with not being able to build a computer that can carry on a stimulating conversation. But if I died today I would face God empty-handed, with no truth to claim as my path to Him and no accounting for my wasted life of searching.*

Wasted life of searching echoed through Latif. Perhaps only the belief that it would someday end made the search seem beautiful or even bearable. What if the search looped on forever without progress, a dusty parade over the same infertile arid grounds?

Tristan rose to retrieve the bottle and Latif said *It's empty*. The old man pocketed it anyway and stood with legs spread for balance, hands hanging by his sides, remarkably stable for an aged drunkard in a moving train. He pointed at Latif. *My grandson is your age*, he said. *Nineteen. Tristan also; my namesake. I told him what I told you: that I have written all my life and told no truths. He led me out of my study and we took the subway out to Queens, to some god-*

damn abandoned trainyard, and he said Grandpa, I'm a writer too. I'll show you truth. *We turned a corner and there it was: TRISTAN, it said, six feet tall in gold and silver and red letters on the side of a freight train, some kind of crazy script I could barely read, all sorts of arrows and curves flying off the thing. And Tris said* This is all that anybody's ever written. The rest is just embellishment.

Tristan's face cracked in a wan smile. *Something to consider, anyway.* He rose. *Good luck, kiddo.* The doors clunked shut behind him.

Latif leaned forward and rode up to Harlem staring at the floor, cracking his knuckles with hungry hands, willing his heart calm. His stop came and he walked out onto his block and instead of latenight quiet Latif confronted earlymorning chaos, the wide street brimming with men and women milling in swirls and young hardrocks stalking back and forth in undirected longstride fury, lips pulled back and white teeth gleaming. A dissonant melange of highpitched agitation, baritone outrage, and moist sadness lingered like gunsmoke over the crowd. Hatchetfaced police hemmed everybody in, positioned in pairs every twenty feet with right hands resting inches from the arsenal of weapons strapped onto their belts. Beneath the arching streetlights, Harlem was writhing in pain and Teef gaped, aghast: What was this?

He walked slowly through the crowd and saw tears glistening in the stubble of men he'd only seen seated and impassive, hands crossed over their beerguts. Mothers hugged young men in doo rags, sobbing about justice, murder, cops. Groups of old men stood silently, hands pocketed and faces sallow, staring blankly at the ground. Twelve-year-olds sat on the concrete, knees tight to their chests, and watched their elders with upflickering eyes.

Spliff, Donald, and Equality stood apart from the crowd, passing a blunt beneath the awning of Good Buddy Chinese Takeout Kitchen. Latif spotted them and cut a wide-eyed beeline through the churling sea to find out what was going on.

Spliff looked at him incredulous. *What fuckin planet you been on, son? Kofi Ogunde cops acquitted on all counts.*

Teef's mouth popped open. *No.*

Apparently, it was nobody's fault the nigga got shot, Equality said darkly.

Suddenly Latif's head ached. *When did they announce it?* he asked.

Four forty-five, said Donald. *Cats been out here ever since.*

Spliff poked his chin gruff at Latif. *Nobody gave a fuck down at your little jazz club, did they?*

Latif shook his head and looked at nothing. *I never even would have known,* he muttered. Two, three hundred people up in Dutchman's and every single one acting like it was business as usual. Motherfuckers must have known, Latif thought. They just didn't care. Goddamn.

That's what I thought, said Spliff. His finger sliced a downward arc, implicating the planet. *We got to realize we at war. You wanna make some music, got to be something we can use. I love the nigga and I hate to say it, but fuck John Coltrane. Put a rifle in that nigga hand and then we'll talk. I know y'all looking at me like* Why this drug-dealin motherfucker acting like he Huey Newton all of a moment, *but I'm dead up. Anybody could be next. And if they find the crack rocks in my pocket, case won't even go to trial.*

Latif took the blunt when Donald passed it.

How long you think folks will stay in the street? he wondered.

Donald curled his lip appraisingly. *Not much longer, unless somebody sets it off.*

Spliff shook his head authoritatively. *Folks got to be shocked to riot,* he said. *Anybody shocked by this a damn fool.*

Latif woke in the sunshine, feeling like a tube of toothpaste squeezed to flatness. The long peppermint rope of his emotions was a dry, crusted mound lying in the sink; so much had happened yesterday that only his body felt anything: stiff, achy, hollowed, bleary. Outside, the street was as deserted as he'd ever seen it, everybody sleeping off the anger hangover. They'd wake up like people after one-night stands, sneaking glances at their bedfellows and wondering what came next.

Latif put on a sweater and his too-light jacket and ambled down the stairs to find some food, walk and eat, think, decompress. He bought a buttered bagel and a coffee at the bodega, glancing at the headlines. The trashy tabloids screamed *Free!* in huge letters, above smiling courtroom pictures of the exonerated cops, and Latif felt validated until he looked at a real paper. On the *New York Times* front page, the trial was just one of seven stories, pictureless. It would blow over like everything else.

I should be happy, he told himself. It mighta been a rough day for the bulletriddled ghost of Kofi Ogunde, but Latif James-Pearson's still alive and intact, dreams coming true. I should be popping champagne, fucking my girl. He breathed deep, trying to stir up enough wind to rouse the exhilaration lining the bottom of his stomach like a sheet of paper.

After "The Omen" and before the first set, Albert had invited Latif down to the Sunday Jam, a weekly session Van Horn hosted at his home. An ever-changing aggregate of young cats gathered there to soak up what they could, apprenticing themselves to an underspoken mentor. Van Horn didn't invite just anybody, and as word spread of Latif's performance, cats at Dutchman's lined up to slap him on the back—harder than necessary, some of them—and congratulate him as if he'd just won the *Downbeat* poll. The kind of guys who always had to answer somebody else's success with a tale of their own made sure to tell him they'd been to The Horn's house too. Other cats grinned with delight and told Latif they hadn't even known he played, were sorry they'd missed it, and had heard he'd killed. As if out of respect for his accomplishment, nobody purchased any dope.

Latif walked down to 110th Street and into Central Park, trying to shake off the clammy feeling and revel in his own badness, but simple sights hit him at symbolic angles, in soft spots free of callused flesh, and reminded Latif that there was trouble, sadness, horror in the world. He lingered at the edge of a sandlot playground and watched young children scream in glee and race in circles on their fat, still-clumsy legs and found himself abruptly and intensely saddened. He felt cowardly in his art, thinking of Spliff's words, pathetic for living in a timewarped jazzworld bubble and—as his trainride with Tristan, forgotten in the folds of the night, came back to him—foolish for thinking that a life of creativity could not itself leave him a broken man.

Here he stood on the brink of entering the world he'd watched so long from shadowed corners, and all Latif could think about was failure—not simply his own, but the larger tragedy of miscommunication, the impossibility of understanding, which seemed to suddenly surround him. It was a mindstate that fortified itself, this sudden helpless sensitivity, this feeling of impotence before the bittersweet embrace of life. Latif walked across the playground, averting his eyes from the small lake just past it on the left because he knew the profundity of glinting water would only deepen his despondence. He watched old folks shuffling along alone and others folded onto benches feeding birds, and his brain coded such pictures faster than he could stop it and translated them into an unknown dirge.

Soon he was thinking of his mother, of her face across from his at breakfast those last few weeks before he'd left, when he'd been nothing but a mask of restless ambition. He'd measured his growing resolve against the softness of his mother's eyes, trained himself for leaving by shutting her out bit by bit. Leda watched him sadly, not understanding why her son was treating her like this. Did he need an enemy so badly? He only answered her in monosyllables, scowled through Leda's attempts to talk until they waned, left her alone in his company.

Latif hunched over, elbows on knees on a park bench of his own, and imagined the tears his mother had shed behind the closed doors of her bedroom onto her queensized bed, asking God what she'd done to deserve such meanness.

He shuddered at his own callousness and pressed handheels against closed eyes, toes curling inside sneakers. How ridiculous was he for trying to pull emotions from an instrument when nothing in life seemed to pull any from him? Why the fuck should the human condition scroll forth from his horn? The only thing he understood was inarticulation, stuttering isolation, how to retreat into silence. Perhaps silence was the natural state of things and struggle was naive. Perhaps silence had been the prelude to his father's departure too. Perhaps that cat was somewhere crying over his lost wife and baby boy, looking at a picture he had taken with him to remember, or perhaps he'd died this very morning. Perhaps there was nothing much but silence and sadness in the world, and that was all there was to play.

The tears were forming. He could feel the water heavy in his eyes, and he blinked to try to make a drop fall, but none would. The moisture glazed his pupils, but Latif could not cry and instead loneliness spread over him in rivulets. Solitude had never scared him, but here in this park, on this gorgeous day, his own physical inarticulation, the sadness that wouldn't drip down his face and relieve him, made Latif feel supremely alone, unknown. He wanted Mona. He hoped to show her he could cry.

Hey, he said into a payphone.

Mona's voice was sprightly. *Hey. How did it go last night?*

Good. Real good. But I'm kind of sad. Can I come over?

He spent the uptown cab ride contrasting Mona's upbeat tone with last night's verdict. When he reached the top of her stairwell, Mona was standing in the apartment doorway smiling. She wore a paintsplattered buttondown man's shirt, not Latif's; robin's-egg-blue paint smeared her left cheek.

Come here, she said, grabbing his hand excitedly and leading him inside to the studio, *I have something to show you. What do you think? Am I close?*

You're very goddamn close, Latif muttered, not knowing what to say. Something in him felt violated, something else amazed. He stared at the canvas leaning on the easel: It was nothing like the way he'd drawn it, but somehow it was right. She's good, he thought. She's very good. It was all there, much more than he remembered telling her: the saxophonist, snakes floating from his horn, the sign, the chain, the stake.

Mona had painted the figure facing sideways and her sense of his balance was perfect; he stood in a classic tenor superhero pose, feet planted shoulders' width apart and back bent slightly like the spine of a question mark, with the bell of his horn pointed almost straight back at him as if he were hitting the highest hardest note there ever was. He was all bubbles, as Latif had said, but Mona's bubbles touched each other, pressed one against the next, bent and shared edges as cells do beneath a microscope. The way Latif drew him they never touched; rather, they hovered near each other and approximated anatomical shapes: a globular hand, a long stretched artless tube of arm. His musician had been bubbles by default, because abstraction was the only way he could attempt to represent a figure. Mona had turned a figure into bubbles.

Latif always drew three snakes, forked tongues extended, facing out away from the musician. Mona, too, had depicted three: scaly, thick, and round. One, its tail cocked and body curled, faced the lefthand border of the painting. Another was just emerging from the horn, mouth wide and teeth sharp gleaming, and the third, his body curving sleek and fast, seemed to be flying straight at the musician. It shocked Latif, but the authority of Mona's work was such that he wondered whether he'd been drawing it wrong all these years. The stake, the sign, were perfectly rendered. The chain enclosed the saxophonist's ankle tightly, visibly squeezed it, but since the tenorman appeared so fluid, the effect was odd: the shackling of water. The colors surprised Latif most: here was his dream rendered in blues and angry rusted-metal browns, yellow snake eyes and green and silver glinting scaly snakeskin, *Jazz Tonite* misspelled as *Jazz Tonight* in bloodred writing on a white and deep-blue sign.

Mona stood carefully outside his line of vision and rubbed paint from her forearm. He knew she wanted him to speak; what could he say? What did the appropriation of his symbols mean? *You had no right to do this* snapped and hissed at *thank you*; they twisted like the serpents of the Hippocratic scepter.

Mona stepped forward and they stood before the painting. He put an arm around her shoulders.

I never imagined a snake coming at the guy before, Latif said.

I wondered about that. I figured if you're blowing demons out your horn, you're the first person they see. They might come for you.

Latif lay on the couch. He didn't feel like crying anymore, for Mona or himself. *That's true*, he agreed. *They might.*

Albert's living room was where the sessions happened. There was a Steinway baby grand piano and a full wall bookshelf, ten feet high and all biography. Van Horn read other people's lives. Nero, William Shakespeare, Frederick Douglass, Jean-Michel Basquiat, Thomas Jefferson, Cleopatra, Desiderius Erasmus, Shaka Zulu, Moses Wellfleet Walker, Confucius: an anachronistic dinner party of history's largest personalities. Pots of food rested over low flames in the kitchen, next to a stack of plastic plates. Marisol woke up early on Sundays and went to her niece's house; Van Horn woke up early to cook downhome recipes reconfigured by the exotic touches of a worldwide palate. Cats grabbed helpings of red beans and a curried rice, mustard greens with pickled lotus root, beef stew over mashed cassava, whenever they got hungry.

The smells drifted into the living room and seasoned the music, but the kitchen was where Albert did his talking. He hung back and didn't play much at these sessions, didn't say much either. What he did say was often couched in culinary wisdom. *Ask him about cooking*, Sonny had advised. And when Latif rang the doorbell at one, exactly on time, Albert steered him right into the kitchen. Latif was dismayed to find the living room already lively with musicians. He'd expected serenity, somehow: for Albert's front door to open onto a Buddhist rock garden replete with slow trickling fountains, for Albert to bless him and hand him a prayer shawl *Let the initiation rituals begin*. Instead, empty plates covered the coffeetable and cats sat smoking and chatting, their legs crossed at rakish angles. On time, apparently, was late. Latif exchanged nods and *how you doin, bruh* with the cats he passed as Van Horn ushered him through the living room and fixed him a plate.

As a species, Albert said, talking as he moved from pot to pot *we barely know a tenth of a percentage about anything. We can barely travel, we don't know bullhockey about medicine or science, and our communication skills are somewhere just past rudimentary. The only thing we've really mastered on this planet*, snatching the lid off a soup tureen with a magician's flair and lowering his nose into the aromatic steam that streamed forth, filling the kitchen *is eating*. He shot Latif an infectious smile and spooned basmati rice onto the plate.

The key to cooking, Van Horn confided as he ladled turkey chili over the rice, looking like somebody's hip grandfather in a white terrycloth suit and beige house shoes *is knowing what flavors complement each other. Cats try to get fancy and throw in every spice in the cupboard, and the taste just gets muddled. What you've got to do is bring out the flavor that's already there. Like putting lemon on fish. Collard greens?*

Latif nodded. There was a warmth to Van Horn's home. It radiated from him and melted the jittery, competitive energy of the other musicians. Latif had expected to be nervous, but what he felt instead was mostly hollow, drained but not purged by yesterday's sadness. He'd left Mona's with the painting wrapped in brown paper, gone home and sat in his room feeling so fragile that nearly anything—a poor irretrievable spoon lost behind the sink, a lone shirt swaying arms-up on a neighbor's clothesline— seemed suddenly eloquent with horror and tore into his heart. Picking up his horn had been out of the question; so was looking at the painting. He'd backed away from that dangerous ledge now, and Latif had no idea where the distance would place him when it was his turn to play; the feeling might return to paralyze him or remain absent and leave him numb.

Albert handed him a heaping plate and said they'd be starting in a few minutes but not to rush: eat, listen, relax. The brothers would be here for hours. Latif wolfed down his food, watching the others tuning and cleaning and tightening their instruments.

It was delicious, and Latif had to fight back his dismay at this delight, at the unattainable honesty which burst forth even from Albert's cooking.

There were only three horn players there besides Van Horn: Latif, another tenor, and an alto doubling on flute. He checked the others out as each found his own corner like a boxer and warmed up, and was relieved to realize that he was the youngest of the reedmen; only the bass player and pianist looked younger than midtwenties. Manhattan School cats, probably, those two; Albert taught occasional master classes there and these kids had that smug bohemian proud-to-be-in-New York student look. Mismatched artifacts of hipness dangled from their lanky frames: porkpie hats, Malcolm X glasses, dashikis. Latif looked down at his own attire: a cream-colored V-neck sweater, sleeves pushed to his elbows, and pressed Italian slacks from Sonny's homeboy's warehouse. At least he looked the part. Last of the well-dressed jazzmen.

Latif stepped up there with the rest of the musicians and the benchwarmer rhythm section cats relaxed to peep game and the drummer counted off the tune and dug in. He was skinny and his playing thin and effete, and Latif clenched his jaw at what the kid was missing, prepared himself to quarterback with insufficient blocking. He looked around, but there was no dissatisfaction to be gleaned from other faces and so Latif forced himself to listen harder, to find what he'd missed. It wasn't that the cat couldn't play, just that his style was so different from what Latif wanted to hear that he had to force himself to recognize the ideas behind it. He wondered why Albert had invited this brother; his sound was as far from Murray Higgins' massive cannonblast drumming as could be. Maybe Albert's neighbors were complainers, Latif thought with a smile.

He carried the smile into his solo, fluttering his sound in

laughter as the other tenor player stepped back and away to give him room. He could still taste the beef stew in his mouth, and Latif felt it knotting in his throat as he batted about the first sounds kittenlike. Playfulness soon dissolved and the chuckle metamorphosized into a different kind of laugh. It was absurd, sinister, despairing, the laugh that erupts from a man as he stands watching his house burn, and Latif didn't control it, didn't know where it was taking him. He grappled for command, able to distinguish this not knowing from the kind which was inspired, which swept you up in exploration and pursuit, the kind to which any intuitive musician bowed immediately.

This not knowing threatened hysteria, and Latif hot-potato juggled the note of sadness he had found and listened to it, tried to match it to the surging feelings he had had in Central Park and in his room, and realized it was lacking, a pale weak sliver, nothing like real life. There was no gravity, no dignity, no nuance to it, only a mounting compensatory aggression. Without wanting to, Latif grew loud, insensible, and nihilistic; the phrases moaning from his horn were infants pushed prematurely from the belly, unready to meet the world. Latif sounded to himself like the worst of what he heard booming from hip hop car systems, anger and bass distorted into frenzied rants that drowned out their own meaning. He squeezed his eyes shut and blew harder, overblew, trying to get to something raw, something he knew was there somewhere, but he was miles away from it and panicking, and he gave up—receded into short low sobbing tone bursts, knowing they sounded hip, and backed out of the solo hot and shamefaced as soon as he could.

He looked around, expecting to see shock on the faces of the others, but there was only standard bandstand body language, nods and small hipswaying, and his frustration grew. Latif wanted his failure acknowledged, gaped at, wanted it to stop the show.

But these cats had no idea what a rough and twisted insignificant approximation of life had just blurted from his horn; to them it was probably just another forgettable and mercifully short solo.

The question it raised slapped Latif senseless: what the hell was he doing here with this unsightly metalwork contraption bulging in his hands? Being a musician? He wanted to throw it to the ground and stomp it, fall on his instrument like a grenade and beat it with his fists until he bled. And in the home of his idol, as he stood and tapped his foot to the pianist's nonswinging collage of better musicians' ideas, and then to another tenor solo as uninspired as his own, Latif realized that being a musician wasn't shit. You had to be a musician and a father, a musician and a rooftop cop sniper, a musician and something. He twitched himself free of the thought, chased it away, but for the rest of the afternoon his horn felt foreign in his hands and bitter in his mouth, like an old lover he had forgotten how to kiss.

You sounded like what you were, that's all, said Albert, crossing his legs at the knee and smoothing the slategray of his slacks. *Somebody who's been pushed up on an unfamiliar bandstand with a bunch of strangers, everybody too preoccupied to listen.* He and Latif sat at his kitchen table with ceramic mugs in hand, sipping Vanilla Almond tea at ten o'clock next Sunday morning as pots percolated on the stove. The crumbs of cranberry muffins Latif had brought speckled the small glass plates in front of them. Every now and then Van Horn would rise and lift a lid, peer at a broth or give something a stir, tap a bit of sage into his cupped palm and then brush half of that into a pot.

It's a shame money and fashion killed the big band, because a three-month tour of duty would be the perfect remedy for you—melt away that what-is-music handwringing with a sturdy shot of life experience. I'm talking about spending every hour next to some of the killingest musicians in the world, not to mention some of the smartest and sweetest cats you'd ever want to know. I used to just sit and listen, which is often better than sitting and asking questions, to whatever any two bodies in that band might be jawing about.

I'll tell you, Albert said, raising his eyebrows earnestly, *those old Asian philosophers and architects who envisioned and designed the special meditative sanctums and classrooms, the places designed for tranquil thought and serious discussion, they understood something. And a tour bus humming peacefully through the countryside at dusk or even four A.M. has been my American equivalent.*

Albert paused. *You've got a touch of that tourbus mentality,* he said, tapping Latif on the wrist and refilling their mugs from the teapot in the center of the table, forearm tendons rippling mighty even with the slight effort of lifting and pouring, *the way you thought to come here and talk life not music. Most young cats want to pick my brain about playing, which ain but so useful because I can't explain it any better than Joe Saxophone might do it for me. It all breaks down to dots and lines, or whimsy and hallucinations. You can kill it with too much intellect or too much romance.*

My girl is always telling me I'm too much in my head, Latif said.

Van Horn smiled. *The mouth is halfway between the brain and the heart. The trick is to use one to find the other.*

Latif looked at him quizzically and Albert leaned forward, elbows on the table, unsurprised the youngster didn't understand. *It's like this: Just from the way you carry yourself, I can tell you have a strong sense of justice, of the way things ought to be. Right?* Latif nodded. *That's a headsmarts thing. So is anger. You can get to sadness from there; maybe you're starting to. Maybe that's why you haven't played all week.*

Part of Latif felt he should sit and contemplate Albert's words before plowing on. But he didn't have forever with Van Horn. *How did you do it?* he pressed.

Well, I sidestepped that particular crisis with the simple gambit of not being nearly so smart as you. Latif smiled impatiently at the obvious untruth, but Albert was serious.

I came from a religious family, he elaborated. *Grew up looking at music as my testimonial, my joy rather than High Art. The only time I ever felt comfortable, expressive, was when I was playing. By the time I got heady about it, I was much older than you and the healing power of music had already become very clear to me.*

I didn't know you came up in the church, Latif said. He'd watched Albert brush away the esoteric questions of young musicians after shows, queries about some forgotten solo or the dynamics of a twenty-year-old recording date, by smiling, *You got to remember, music is all about love,* getting a laugh and leaving it at that. But Latif had never associated the spirituality of Albert's music with any particular religion.

In it but not of it, Van Horn said, standing and flicking the front burner from low to warm. He glanced over at Latif. *Is your family musical?* he asked.

My mother sings in church, and she got me started on horn lessons. But not really.

Van Horn nodded. *It always astounds me how many of the cats I've met throughout the years come from musical families, with a mother who teaches piano back wherever they're from or a father who played cornet in marching bands or blues guitar in pickup combos and so forth. Not to mention enough siblings and uncles and cousins all on different instruments to make any family gathering an all-out jamboree. I've always envied that, because I grew up having to practice on the sly, if you can imagine such a thing. My father was a minister, the Reverend Telford H. Van Horn, and he soon cursed the day he bought me my first instrument, a schoolboy clarinet.*

Uh-oh, said Latif, leaning back into his chair as Albert's voice went storyteller. He had a style of speech so natural and easy that listening was effortless and yet you felt as much a part of the story as he was. *It wasn't that The Rev disapproved of music as such,* Van Horn explained. *Quite the contrary, his congregation sang as loud and long as any in the city, and he even encouraged me to practice for the first few years. It was when I started getting serious about playing, around the age of fourteen, that he and I began to clash, and it was not so much an issue of music as of spirituality.*

Now, I make no distinction whatsoever between the two, and that was precisely the problem. To me the act of making music is a tribute, an approach to God. Even an attempt to follow in those footsteps by creating something. And it's a collaborative effort; I feel the hands of something greater on me when I'm playing at my best, and that's the way musicians the world over feel about their craft, Hindus to Jews. Teef nodded slow, a wordless amen corner.

It's a damn lucky thing I wasn't yet thinking along those kinds of lines when I lived beneath my father's roof, however. We had plenty to argue about just within my contestation that music was the form which my relationship with The Divine was meant to take, without me mounting what he would have no doubt perceived as a challenge to the fundamental sanctity of Christianity Itself on top.

The upshot of it all was that The Rev forbid me to play what by then was no longer a clarinet but a tenor sax, saying that I would not blow another note until I learned to put things in their proper perspective and understand that the Good Lord had put me on this earth to do His Work and that His House was the Church and not the concert hall or nightclub, that He had taught us how to worship Him and it was not with any fool saxophone but through Good Works and Prayer and adherence to the Word of Holy Scripture, and didn't I know what would happen to my Soul should I ignore the Teachings of the Lord and not Repent my Earthly Sins?

I know, I said, but what I thought was, I know that you can't show a different page to a man whose book is closed. And I set about earning the money to buy myself a horn. I scraped together enough to put a payment on a tenor, and I went down to Ms. Jacqueline McKinney's Music Shop with my friend and high school bandleader, Mr. Terrence Taylor, and he explained to her that I was a talented and trustworthy schoolboy for whose character he would gladly vouch, and she looked me over hard and finally agreed to let me hold the tenor while I made my weekly payments.

I had to be very careful never to let The Rev see my new horn. He had the old one locked away somewhere, right next to my old slingshot no doubt, and as far as he was concerned the matter had been dealt with and was closed. I never mentioned music again and he assumed I had forgotten all about it—something I'm sure he did only against his better knowing, for even a fool knows that such things are not so easily forgotten, and my father is no fool. But I let him go on thinking it had only been a phase and practiced before and after school and often during, hav-

ing arranged with Mr. Taylor to store my instrument in a locked closet in his room, to which he kindly gave me a copy of the key.

To The Rev I was suddenly and for the first time No Trouble At All: careful, quiet, and an obedient churchgoer. *Really, I was a million miles away from him at all times; I'd learned the trick of going through the necessary motions without having to think of anything I didn't want to. I absented my mind from my physical circumstances, as I've since read that torture victims also learn to do, and sent it hurtling toward whatever music I was working on or working out. The Rev never guessed how far he had pushed me from both himself and his religion by positioning them in opposition to my need to play. It was years before I was even able to think his God and mine could be the same.*

How did you get out to play? Latif asked.

That was trickier, smiled Albert, a sneaky kid's grin covering his face. For a moment Latif could see him back then, peach-fuzzed and a little pudgy, dodging his pops like any kid with a for-bidden hobby. *I had to finish my homework before I could go out after supper, and I was subject to a ten-thirty curfew even then, so what I did was catch part of the first set, go home, and sneak back out around mid-night to hear the closing number and find out where the jam session would be. On Fridays I was allowed to sleep at a friend's house, and I usually got someone to cover for me and stayed out listening all night. A few of the local musicians knew my father, and I had to beg them not to tell him that they'd seen me, which they were happy to do once I ex-plained my situation. Most of them came from musical families, as I've said, and thus they saw me as an orphan and adopted me.*

Winston Rodney, Albert said fondly, aiming a closed-lipped smile at the ceiling and tapping his hand against his knee. *Bass player and an old high school buddy of my dad's. He's the one who not only began taking me with him to afterhours jam sessions, but also found it in his heart to drive me home at four or five A.M., talking all the way* cross town about the finer points of what we'd heard or he'd played and leaving me with the admonition to hurry up and catch some Zs before you got to get back up and go to school, cuz you know if you don't bring home A's your daddy gonna whip your butt.

And it was Winston who introduced me way back then to many of the local circuit's luminaries, cats like Abraham Apollo, Redfoot Keefe, and Deadeye Willie Waterhouse, so called because he'd been an Army sharpshooter in younger days. Cats like Gabrey Masselin and Lucas Price, whose names aren't widely known outside of Pittsburgh but who could burn with some beautiful stuff when they felt like. And it was Winston who took it on himself to sneak me into the concert halls with his backstage musician's privileges when the big touring bands came into town, The Emperor's among them, so I could check out firsthand the stuff I'd only heard on the records I bought and borrowed, records I only played in Mr. Taylor's room and at my girlfriends' houses to avoid The Rev's suspicion.

And Winston was also the one who first asked me did I think I was ready to sit in, and when I said yes he said, I think so too, and offered to take my horn after school and meet me with it later at Small Talk. I realized when I got there that I'd been set up. I walked in with Winston at one A.M. to see a lineup of the city's finest musicians waiting on the stage: Abraham Apollo at the piano, Deadeye Willie Waterhouse behind the drums, and Shelton Langley and Lucas Price respectively on tenor sax and trumpet. Winston swung his bass onstage and said, When I asked if you were ready, I meant are you really ready, drawing laughter not only from the band but from the two dozen other musicians and scene-regulars sitting at the tables with their drinks and cigarettes in hand. I got onstage and Winston clapped me on the back, saying And I think you are, so here we go. Let's see how big your ears are, and they proceeded to tear into one hell of a burner.

What I did was keep up. Not just keep up but do what martial artists do and respond to the attack, as it were, by redirecting the attackers' energy back at them. *They gave me speed and I gave speed back double time. Winston dragged on purpose but I paid no nevermind. Willie turned the tune around three times and I kept with it, so finally he just dropped out on me. But man, I'd been watching him play every week for two years by then and I could feel it coming from the way he started building up momentum on the crash and ride cymbals. I knew he would grab a hold of them all of a moment and leave me wailing without anything behind because the rest of them would cut out too when he did so.*

I finished my phrase and just as he cut out, I cut out too. It sounded like we'd planned it. I turned and winked at him and Winston said Whoo, show us what you got Al baby, *and they all grinned and I started back where I'd left off, bright orange and fast as hell, and Willie came back in and so did Lucas and Shelly and we brought it to the out chorus.*

We played five more tunes and I managed to make it through all the tricks and turns they threw at me and play a little something too while I was at it. My socks were squishing in my shoes by the end: That's how hard they worked me. I traded speed and power with Shelly four for four and eight for eight, but I wasn't so much thinking about cutting his head as I was just soaring on my own. I think the happiness I felt just being up there served me well, because I came off like a noncombatant not out of timidity or confusion but rather like somebody who was beyond that kind of thing. Like you the other night. Latif's smile looked more like a grimace.

After that I never came without my horn, said Albert *and out of tradition and also as a running joke those guys never let up on me for a moment. Everyone would shout out* School's in session! *whenever I stepped in to take my turn.*

Van Horn chuckled. *So you see, what I put you through was downright friendly next to the way I had to cut my teeth trying to cut those dots. Though I did lay a little headgame on you off the bat.*

Mmm-hmm, Latif confirmed with overblown churchy conviction, making Albert laugh.

Never underestimate the value of high stakes, said Albert. *The reason I came in that night with Winston and blew like that was because in my mind those sessions were not just about proving myself or even getting next to somebody. My goal was a lot more real: to get the fuck out of Pittsburgh on the next thing with an engine, motor, or turbine. I would have stowed away on a carrier pigeon if I'd had to.*

And as it turned out, all that was preparation for the night a year later when The Emperor's Big Band came to town in need of a tenor man to replace Alvin Reece on the next leg of their tour, from Pittsburgh to Wheeling and then over to Virginia and down through Chattanooga, Knoxville, and Memphis, more than thirty dates in all. Reece's wife was sick and he'd had to go back home to New Orleans suddenly, so what was needed was at least a stopgap fill-in and at most an indefinite replacement. Someone in town, and I was not surprised to find out later on that it was Deadeye Willie Waterhouse suggested that The Emperor take a listen at me, and lo and behold into Small Talk walked the man himself.

I didn't see him until after we finished the set, and no sooner had Winston introduced us than Emp said I like what I hear, young man. I was told to listen for you and I am not disappointed. You playing a lot of horn up there. *We had just closed with two of his compositions,* Monarch's March *and* Alchemy, *and Emp asked me how much of his songbook I was familiar with. I told him I knew practically everything he'd put out on a record in the past ten years and that I'd transcribed several of his piano solos and a few of Alvin Reece's parts as well.* I was hoping you would say something like that, *he said.* Tell me, how would you like to come on the road with me for the next few weeks and maybe longer, depending on how things work out?

There's nothing I'd like better in the world, *I said.* Shoot, I'd leave right now with just the clothes on my back if I had to.

It wasn't until Tennessee that The Emperor finally got around to asking me my age. I was pretty tall and acted older than I was on account of keeping so much older company—like somebody else we know—so naturally it threw him and everybody for a loop when they found out. We were sitting together on the bus, and when I told him he thought I was kidding. After I convinced him that I wasn't he stood up and said Attention, attention, *loud enough to wake the cats sleeping in back* it is my pleasure to introduce to you the eighth wonder of the world. Get ready to feel like old men when I tell you reprobates that our new tenorman here, Mr. Albert Van Horn, is all of seventeen years old, out here on the open road and fitting right in with the greatest band in the world like he was born to do it.

I got a full round of applause and also the nickname True, as in truant, due to the joking speculation that I had skipped out on my final months of high school to join them on the road. Everybody had already known I was a neophyte and taken special pains to school me on everything from the history of the places we were passing through to how The Emperor ran the band and general aspects of life on the road, including and particularly women, but when those cats found out how young I was they began to take even more seriously the responsibility to bring me up to speed and fast.

The way they took care of me was really something. I was barely making any bread back then, and after drycleaning my bandstand suit and sending Ms. McKinney her weekly payment, I could barely afford better than hot dogs. I'll never forget how wonderful guys like my roommate Milford Montague and our drummer Doxie Tillerman were to me. They'd invite me out to dinner with them, knowing I didn't have the scratch to go where they were going and taking care of me instead. The band was like a family; some cats might be your brothers and your uncles and others more like second cousins, but still in all you were related.

Albert crossed his arms over his chest. *I still worry whether I'll ever be able to teach anybody as much as those cats taught me.*

Well, Latif said *you can try. I need everything you got to give, and fast.*

What you need is patience, said Albert. *Take it easy, greasy. You can't always be getting better.* He studied Latif. *All you young cats nod your heads,* Van Horn said gravely, *but none of you hear me. That's alright, though. You'll learn when you have to.*

FLATNESS | SCRAPING | SNAKES

The doorbell rang for the first time at twelve and for the last by quarter past. This session was bigger than Latif's first: half a dozen horns and three cats each on bass drums and piano, rotating so that each of the nine possible rhythm permutations got some run. Latif kept to his kitchen table seat as everybody ate and mingled. He chatted a little bit but not much; what could he say to these cats? Most of them diddy-bopped around the city and the country and the planet, dipping in and out of bands and hooking each other with gigs. They spoke in first names only, telling stories about Don and Tony while Latif wondered Moye, Pullen? Williams, Hart? and couldn't ask. Half of them, as he'd thought, had met Albert during master classes at Manhattan School or Berklee College of Music in Boston, where Latif had considered applying for about four minutes, until he told Wess and Wess said *That's great if you want to sound like a Berklee cat.* Berklee cats worked, though.

Latif sat out the first tune like a surfer straddling his board, watching small unridable waves roll underneath him. The only soloist who got his shit off was the trumpet player, a stocky untall cat—what trumpet player wasn't?—with rings on seven fingers which threw light across the room when he fingered his pedals. Latif watched the band thump through the tune and noticed Albert wasn't even in the room and got to thinking: Maybe playing with the Van Horn Quartet had ruined him for other musicians. Having Murray and Amir and Sonny behind him and Albert watching like a patron saint was very different from—he stopped, knowing he was bullshitting himself.

He'd blamed everyone and everything for what had happened here last week. Decided he was just burned out like every other New Yorker and taken Tuesday off and slept for fifteen hours, woken up and played like a doddering old man whose stories piddled into mumbling senility. Cursed the New York Police Department and Spliff and Tristan and went to dinner Thursday night with Mona before work and sat in an Upper West Side cafe chewing morosely on French bread and animosity. *I'm not playing*, he said, mouth moving dead around the words. It was a disclaimer, Mona realized a few minutes later. *I'm not playing* meant *I'm not responsible for my actions; I'm about to start being an asshole.* His tone became acidic and his manner harsh; he answered her as if she'd interrupted matters of portent with stupid questions. Like all of this was her fault.

This is how it ends up, she thought. They get a little close to you and before long you're the only person near enough to hurt. And here she was letting him, becoming Mona at fourteen again, locked into a mode where shit was all there was and taking it was all you did and it was bad but you got good at it and that was life. Mona hadn't had the chance to walk out back then—walk out into what? They just followed you, yelling.

This is one hell of a solo you're playing on me, Mona almost said as they sat cutting and stabbing at their meals, eyes on their plates. She wondered just what it would take for her to leave, what nasty word or insolent expression would make her calves tense instinctual and slide the chair back.

Latif sipped his water and wondered whether he should say some of the things he felt, flip Mona's whole sharing-giving-knowing shit around and tell her that at this moment, he felt for her the same thing he did for Dutchman's and his horn: an inextricable connection so great that it was indistinct. It might have been love, hate, or need; he couldn't tell.

He'd stared at the painting for hours that day and thought about *The Picture of Dorian Gray*, a book Wess had given him the summer after high school in which the portrait of a man absorbs his sins and leaves his body unspoiled by age or sin. Mona's picture only bounced his maladies back at him, and the longer Latif looked, the more wrong colors and ideas he noticed and the angrier he got. Below Mona's presumptuous blind-guess artlessness was his own, and it glared at him until Latif didn't know whether Mona had been desperate and crazy or just cruel to paint his dream. He'd stood up and stepped into his pants and cinched the belt one-handed, already late to meet her and unhurried. He moved to hit the lightswitch and then changed his mind. Latif wanted the painting to be waiting for him when he got back.

He thought of it now and peered into his hornbell, looking for snakes as the rhythm section switched up, snare rattling with everybody's movement over the wood floor. No snakes. He would've settled for a fangful of venom just to feel something, but the horn was hollow as a cave. The new musicians settled in and the horn line made room for him. The tune was a fast blues and when his turn to play came Latif was still thinking of snakes and the time Mona had asked him if he ever felt out of control, deciding that if he lived through this session he'd call her and say *Yes, I'm out of control now; I don't want to treat you this way but I can't stop myself.*

The drummer was playing fast and light; he was the type of cat who hadn't realized yet that there was more to the trap set than the snare, hi-hat and bass drum, that the toms and floor toms and the crash and sock cymbals could be used for more than just effect. Instead, he'd mastered one corner of the kit and was content to play it with great intricacy.

Latif came in fast, after a marchingband snare fill, and immediately found himself ensnarled in his own bullshit. What made it worse was that it was the kind of bullshit that covered for itself, that fooled nonplayers and even some musicians for a minute because it was frenetic, nimble: nutritionless ear candy. Latif was making no decisions, playing every note, filling up whitespace like a blabbering idiot. He rocketed through the air executing meaningless tricks and felt that everything he knew, all the speed and style he'd picked up, was useless. So what if he knew how to fly the plane; he had no bomb to drop. He could play these flashy lines forever and feel nothing. He might as well be lying on the couch watching TV and eating frozen pizza.

Van Horn beckoned him into the kitchen when the tune was over and sealed the doorway with his frame. *Number one*, he said, pep-talky *you know you're bullshitting. Nobody has to tell you that, and that's good. All it takes for a lotta cats to convince themselves otherwise is some handclapping or a nice write-up. You're too honest for that.*

Latif leaned against the wall and hung his thumbs from his belt. *Great*, he said.

Listen. Writers get writer's block, ballplayers slump, dancers sprain their ankles. The important thing is not to panic. The same old stuff that got you here will get you out. You wouldn't be here in the first place if it wasn't some damn fine stuff from the beginning.

I feel like everything I know is trickling out of me, Latif said, grimacing. *I swear, if there was anything that would kickstart me even a little bit I'd take it, even if it killed me.*

Don't joke about that, Van Horn snapped.

Latif sighed. He knew he sounded immature, alarmist, willfully ignorant, but something self-destructive in him pushed relentlessly ahead. He felt the way he sometimes did after a quick couple of drinks, when a slight buzz demanded loudly to be reinforced and he drank with determination. After a third drink the feeling always faded and drinking bored him, but for that raging half-hour, Latif plunged toward obliteration with intensity. *Wess told me once about this French poet who just stopped writing at nineteen,* he said. *Just disappeared into the countryside and never wrote again. That's what I feel like doing. I don't know if I have anything to say anymore, much less how to say it. I pick up my horn, Albert, and I feel like*

I'm sign-languaging a poem with my hands all burnt and bandaged up in gauze.

It's not that you can't play, said Albert. His voice was soft and funeral serious. He pressed his hands together in a prayer position and pointed his fingertips at Latif. *And it's not that you have nothing to say. It's that you won't say it. What are you afraid of? What's so ugly that you can't play it?*

Latif had no answer. He was dying to play; how could Albert not see that? *What are you afraid of?* Was Albert calling him a coward, even as Latif paced back and forth in his own cavernous head and wondered what mortal sacrifices he could make to get this music back?

He mumbled an I-need-to-think goodbye and Van Horn nodded and Latif walked out the house and toward the water wondering what people did, people in general who didn't play music or write or paint or draw or dance, or have religion. How did stockbrokers and bartenders reckon with the world; how did men decide to start families? Was it the same love that made a man get married as made him blow a horn or pluck a bass? Did the raw desire to create, the only force in Latif's life he'd never doubted would guide him forever, did that certainty manifest in some men as love for another person, a woman? A son?

Latif couldn't imagine knowing that he wanted to be with someone for life, bound to her, the love between them superseding what he felt or used to feel when he picked up his horn and blew his soul. He had been a son, he had seen husbands and wives. His own father had not been so bound to either wife or son that he hadn't moved on in course of time. His own love for his mother hadn't filled him; he'd been hollow until he found this music and what was love anyway without a vent hole, a way to proclaim it, sing it, celebrate it, and interrogate it? Latif tried to imagine being happy, so happy that he didn't need to testify to it, and could not. Nor could he envision a despair so deep that proclaiming it, beating it out of the underbrush with drums and shouting, would be impossible. Nothing scared him that much. Only the thought of being without drums and shouting.

He reached the water and the sun was setting. Plastic baby carriage wheels clicked across the stone pathway behind him and Latif rested his elbows on the railing and stared. Everything around him whispered with music and he felt suddenly like an abomination, a mistake of nature, horribly deformed and staggering with crooked legs and twisted eyes through the wholenumber harmony of life. The water rippled evenly, a plush-plush walking bassline rising and ebbing along its own axes of movement. The trees swayed and stood when and where they should, and Latif bent over the iron fence wanting to vomit up his lungs as an apology, a penance for falling out of synchronization with the world.

Maybe she's working late, Latif said, looking at his watch. He and Sonny sat drinking at the only table in Dutchman's that wasn't still piled with inverted chairs from last night's sweep-up. Latif was unsurprised that Mona hadn't shown; she'd walked through his unlocked door at six-thirty yesterday to go to dinner and found him lying naked on the floor, an ash cigarette balanced vertical between his lips and a half-empty pack in his left hand.

I've got a new painting for you, Latif said in response to her sarcastic *Ready to go?* The ash toppled onto his lips when he spoke and he ignored it. *A guy who keeps blowing and blowing on his horn but nothing comes out, and instead his head gets bigger and bigger until it explodes and splatters all over the walls. Then the snakes come out and lick it off.* He spit the cigarette butt in the air, loudly, raising a cloud of ash. The filter landed on his chest. He craned his arm and bent it at the elbow so his fist was over his face, then tilted the pack until a cigarette slid out. He caught it with his lips.

Mona, bored and annoyed by the whole scene, said nothing. Latif knew she was coming, she thought; he'd wanted her to find him like this. She wondered whether he had studied the apartment like a set designer and made minute adjustments for her: arrayed himself at just the proper angle or draped and redraped the clothes littering the usually immaculate room so that her entrance would play perfectly. She had no patience for this juvenile shit, these human dioramas Latif constructed to let her know he was in pain, in need of sympathy or closeness or distance or support or whatever without opening his mouth. She glanced at her painting, leaning up against the window, and noticed a pair of orange-handled scissors balanced open on top.

I take it we're not having dinner, Mona said after a minute. *So I'm gonna go now.* She put her hands in her coat pockets and turned slowly toward the door.

I probably need to be alone. Latif sighed, in a tone Mona knew was supposed to sound contrite and troubled. Apology and excuse rolled into one.

Well, do me a favor and just cancel next time, said Mona, then panged with regret that she'd sounded so harsh. *You can call me if you want to talk*, she added, softer.

Around eleven he had, and Mona listened to the streetnoise behind him thinking how ridiculous it was that her man considered a corner payphone his home line. He likes having no phone, Mona thought. That way she was reachable and he wasn't.

I don't know what I'm supposed to do when you're like this, she said into the receiver, pacing her studio. She'd gone home and taken a bath and now she was trying to get up the gusto to work. Instead of her mother's elusive baby blues, though, Mona closed her eyes and saw Latif's despondent darkbrowns, staring at her from his grimy floor.

Neither do I. You shouldn't have to deal with that. Latif was weird about patching things up on the phone. Standing in public with his quarter running out, wary about cats on the block somehow knowing he was holding weight, Latif was sometimes refreshingly candid and other times inclined to say whatever he thought Mona wanted to hear. Either way, they argued in shorthand and nothing seemed real. This time Latif had stood unspeaking for what seemed like minutes, the payphone receiver microphoning life as it screaming by, and Mona had held back, pulled the conversation into none of the dark territories encroaching on her heart. Instead she listened to Latif think, and when the quarter dropped and forced him to act he spoke over the operator's automated voice. *Have a drink with me and Sonny after work tomorrow?* knowing she didn't like Sonny Burma and for good goddamn reason. But there was pleading in his tone and she agreed.

So where was she? *She'll show up*, Sonny assured.

Latif grimaced around the cocktail straw he was chewing and leaned his head against his fisted hand. As his identity faltered, Latif resorted to overwrought gestures to make sure his frustration, and thus his seriousness, was duly noted. *Sometimes I wish I had somebody like Marisol,* Latif confided. *Somebody who'd just shut the fuck up and get my back like it was her job.*

They don't grow those domestically, smirked Sonny. *You got to import. And unless you're a genius like Albert she's an idiot for sacrificing herself. Even if you are.*

Maybe that kind of support brings genius into bloom.

Even if it does, man, you'd hate it. Marisol used to go around saying I no love man, I love musician. *She might as well be Albert's personal assistant.*

Well, I've got one other fantasy relationship up my sleeve.

Let me guess, said Sonny. *The two great artists living together in mutual badness, wedded to art and each other in a symbiotic bohemian bliss quite different from anything you've ever actually seen.*

Latif nodded sheepishly. *Throw in that homegirl sucks dick like a champ and you've pretty much got it.*

Whenever you needed her, she'd be busy. And vice versa.

I could deal with that, Latif said. *Mona's always telling me I don't make her feel needed. I'm like what the fuck do you want me to do, need you more than I need you?*

How's her stuff, anyway? She really on some artist shit?

It's good, but no. She's on some ol Emily-Dickinson-die-with-a-house-full-of-poems shit.

Sonny chuckled. *She's probably sitting someplace right now telling somebody that her boyfriend's on some ol Vinny-Van-die-miserable-and-obsessed-with-his-work shit. That's the stuff you got to watch, Teef, like my man Rubberlegs Williams used to sing.* Latif smiled recognition, though he'd never heard the tune. *You only have so much energy, and if the music takes it all then where are you?*

But if the music doesn't take it all then where's the music?

The music's gonna be alright. The music's gonna get played with or without you, just like Albert says.

Latif smiled. *He told me that last week. Mona says it all the time now, even though she has no idea what the fuck it means. Maybe I don't either. It just makes me feel expendable.*

Man, you got it twisted. The idea is that there's a whole tradition keeping you afloat, and if you drop the ball somebody's gonna pick it up.

. . . So it doesn't really matter what I do. Great.

Sonny pointed his finger at Latif. *You need another drink, boy. Remind me of my cousin's kid. Decided he was gonna be a rapper and now every day Russell Simmons doesn't stop him on the way to school and offer him a deal he gets angrier. Mufucker, you nineteen years old. When I was your age, I was wearing my daddy's suits to gigs. Had to keep my elbows bent all night so the sleeves wouldn't cover my hands, and the jacket buttoned so no one would see that I had the waist folded over and pulled up around my ribs. I'd even put on four or five pairs of socks and wear his shoes. Every check I got went straight into the tailor's pocket.*

Albert seems to think the road would straighten me out.

Sonny shrugged equivocation. *Thing about the road is that not only does it make clear who's bullshitting—something the bandstand lays bare anyway—but also why. Everybody's analyzing everybody, whispering crosscurrents of shit-talk and familial concern. Lotta interpersonal polyrhythms to decode.*

Sounds like it could be a nightmare, said Latif.

All depends on the band. The more you understand about each other, the better y'all might sound. Or the worse. You might have a cat who never wants to stop playing; gotta figure out if he's the most serious dude around or the most trifling. Amir was with a pianist like that in Charlie Sanchez's band; he said it took them all a couple of months to figure out that homeboy's reluctance to stand up from the pianobench didn't stem so much from straightshot ebony-and-ivory love as from a fear of having to relate to motherfuckers any other way but through those keys. The finest waitress in the club walked by, plump ass eye-popping even beneath straightlegged black uniform pants, and they paused to give her smiles and stare after her.

It's all about finding a balance on the road, Burma said when she was gone. *Ol Mr. Play-All-Night might seem as deep as holy hellfire as he tries to cajole cats into joining him for a postgig session in the hotel lobby, offering to play time for the absent drummer out getting laid. Or when he stays at the club by himself, linebacker shoulders up around his ears as he puts down those two-handed meaty trinkletinkles on the dressingroom piano with the door open. He knows those sounds are bound to draw in some young lingering drummer only too happy to accompany Play-All-Night's Latin lines on a beer bottle and a spoon until dawn shows its asscrack.*

Sounds like Play-All-Night's gonna be one hell of a musician even if he is socially retarded, Teef opined.

Maybe, said Sonny, looking left and right and then returning to his interrupted point, *but if he keeps dragging his woodshed everywhere like it's a porta-potty then he's gonna miss some other shit that he can't grow without. Maybe while he's in the lobby the bassist, tenorman, and roadmanager are huddled over some latenight-menu room service, TV in the background playing time, having a session of their own. Maybe the bass player intros by pizzicato bitching about the leader underpaying them—which Play-All-Night doesn't even know, let's say, cause this the first band he's been in.*

Maybe from there, they stretch the convo into an analysis of generational jazzworld discord, or backflip into band business and break down how the new arrangement sounds or discuss new tunes to bring the leader. Sonny sipped his drink and smiled. *Or maybe they're just talking dumb shit—but the dumb shit is important too, because you learn to flow from topic to topic together, as a unit. One time, I remember, we spent* an hour discussing interspecies fighting—who would win if a polar bear and a hippopotamus should somehow meet under neutral sportsmanlike conditions. Or a shark and an elephant in five feet of water. And then the saxophonist's gaze fell on a framed photo of our bass player's son, always the last thing to go back in his suitcase, and boom, we're building about raising kids and how to make a marriage work in the face of travel and all this ass out here. You dig? Latif nodded.

And a cat like Play-All-Night, his only contribution to all that is an Art Tatum impression rising from the lobby like campfire sparks, reaching the thirdfloor window still glowing. Amir told me that after a while, there was a sort of unspoken thing in the band where everybody kind of wanted to stay up talking until Play-All-Night quit and went to bed or joined the cipher. But he never did either one, and everybody wound up exhausted all the time from trying to outlast him. On top of which, you're never alone on the road except right before bed, so even when you want to crash you end up puttering around your room or calling your girl in New York or, if you're me, jerking off to the sounds of the blacked-out adult movies because you're too cheap to pay for porn.

Into their cloud of laughter shuffled Larry Calvin, gaunt and ashy-fingered, hands dangling at his sides bare of his trademark rings. Lo-Cal Larry Larr, said Sonny, jubilant. What's poppin, partner? Haven't seen your ass in here for weeks.

That's because he's supposed to be at City Hospital, said Teef sternly, fixing Larry with impassive eyes. Say Brother gave him half the money for a one-month treatment that ain't over til next week. It was the dealer's conscience-balming policy to pony up a portion of the rehab bill for any longtime client who decided it was time to kick. I'm in the leisure service business, Say Brother would say. I ain tryna make no junkies. If a cat on Say Bro's clean list tried to cop, Latif was supposed to refuse the sale.

Come on, bruh, said Larry, do me a solid. I got a gig lined up at Free

Will tomorrow and I need my medicine. Gotta blow my head to blow my horn that good. His eyes drifted over to Sonny. *You know what I mean, Burma. Say Brother will never know, Teef. That's my word.*

Latif regarded him from beneath halfmasted eyelids, too sympathetic to Lo-Cal's plight to turn him down. It wasn't the first time Latif had heard this rap; plenty of musicians seemed to agree smack was a toxin but a fuel. He gave Larry what he needed and they watched him vanish like a specter.

It's true, Sonny said when he was gone. *He's almost listenable when he's high.* Latif nodded. How many nights had he watched Sonny negotiate the supreme mathematics of the blues, swing the band like a babe in arms, twenty minutes after the needle slid beneath his skin? How many times had Latif made deliveries to loft apartment jam sessions, stuck around to sit in with a borrowed horn and watched the night brush morning in a swirl of creation and consumption?

Some cats just hear better high, Sonny continued. He lit a cigarette and so did Teef. *The colors in the music come out more distinctly. It's like a sunbeam through a haze; you can't see nothing but fog all around you, but when that beam breaks through it's like the sun has never been brighter. You hear pure blocks of sound.*

Sonny's eyes brightened and Latif turned in his chair to see what he was missing. *Well, well. Better late than never.* Mona walked toward them through Dutchman's, swaying her hips and smiling. A hint of lechery glinted in Sonny's eyes as Mona bent forward in her lowcut dress to kiss him hello. Teef felt a twinge of pride.

Sorry I'm late; the subway's all fucked up. What did I miss?

Not much, said Latif. He smiled to let her know that last night's despondence was behind him, hoping he looked more convincing than he felt. Mona squeezed his hand and he relaxed.

She was certainly remarkable sometimes. Nothing in her carriage suggested the scene she had walked out on yesterday. Watching her almost made him forget himself.

Just waiting for you to show up so we could get into something deep, winked Sonny.

Well, it just so happens I've got something deep to talk to you about, said Mona, crossing her legs and reaching for Latif's smokes.

Oh yeah? said Sonny mildly, lifting the tablecandle to her lips. Latif pinched Mona's thigh beneath the table and she looked at him like *I know and I don't care.* He'd been pleading with her not to do this since they met, and now it looked like his bargaining power was gone.

Baby— said Latif.

Your brother Marlon misses you, said Mona. She exhaled smoke. Sonny's lip curved like she'd made a joke. *Says who?*

Says Marlon. Mona leaned forward, elbows on the table and breasts squeezed between them, cigarette cocked next to her ear. *How do you think it feels to have the person you trust most disown you just for being gay?*

It's more complicated than that, Mona, said Sonny, slow and deliberate, like he was talking to a ten-year-old he didn't like. He stared down and traced a line across the table with his cocktail straw. *And frankly, it's none of your business.*

It may not be, but nobody else is willing to tell you to stop being an asshole so I'm making it my business.

Sonny glanced at Latif and tried to play it off: slouched in his chair pretend-bemused and said, *Your girl is whylin, bruh.*

Mona leaned further toward him, until her chair was pitched up on its frontlegs: secret-sharing distance. She put her hand on Sonny's arm. Latif watched him soften at her touch and was impressed despite himself. *Listen,* Mona said. *I know what it feels like to lose touch with family and convince yourself that you don't care. Let me tell you something, and then I promise I'll shut up. When I met Marlon I was just learning to paint. We'd go for coffee after class at MOMA and sit and talk for hours. He made me feel like I could be an artist, like I was searching for myself in the right place. He showed me some things I'll always be grateful for, the same way I'll bet somebody showed you things when you first started playing the piano. The same way I'll bet you showed Marlon things when he was growing up. He misses you, Sonny, and I bet you miss him.*

He's my brother, said Sonny. *Of course I miss him. But that's not the point.*

What is the point? asked Mona quick. *That you hate fags? Or that you're too stubborn to say you're sorry when you know you're wrong?*

Sonny stared off, scanned the portraits on the walls, spoke without looking at her. *This is the first time anybody's mentioned Marlon to me in years,* he said. His one-note laugh was a rusty knife scraping the air. *Sometimes that pisses me off. Makes no sense, huh? Getting angry because your friends don't bring up something you told them not to?*

A lot of things make no sense. Mona smiled; Sonny smiled back, reluctantly, and Mona pressed her advantage. *This is really the last thing I'll say: Anytime you decide you want to see your brother, I'd be happy to arrange it.*

Is he still dating whiteboys? asked Sonny. *No offense.*

Mona shook her head. *No. He's been with a Haitian man for two years now.*

Huh, said Sonny. *Well, don't hold you breath. But thanks. I'm glad to know he's got a friend like you. Alright. Enough. New topic. Who's drinking what?*

Mona was quiet in the cab up from the bar, arms folded stoic. Latif wondered if her mind was on Marlon Burma or on him; he got his answer the minute they were back uptown in the disheveled stankness of Latif's neglected room. Mona sat down on the unmade bed and didn't take her coat off. *You know what?* she said. *You're never depressed in public. With Sonny, you're fine, and then as soon as we get in the cab I feel you sinking back into your own world.*

I pretend better in public, said Latif. He didn't want to join her on the bed and there was nowhere else to sit except the floor, so he paced. *You want me to pretend for you?*

Sit still, thought Mona; why can't you sit still? *I want you to treat me as well as you do total strangers*, she said.

He stopped abruptly in midstride and turned to face her. *We are strangers*, he said hardvoiced, turning up the volume. *You don't understand me and I don't understand you, okay?* Latif threw up his hands like Icarus. *I don't even understand myself. I'm sitting here with my horn like a fucking kid at his father's bedside, holding his hand and waiting for him to die, and I'm sorry but that's all I can think about right now.*

Mona nodded through his last few words as if she'd heard it all before. *Yeah yeah yeah*, she said, and Latif winced at the venom in her voice. *The great tortured artist who can't play. I'm sorry, but do you know how boring that is?*

The word cut him, sharp with unexpectedness. He knew he was temperamental, caustic, an occasional asshole, but in all his mirror-searching Latif had never felt bored—that was half a step from giving up. It was cruel, that word; it slapped his whole life flat. He stared at Mona, hurt. Her eyes flickered sadness, in apology not only for what she'd said but what she knew she was about to.

In a tone somewhere between reluctant truth-teller and

weary victim, Mona went on. *That horn is a cop-out, baby. Your fa-*
ther's gone, you've spoken to your mother what, twice, since you moved,
you hate your sleazy job and you think your biggest problem is your
horn? That's an effect, Latif; that's not a cause.

Mona sat still on the bed, tucked her hands under her thighs
and watched him. Latif was silent, standing awkwardly with one
arm bent behind his back and his stare frozen to the floor. He was
listening and he was hurt, she thought; he might crumple into a
pile of limbs or reanimate and scream. Mona hated when things
got loud, and so she spoke like people walked on frozen ponds.

You're fighting so hard not to need anybody, Latif. He didn't move.
You think if you stay closed off, bad things can't get in. But how will good
things? She bent a little bit, trying to duck into his line of vision,
but he refused to look at her. *From the day we met, you've been giv-*
ing me reasons why I can't be close to you. I'm white. I'm not a musi-
cian. She gestured at the painting. *I'm overstepping my bounds when*
I try to reach out to you. Well then, why are we trying?

She stopped and felt tears welling unexpectedly, wiped a wrist
below her watery nose and smeared a tear into her ear and felt the
tiny drop incavernate there. Latif looked up and blinked; the sight
of tears always muted his feelings, directed them outward, melted
them into remorse. He hoped, suddenly and desperately, that
Mona had a reason.

I don't know, Latif said in a small, choked voice. *Why are we*
trying?

Because we're people, Mona said through trembling lips. *People*
need each other. We're the same.

Latif craned his neck to the ceiling, pressed his eyes with his
handheels until his mind danced with colordots; he watched them
dissipate and thought about her words. How come white people
were always the ones coming with that we're-the-same rap? Did
they want to let you know you were as good as they were, or

reassure themselves they were as good as you despite their cruelty? How dare Mona tear him apart like that, tell him he was boring and self-deluded and rigid, a total fuck-up, and then try to make up? Why did she want to worm her way into his life if he was so terrible? Maybe Mona was just weak and needy and wanted everybody else to be too—didn't have a tradition to hold up and aspire to and chase after, nothing of grandeur and nobility to enliven and torture her and so she wanted to tear at the only thing he had of meaning and—

We're not the same. He looked at her with bleary eyes and Mona was stunned at how mean Latif suddenly looked, how hunted. He pounded his chest twice with his right fist. *This is my life,* he seethed. *I've got nowhere else to go; I've got to deal with this or it will kill me.* He stopped and looked at her, eyes wild hard, then sneered *I'm not painting my fucking mother here.*

Mona shook her head in slow shock that Latif would lunge so viciously, hurt her so deliberately. She stepped toward him: *Fuck you,* Mona spit, then slapped him hard across the face and gasped and stepped back quickly in surprise and fear, the hand that did it pressed now disbelieving to her mouth.

She gaped at him with naked fright, and her expression made Latif angrier than the fact that she had hit him. His words had beckoned violence and he knew it, perhaps even wanted it, but this look was something else: Mona thought that he would hit her back. She looked at him like he was an animal, Latif thought, a goddamn wild animal. He stepped toward her and she flinched, and seeing it Latif snatched up the closest thing to him, an alarm clock, and raised it behind his head.

You think I'm gonna hit you, Mona? That what you're waiting for? He whirled the other way and heaved the clock at the open window. It punched a jagged hole through Mona's painting, through the saxophonist's chest. The canvas toppled and fell upside down onto the floor, the huge tear flapping.

Both of them stared at it. *I'm sorry*, said Latif, hardbreathing through his nose bull-like. *I didn't mean to do that.* Mona stared furious, sharks cutting through the blueness straight at him, then darted her eyes at his horn lying in the corner.

No, he said. *Uh-uh. Not in your life. I ain't Smiley. I'll put my foot dead deep up in your ass.*

I learn from my mistakes, said Mona, recoiling bitter, angry that he knew. *At least I thought I did.*

Better write it down this time so you remember, said Latif. *No more nigger boyfriends.*

I didn't say that! Mona screamed. *You said that!*

Latif walked to the window and looked out at the alarm clock lying lonely in the street. *Yeah*, he admitted. *I did.*

His anger was gone; he looked at Mona now and saw a distant symbol, saw himself one in the convex mirror of her eyes. It was simple that way. Simpler. He wiped sweat from his brow onto his pants and collapsed into an Indian-sit on the floor, arms dangling loose over his knees, head bent forward.

This isn't me, Latif said. He sighed and the breath shuddered out of him. *I'm sorry. I'm just so fucked up right now . . .* He looked at the floor. They were silent. Finally, Latif heard Mona walk toward him.

I'm sorry too, she said. *But I'm sick of playing missionary to the dark fucking continent. When you understand yourself a little better, give me a call.* And the door slammed behind her.

Latif stayed where he was and nausea rumbled his stomach, threatened to rend his guts and the day's nourishment and leave him as empty as he felt. He looked around for something to puke into and found himself wondering what it would feel like to throw up in his hornbell, defile it with what was inside him. Soon, though, the nausea ebbed and a new urge asserted itself, one he couldn't identify, a craving which contradicted the compulsion to purge. He touched his shirtpocket and felt the pack of cigarettes but knew that wasn't it. Touching the cigarettes was an associative gesture, a reminder of the moment outside Dutchman's when he had first needed a smoke although he'd never had one. Latif felt his heart bang beneath the menthol softpack and panicked when he realized that his body was asking him for heroin.

Latif sat on the floor of his room, under the mirror, and did it without flinching, casually precise like it wasn't his body. And it wasn't as the surge of warm electrics radiated through him, coloring his thinking; he knew how he must look and wanted to laugh at finally being inside the joke of what's really going on while all the world sees nothing but a stoned musician nodding vagrant rhythms. The tuning fork vibrations of every muscular decussitation, heartbeat, and neurological pinprick tingled and resounded through his body; it was an ecstasy so self-contained that even the slightest movement might have pushed him over the edge of sensory overstimulation; lifting his leg or brushing a palm against the hardwood was unthinkable. Everything was unthinkable; the only data pulsing in the blunted clot of Latif's brain was an unassimilated unreadable appreciation of a universe in which one could breathe this slow and feel this good.

Three hours later he twitched an eyelid, blinked though a crust of snot and tearsalt at a gleaming point of light across the room, dim through his undilated eyes but steady glowing. It was a refracted sunbeam dancing on the fingerpedal of his horn, and from this northstar Latif mapped out the constellation of his instrument, squinted it into focus and snaked mind tentacles around it and squeezed forth a sound, a rustybrown flat tone sheet that hummed toward him in a straight slow line, cleaving through space shedding a halflife vapor trail. He held it, amazed, afraid that if he looked away, unclenched his jaw, blinked, it would vanish. When the tone had almost reached him, Latif scraped up the courage to try altering it; his next thought made it dip into a lower register and fatten to a deeper chocolate brown, and Latif watched, listened, euphoric. These sounds were purer than any he had ever heard. They were whole. He willed a simple melody into existence and watched it chase its tail, then blinked and made another sound dive through it like a ring of fire—orchestrated an array of interplays until the room dizzied with multicolored ribbons of music rippling together and apart, dancing to his thoughts. It was a feeling greater than any music he had ever played, an apex of expression so innate and natural and affirming that Latif couldn't imagine the anxiety of separation, the fear of inarticulation, that had plagued him for so long. Thoughts and music were the same; it was merely a question of bypassing translation, automating the conversion as he just had.

Blocks of sound: All of a moment, Teef understood what Sonny meant. Before the miosis into bass saxophone piano drum there was a solid chunk of music like a sculptor's uncut stone. The musician found the form and fault lines, chiseled the block into a statue. Until now Latif had been trying to build a statue from the ground, piling up rocks instead of chipping at the block to shape the space around it. He lifted his hand to his head to rub in the epiphany and found his domepiece wet with sweat. His joints hurt; he felt achy and crawled shivering to bed. Smoking a cigarette calmed him. Latif slept.

He dreamed that some musicians were time bombs, strategically developed secret cyborgs built by the conspiracy and programmed to play jazz, to be heroic blowers of the now. And after years, recording dates, world tours, interviews, band breakups and re-formations, innovations and compositions, when the club was packed with as many of the kind of people who found hope and validation in the music as could fit inside, the kind of people the conspiracy wanted dead, the musicians would explode in flame and razor shrapnel, killing everyone.

There was no way of telling which musician, which genius of the form, might be a killer. There was speculation; some music buffs claimed they could discern a hallmark timbre in the cyborgs' playing, a certain commonality of phrasing, but men who claimed this had been known to die like all the rest. People knew that it might happen but they sat in jazz clubs all the same; they chanced it and they listened. Musicians took the biggest risks of all, spent half their lives at ground zero and never knew which of their bandmates might explode. Latif ran from Wessel Gates to Van Horn to Sonny Burma and suddenly each one had a serial number on his wrist, each one clicked mechanically from the neck and hummed suddenly electric, and he ran from all of them, barefoot through an endless tunnel washed in dull fluorescence, but the humming wouldn't stop. He threw a hammer through the ceiling and the lighting died. He stopped and saw the nightsky glinting through the hole and heard birds twitter but the humming was still there. Latif realized he was a timebomb too and woke up screaming.

He never stopped. His body shrieked with pain and need if he ignored the dripping nose and eyes, the sudden sweating hotness and shivery yawns and clenching stomach which meant it was time to fix himself another hit. The kid got bad so fast. Cats said it took a month or more of dabbling before your body fully forgot how to function without regular infusions of poison, and as day one blurred into day two and then day three Latif told himself he was only fucking around. There was still time to pull out, write up this binge as an experiment and let the results, the revelations, reinvigorate his music. Latif had no point of comparison for his consumption, no way to know if he was going overboard. The facts he could recall were masquerading anecdotes he bent to serve his need to feel alright. Sonny had told him that what did most cats in, made their habits balloon until unmanageable, was hanging out with other users. Just hearing cats discuss their need to score could have you salivating for a fix, even if you knew you didn't need one.

Latif took solace in the knowledge that he was alone; no fraternal aggregate of laughing musicians was here to glamorize the act, to normalize a physical process which still partly horrified Latif even as he performed it on himself. He latched onto Sonny's words and squinted until he could not see past them and the reassurance they provided, and five days passed in a constipated binge of sensory pingpong, Latif bouncing between bliss and anguish without once leaving his room. He had so much smack that it seemed for a while as if his reserve would last forever.

The insight he'd glimpsed after his first hit still filled Latif with hope; he'd found what he'd set out in pursuit of, and he wanted to return to that place of discovery. He knew addicts were forever trying to recapture the magic of their first time, but Latif pursued it nonethless, with the same single-minded rigor, the same sense of purpose, with which he'd hefted his horn those first few silent weeks in New York. He was back in the woodshed.

Murray Higgins had nothing on this drug as far as time went. It borrowed without returning, burrowed without surfacing. Latif and his horn and the objects in his room became a still life, forms on which the changing light played as the sun rose, peaked, waned, set.

Latif ate only once, on the second day, couldn't keep the food down and never had the urge to try again; an almost full styrofoam container of Szechuan chicken and vegetable fried rice sat rotting on the floor and so did he. *Don't get high on your own supply*. The back of Latif's mind generated dull thoughts; they floated unnoticed for hours before osmosing into his consciousness and taking root: Say Brother must be looking for me. I have to get my shit together. I'm almost out of smack.

Only Sonny Burma knew where he lived, and Burma had come knocking on the door a day ago. Latif had heard his own name vaguely through the haze of mellow madness and thought at first he was hallucinating. When he realized it was Sonny, Latif had wanted nothing more than to explain what he'd done and ask for help, to tell Sonny that he knew now how to play and couldn't even lift his horn, that he had driven himself to the brink of insanity in desperation and discovered what he'd been in search of, a master key that unlocked the relationship of mind to music and erased time space and saxophones, but it had trapped him. It had been a trick. He was entombed now in a one-room purgatory world, diluting his blood with a drug so insidious that it prevented him from putting any use to what it taught him.

He wanted to tell Sonny but he feared what Sonny might say, who he might tell, what a cat like him whose own habit never seemed to fuck him up at all might think. Teef couldn't move to let him in regardless; he sat on the floor holding his mirror in his lap and closed his eyes to Sonny's banging, eyelids humming, afraid to get up. The imaginary breeze against his skin was almost more than he could bear; it whistled evilly against the holes in his arm. The tickling was maddening, and finally Latif gave in, raised a shaking hand and scratched and couldn't stop. He tore himself apart for hours in a steady absentminded clawing rhythm until his flesh was red, sticky, and raw, and blood was caked beneath his nails.

What could pull him out of this, and would he let it? Behind his humming eyelids Latif saw the black cord of the tradition coiling around him like a python, squeezing him until his bones snapped and his lungs popped, unhinging its agate mouth and swallowing him whole, forcing him in lumpy peristalsis gulps into its gullet to the rhythm of Sonny Burma's fist against the door.

Sonny was gone when he got up, had been gone forever. The sickly coldness of the window's light told Latif that it was early morning, six or seven. He must have zoned out wild long; the last image pasted in the scrapbook of his brain was the glow of a sunset, set to sounds of dusktime double Dutch. Latif felt strangely normal, hollow and crampy but sturdy on his legs. Perhaps the storm was over, he thought. But the eeriness of his own body-calm told him this was more likely the hurricane's eye.

Latif stood and walked a slow stiff-legged loop around the room, stretching arms and back. He scratched his head and dandruff fecundated his shoulders. Latif loped to the sink, washed his arm and dried it delicately with a towel. He settled in a catcher's crouch in the bedroom's center, poised on the balls of his feet with his lefthand fingers splayed against the floor for balance.

He blinked in the light, trying to acclimate to his sudden lucidity. Latif didn't trust himself right now; he had to keep watch to ensure that the orders he gave his body were carried out, had to keep himself too busy to get high and hope he remained steady. The best thing to do would be rejoin the world outside, he thought, assuming it was still there. He nodded an affirmation of this plan, adopting a military curtness with himself. Shower. Get dressed. He tried to do some pushups but found himself too weak and ended up lying facedown on the hardwood with his palms pressed flat and elbows pointing in the air, smelling the stale sourness of his body through the soapsmell of the shower. He could feel the soreness in his arms, the rawness from scratching covering a deeper, sharper pain. He rolled over and looked at his watch: nine-thirty. Hours to fill before the club opened.

He would tell Say Brother that a family illness had called him out of town without warning, that he had been in Boston at his mother's bedside all week long, and he would apologize and eat the loss, pay Say Bro's cut out of his own bank account and continue to do business as usual. Part of him knew this was a fantastic idea, to do business as usual once the vendor had become a customer, jumped the million-volt electric fence and landed on the junkies' side amidst discarded needles and the bootlegged economics of dependence, but he let himself believe it all the same.

Business as usual. Business before pleasure. Business never personal.

Latif bolted his horn case and picked it up, then changed his mind and set it down. He put the rest of the skag in his coat pocket and shut the door behind him. The routine competence of his body was a sudden marvel to Latif; the graceful independent way his feet shimmied down flights of stairs, the balance with which he swung open the building's door and slipped outside before it swung back shut.

Spliff was standing by the payphone with his pager in his hand. *Yo, your girl was looking for you, b.*

Latif visored his eyes with the flat of his hand and glared. *She was? When?*

Yesterday, like in the afternoon. Told me to tell you call her.

Thanks. Hey. Three long strides and he was next to Spliff. *Here. Put this in your pocket.* He closedfist-passed the bag of smack. *It's already cut but you could step on it again. I can't be holding it right now.*

Spliff screwfaced him, perplexed, but Latif just walked away, moving fast now, strength returning. He felt like a man making arrangements for his own funeral, and thought suddenly of a werewolf in a movie he'd once seen who chained himself down frantically as the full moon rose, knowing he would soon become a killer. Time was limited; soon Latif's body would claw and wrack, knot and twist in hunger. Until that happened this was nothing: empty rhetoric, meaningless charity. He was a Sunday morning sinner sitting in a church; the question was where he would be once Saturday night rolled back around on goldrimmed tires screaming whiskey.

HALFSTEPS | BETWEEN THE DEVIL AND THE DEEP BLUE SEA | TEARING

Latif zigzag staggered down Manhattan like a tourist, passing personal landmarks: Free Will on 125th and Lenox, Smoke on 106th and Broadway. One of Burma's girl's apartments in the nineties, where he and Sonny had once stopped in for an afterhours meal of tunafish sandwiches, beer, and homemade apple pie. Mona's office building. By late afternoon he was sweaty and exhausted, sitting in a little park around the block from Dutchman's, nothing more than the space between two buildings, fenced in with picnic tables and a swingset, three trees and two inches of gravel on the ground. Sonny liked to go in there sometimes and smoke a joint, gently pendulating on a leathermetal swing like a big kid. He and Latif shared an affinity for swings; *What kind of musicians would we be if we didn't swing?* Sonny always joked. From the swingset in the back, shaded by the trees and practically invisible, you could watch people going by outside without their knowing. Latif sat and dangled his legs, the childsized swing pushing his thighs together flat.

It was almost five. Murray Higgins would be at the club by now, at least, looking at baseball. Latif had never said much to the drummer. They smiled small knowing smiles at each other but conversations sputtered; it was a liking which failed the test of words rather than superseding it. When they did converse, Latif clung to any topic that proved viable for as long as possible, forestalling the abyss of silence which he knew to expect once its vectors expired. He'd felt a certain closeness with Higgins since playing with him, but one on one Latif was always ill at ease. Murray carried himself more like a prizefighter than a musician and he was a massive man, wide and tall and thick and by no means a gentle giant. *The kind of guy you're glad is on your side,* were Sonny's words.

Burma and Amir would rollick in laughter whenever one of them alluded to what Murray had done in Selma or Decatur years ago—stories which had been passed down to them by Albert and were only referenced, never told. Latif could gather only that in each case Higgins had left some local Jim Crow cracker badman wishing he'd left well enough alone. Murray was a loner for the most part, a silent partner in a social band. They all liked him, and sat and joked and drank and smoked with him, but as often as not Higgins would elect to do his own thing after shows and on the road. Only Van Horn, after almost forty years together, was truly close to him. He had met the drummer's family, visited his neighborhood. And they had both come up on tourbuses.

Murray was the oldest of six children and his father's only son. He'd grown up poor in Oakland, light-skinned and wavy-haired at a time when high-yellow pretty boys had plenty to make up for, plenty to prove. Higgins had proved it all and then some; at thirteen he was six feet tall and had gotten into so many street fights, bars, and high school girls' drawers that his daddy had enough and found the money somewhere to send Murray to a military school in the Northeast, where he discovered marching bands and drums and boxing and forgot about most everything else for the next five years.

Albert met Higgins at a jam session at Spirits, traveling through Atlanta while he was still a sideman with The Emperor. From that very first night hearing him play, Van Horn told Latif, he had known Murray was the man to lay down the sound he'd been hearing in his head, the special rhythm groundwork that would free him to explore his own instrument in ways he'd only just begun to think about. They went out for a drink and Van Horn told Murray he was getting ready to put together his own group and that he heard some things he liked in Higgins' sound. They kept in touch by phone and mail as each one crisscrossed the country, exchanging tapes and other vital information. And when the time came Higgins was right there waiting, the first official member of the group.

Dutchman's was quiet when Latif walked in, employees finishing their set-up chores and lollygagging by the bar and Murray Higgins sitting in a way-back booth, the worst seat in the house, with a straight scotch in one hand and the *Amsterdam News* folded in the other. Latif nodded hellos as he walked through, then slid into the booth across from Higgins. *Hey, Murray.* It was only when he was high that Higgins was a cruel bastard, Sonny said. *His Irish side comes out.* With friends he stayed mellow, but in strangers' mannerisms Higgins found insult, and acted in keeping with the due rights of a man wronged and with state boxing regulations. If that meant the whole band had to hightail it out of the Deep South just ahead of a white mob—as Sonny said he'd heard had happened when Murray was playing with Brother Landis Hand back in the day—it didn't bother Higgins much.

Hey, Teef. Murray's voice was grainy, guttural, heavy with the kind of gutbucket soul that epitomized the world's conception of how jazz musicians sounded. *Murray is those drums,* said Albert lovingly, and it was true. He cackled snarelike, rattling sharp, told jokes with cymbals in his voice, defended his trap set from the occasional grabby overcuriousity of fans with deep tom-tom resound. Now his fleshy horizontal right fist sliced toward Latif in greeting like a giant mallet head.

Hey. Teef met Murray's fist with his own and leaned back into the corner of the booth, throwing his left leg up onto the cushionplastic and faking relaxation. *So what's new in the world today?* He offered Murray a cigarette.

Murray with the cigarette unlit between his lips said *Nun much. Says here that forty percent of all restaurants and bars fold within a year of opening their doors.* Jerking his thumb at the drink bank,

Murray spoke low and confidential. *One day these guys are gonna wise up and realize they're housing their own competition. Start charging you rent. Say Brother laughed at me but I'm not kidding. There was a time when it was legal to smoke a joint and illegal to take a drink in this country, so who knows what will happen next.*

He-hey, Sonnay! It was the bartender. Latif swiveled his head and sure enough. Burma lifted off his houndstooth brim and leaned forward to shake hands. He picked up the Bass Ale waiting for him open on the bar and raised it to meet Murray's glass as he strolled toward him. *Mister Higgins.*

Doctor Burma, the drummer responded in the same ceremonial tone, and then Sonny was standing over them.

Well here this motherfucker is. Where the hell you been, Doctor James-Pearson? Whatchu mean just disappearing on us like that all of a moment? Sonny sat down next to him and sipped his beer.

Latif's face flushed; he was a terrible premeditated liar and even before he spoke he thought he glimpsed suspicion underneath the casual question. *I'm glad you gentlemen missed me. I had to go back to the Bean a minute.*

Oh yeah? Everyone's alright, I hope, said Sonny.

Yeah, yeah, everybody's fine. My mother just sounded like she missed me, so I hopped a bus. Surprised her.

Sonny smiled. *That's nice, man. Next time let a brother know. Cats been looking for you all week.*

I told em you were probably just so deep in the shed you couldn't find your way out, Murray said, winking.

Uhmm. Sonny put his arm around Teef's shoulders. *This cat been in there so long he's half birchlog.*

Murray laughed and drained his drink. *More cats need to get in there with you*, he said. *These young bullshit motherfuckers just pretend they wanna learn. Ask me questions then don't listen to the answers. Just yesterday some rapper-looking kid made a face at me like I had farted*

when I told him I played eight or ten hours every day when I was young.
Sonny laughed and Murray maddogged him and made a fist.
*Don't sleep, Doctor Burma. If these kids keep making me feel like I'm
dead and stinking, I'm liable to demonstrate otherwise by punching a hole
through one of their chests.*

Shoot, said Sonny, *meanwhile I'm listening to the scoldings these old
academic high art music critics putting down and feeling young like a mug.*

That's the kind of thing will drive a cat to drink, Murray agreed,
standing with his empty glass in hand. *Y'all need one?* Sonny and
Latif declined, and Higgins ambled toward the bar.

Boy, you look like death eating a sandwich, Sonny said when he
was gone. *You sick or something?*

*I copped a touch of flu up in the Bean. Couldn't hold down any food
the last few days.*

*Your hands are shaking. You want some peanuts or something from
the bar? Some orange juice? Hey Louie!* Sonny shouted.

Naah, naah, I'm fine man, really. I don't want no food. Sonny offered him the pack of cigarettes on the table, Teef's own, and lit
the stoag Latif selected. The chrome lighter popped open with a
satisfying chunky sound. *How's your man Wess doing?*

He's alright. I don't think he's gigging as much as he'd like.

*How come he didn't move down here years back like every other mu-
sician from the Bean?*

Latif shrugged. *He's got his teaching thing, his friends, his students.
He's an educator. Boston's as big a city as he needs.*

Higgins' raucous laughter floated over from the bar. He'd
joined some kind of card game the busboys were playing. *Come
on slim, throw your bet*, he roared. *I'm takin all you niggas' rent bread.*

Sonny's eyes were far away. Latif watched him refocus and
braced for something heavy. He tried to steady his fingers on the
cigarette, but the more he thought the more they quivered, shaking ash onto the tabletop. *Let's cut the bullshit*, Sonny said. *You*

didn't tell Say Brother you were leaving town. Didn't call from Boston. Broke up with Mona. And the last time Albert saw you, you stormed out his house talking some crazy shit about doing something to give your mind a jumpstart. You know what I'm talking about. He met Sonny's solemn don't-make-me-say-it stare and nodded *Yes, I know what you're talking about.*

Obviously mufuckers gonna worry, Teef. We were afraid you went off and did some stupid shit, in a frame of mind like that. Mona too. Sonny paused, looking at him, trying to size him up. Latif knew it was a chance to ask for help. He traced the rimtop of a shotglass on the table with a thumbnail and tried to bring the words together. He took too long and Sonny prompted him. *So did you?*

All he had to do was whisper *yes*, but he couldn't. Some part of him begged to be allowed the dignity of coping on his own. Latif wanted to cry at the sad absurdity of his not wanting to cry, the pride, if that was what it was, that prevented him from doing what he knew he should, which overcame all else and made him look back up at Sonny with a reassuring solemnity of eyes and firm his mouth against the inward quiver and say *No, I'm cool. I didn't do anything stupid.*

As the stalebreathed words escaped, Latif glimpsed the ridiculousness of his denial. He was a little kid with shitlogs weighing down the plastic waistband of his playpants, stinking from across the room, whose mother nice as can be comes over and bends down, *Sweetie, did you have an accident?* and the kid says *No Mommy*, embarrassed and afraid to forfeit the prestige of wearing big boy pants, and so he opts for flat denial, the most preposterous denial possible but he sticks with it and his mother says

Are you sure, Latif? Latif stood up and patted Burma on the shoulder. He had to get out of there before Sonny stopped pulling punches and simply accused him with the truth. The only place he could plausibly hide was the men's room.

I'm sure, man. Everything is fine. I gotta take a leak.

He pushed open the bathroom door, walked on his heels over the just-mopped white tile, and leaned his palms against the sink walls, elbows locked and shoulders up around his ears. His face was gaunt and heavystubbled in the mirror and he cupped his hands and carried water to his cheeks and temples, rubbed it through his scalp, held his wrists beneath the faucet so the stream could cool his blood. Here you are, he thought. This is your life.

If only what he'd told Burma had been true: a week in Boston with his mother. The light parenthesis beginning to crease the left side of his mouth, magnified to a deep pleat beneath the bathroom's cheap fluorescence, matched his mother's face exactly. Home was only a four-hour busride away, cheap and running every hour on the half from dawn to midnight out of Fortydeuce street, but Latif had never gone, had barely spoken to his mother since leaving. He loved her but he had nothing to say; he was on his own and it was too soon to start straddling the ditch he'd dug between then and now, Boston and New York, provincial stagnation and cosmo opportunity. He had to fortify himself here on the other side first. He didn't want to know what his hometown friends were doing or send back any news of himself until he had some progress to report. He didn't want to feel welcome there, connected to the old neighborhood's life, didn't want to acknowledge that there was still a place for him on the old streetcorner. He told himself returning to his mother's house meant crossing a burned bridge, even though Leda made it clear she missed him every time they spoke, that she forgave him for leaving as he had.

The bathroom door creaked and Latif turned from the sink to see Van Horn standing behind him with legs firmplanted at shoulders' width, his mouth set hard. He looked ready to absorb a punch.

Congratulations, Teef. He walked over, grabbed Teef's arm and pumped his hand. Latif sucked his teeth and winced in pain but Albert wrung it harder and the sting shot up and down and through him from his elbow to his wrist. *Solved all your problems just like you thought, huh?* Albert's eyes were wide, furious, and he squeezed Latif's hand harder and harder. *Mind's all clear now, right? You can really listen. Now you're a musician, baby. You can play like me now, probly better.*

If I could play like you, Latif gasped, lip trembling, *I wouldn't have done this.*

Van Horn flung Teef's hand away and his wristbone banged against the sink behind him. And then Albert was on tiptoes in his face, shouting at Latif with hands on hips. *Well, motherfucker, you ain't never gonna play like me! You ain got it, nigger, so why don't you go ahead and kill yourself?*

Van Horn dropped down and turned his back, then heelspun and flung a limp hand in the air. *Or better yet, I could call Say Brother down here and have him put a gun in your mouth.*

Go ahead, said Teef. *That's probably the best advice you ever gave me. Fuck would you know how I feel, Albert? You never failed in your life.*

You ain't fail neither til you started doing this shit, Van Horn retorted, catching Latif's forearm and slapping it hard with his open palm. The sound echoed. *You think this is how come I can play? You believe Sonny and all these sick niggers out here trying to make themselves believe they got a reason for shooting poison in their veins? You, of all people—you seen motherfuckers sucking dick for this!*

Latif glared at him, head throbbing. *From one junkie to another, huh?*

You goddamn right from one junkie to another. From a junkie who's been clean for thirty-seven years and—

Well, I don't have some crazy bitch to save my life then run it for me, Albert, Teef snapped. *I'm on my own out here.*

You sure are, said Albert, mouth pinched bitter. *You sure are.* He walked across the room and posted up against the other wall, a smoothsoled foot braced on it and a hand clutching his knee. *And long as you wanna get nasty, let me tell you something else. You're killing yourself for something you don't even believe in. You couldn't possibly respect this music if you think a drug can make you play.*

Latif walked slowly to the door and leaned against it, face cupped in his hands, and the tears came. He crumpled at the knees and eased his body down the wall, a shuddery squat of arms, shins, elbows, saltwater, and snot against the floor. *I'm sorry*, he sobbed. *I don't know what I'm saying.* Tendrils of saliva stretched between his lips like an accordion and he spoke in a broken whisper. *I need help.*

Van Horn squeezed his eyes tightclosed and dropped his head, pinching the bridge of his nose and then rubbing his temples with a thumb and finger. *I can't help you, Latif. I'm too angry and I don't have the strength.*

I want to go home, Latif said. *Please.*

Van Horn stared at him and sighed. *You don't want to put this on your mama, Teef. Trust me. Anything's better than that.*

I've got nowhere else to go, Albert. The tears were falling hot and thick. *She and Wess the only family I've got.*

Albert crouched and leaned in close and pressed his palms together. He dropped his head and looked up over his own crinkled brow. The browns of Albert's irises touched the bottoms of his eyelids, floated stark atop the whiteness of his eyes. *Alright*, he said finally. *No reason you should listen to me now. I'll square you with Say Brother if I can.*

Albert sighed through his nose and squinted at the ceiling. *What you need*, he said dryly, standing up *is a crazy bitch to save your life.*

It's true, said Van Horn gravely, steering the big old Cadillac uptown. The wipers moved across the windshield syncopated, beating back a light rain. The car was on its way to Harlem to pick up Latif's things: Albert wanted to watch him leave town with his own eyes. *I'm not ashamed to say I owe my life to Marisol. I was good and messed up when she met me, down in Brazil on a gig I did with a singer named Anderson Hainey right after I left The Emperor.*

I barely made it down there, I was so tore up. We flew out of San Francisco and I literally walked out of the hospital and hailed a taxi to the airport. If Higgins hadn't been on the gig as well, and if he hadn't promised to meet me outside with some junk, I might not have risked being in a foreign country without dope and consequently would not have gone, met Marisol, or lived. The way it all went down proved to me that the Creator has a master plan like Pharoah said, because at the rate I was going I might not have survived long enough to make my contribution to the world. He paused to let that sink in, not that Albert anticipated much reaction. Teef was slumped against the passenger door, his cheek pressed to the cool window, his eyes barely open.

All I did was play music, shoot dope, and drink, and I wasn't even playing so much music when I played. I just went through the motions, collected my weekly paychecks from Emp and did my thing. I was practically an animal, slaving to supply a monstrous appetite and thinking of very little else. When I did think about what I was doing it made me so depressed that I had to forget, and my mind would beg me for a fix right along with my body because what I'd become was too sad to address. Little did I know when Milford Montague first put me next to some dope that it was any different or more dangerous than grass or alcohol. I was so young, and he and the other people we were with treated it so casually.

Albert shook his head. *I'll never forget that. I was about twenty-two and we were somewhere in the Midwest. I don't remember where exactly, but we'd played Chicago the week before, so probably one of the big college towns like Madison, Wisconsin, or Ann Arbor, Michigan. Milford and I met two fay college chicks at the afterparty and went for a drive, which usually meant that although she didn't want to come back to your hotel room by herself, the woman in question was comfortable messing around with you in her own automobile while your friend and her friend did the same thing in the backseat two feet away.* He laughed: nerves. Latif looked bad and Albert wanted to keep him awake. *You listening?*

Fucking white chicks in the backseat, Teef mumbled.

Right. Except that on this particular occasion one of the young ladies instead pulled out some horse and I watched as first she and then her friend and then Milford proceeded to snort it. It looked no different from cocaine, which I'd tried and hadn't cared for but neither did I have any strong aversion to it, so when it was my turn I followed suit and that was how I started. The next morning Milford and I were up early, calling these chicks back to get more stuff, and it was on from there.

Two weeks later I changed over to needles, and that was when I knew I was in deep, because I'd hated and feared needles my entire life, dreaded my annual physical for days in advance when I was young and always declined to give blood when there were drives at school or elsewhere. In the car Milford said he had done horse before, but when I cornered him later that same night and threw him up against a wall and shouted What the fuck was that, *already wanting more, he broke down and admitted he had only said it to seem hip to the girls, whatever that was worth. The fact that he was as scared as I made me forget my anger toward him for fooling me into trying that shit, but a month later it didn't matter anymore because Milford Montague overdosed and died in the back of a nightclub in East St. Louis.*

Shit, Latif said, sitting up a little.

Only I knew what had happened, and I kept it to myself. We were roommates and they found his hotel key and called me. I went down there and identified the body, dealt with the paperwork and so forth, but when it came time to inform the band I told them Milford had had a congenital heart problem and that was what had killed him, plain and uncomplicated. I did it for both him and me; I didn't need either one of us associated with dope, alive or dead. The Emperor didn't have any strict prohibitions against anything, but I knew he would have had something to say if he'd found out, and I was already so twisted in my thinking that all I wanted from him was money for my dope. I educated myself frantically about the drug so that it wouldn't happen to me, which should tell you something about how addicted I already was; my homeboy and bandmate dies and rather than thinking about quitting, my mind is on learning to use the shit correctly.

Albert exited the West Side Highway and drove slowly through the Harlem backstreets, left hand on the wheel and right stroking the middle of his upper lip absently. *The band was devastated,* he said, *but we went right on working; couldn't very well cancel our tour. I feel sorry for anybody who came to see us at that time. Nobody much felt like playing or traveling or anything. Which also meant that nobody noticed for a while how messed up I was, that I was always either high or crazy low, and that my playing was getting distracted and flashy; I would lose my focus and then snap back to attention with compensatory theatrics which sometimes worked beautifully and oftentimes did not.*

By no means was I the only junkie in the band, as I found out in the coming weeks to my surprise, dismay, and relief. And thus began a whole new phase of my education about the dynamics of the band and of the life, one I wish I never had to go through. The unspoken rule, as I found out, was simply that if you could play your parts and be on time, anything else you did amounted to your business and your problem. He squinted out the window, reading numbers. Latif had given him only the building address; before he could tell Van Horn a cross street, Albert had waved him into silence: *I'll find it.*

In the course of the next year, though, my problem became the boss's business. Emp called me into his hotel room one night, and sitting on the edge of the bed in a pair of charcoal-gray slacks and an undershirt, he calmly and kindly explained that he could not have me on the road or in the studio in my condition. He said I would always be welcome back when I was ready, advised me to get help, and told me that if there was anything he could do to help me just to ask. I asked him for some money, and he apologized and said he couldn't in good conscience give me any for fear that I would only hurt myself with it.

Albert pulled up in front of Latif's building and double-parked. *Thanks,* Teef muttered. *I'll be right back down.* The stench pounced on him when he unlocked his door; flies buzzed the Chinese food container and red drops dotted the floor like he'd been painting. Latif snatched a duffel bag from the closet and stuffed it with fistfuls of clothing: a tangle of pants, shirts, socks, the belt he'd used to tie off. All of it was dirty. The needle lay on the floor; he picked it up with two fingers and dumped it and the rancid number-four lunch plate into a plastic bag, tied it and threw it in the hall and turned his attention to his horn, lying on the bed. He didn't want to bring it, but he knew it was an essential traveling companion if his facade of normality was to be believed by anyone who knew him. With quick, inattentive gruffness he undid the mouthpiece and packed the instrument into its case, then slung the duffelbag over his shoulder and looked out the window. Spliff was nowhere in sight and the rain was coming harder. Latif slammed the door behind him, walked slopebacked down the stairs to Albert's car, and dumped his life into the trunk.

So there I was, Albert went on, sliding the car out of its spot and swinging it downtown toward Port Authority Bus Terminal, *broke, jobless, and addicted, stuck in San Francisco. Higgins came over from Oakland to see me. We were still talking about the band we wanted to get together, but nothing was much further from reality right then.*

Murray was in far better shape than I was, although he had a habit of his own and still does, but then as now Higgins was just so goddamn strong that nothing seemed to jack him up too badly. The only thing I had going for me was the fact that it was not yet common knowledge why I'd really left The Emperor, even in musicians' circles, and thus my services as a sideman were still somewhat in demand.

The Brazil gig, which I almost missed along with the rest of my life on account of shooting some bad dope the previous night at a bar in San Francisco, was when things began to turn around. Marisol had come to see the festival with her parents, and they were staying in the same hotel as we were. I met her in the bar the first night, after the concert. She spoke almost no English. You genius, she told me. The way you play like magic. She was right about that night: After my near-overdose, my body hadn't wanted any heroin at the airport and I'd been straight for a day or so and played my best set in a year—then celebrated by shooting some local shit with Murray in his room.

For that reason alone, I don't remember much of our initial conversation, except the rapt attention Marisol paid to the slurred who-knows-whatness I was talking. She was small, energetic, and very beautiful, with long black hair and calm black eyes, and we stayed at the bar until it closed and then went upstairs to the roofdeck. I was drunk and still high, and Marisol had to lead me up the stairs when I stood from my barstool. We fell asleep together in my room, woke up at four the next afternoon, and kept on hanging. I found her very easy to talk to, even though or perhaps because she spoke so little English. I didn't speak slowly or try too hard to make sure she understood, just rambled on and on and watched her eyes to check out what she thought, caught, and missed.

She didn't miss much, as it turned out, and I held nothing back. By the second night I was crying on her lap, taking off my shirt to show her my track marks, telling her how close to death I'd been only a couple days before and how close I still felt even now.

And Marisol said, Albert, I gonna save your life. I gonna give you help. *I swear, the way she said it, I believed her. Her face was set so firm, as if now that she'd decided it was good as done. I've asked her since then what made her say those things, and she told me that one hundred percent of her mind, body, and soul were in those words, and she knew she was leaving everything behind and coming to America with me. She also told me that both her grandmother and aunt married their husbands within a few days of meeting them and lived happily ever after, and that her mother met her father on a train the day he was leaving Brazil to go to university in France, fell in love with him, and showed up unannounced in Paris three months later with only a name to go on. Needless to say, she found him.*

What Marisol told me that day, as I lay sobbing and hugging her knees in my hotel room in Brazil, was that her family was rich and her grandfather had left her part ownership of a leather processing factory he'd founded. And just like that, by the next evening in fact, Marisol cashed her assets and flew us both to Stamford, Connecticut, which is where the best dope rehabilitation center I had ever heard of was supposed to be. That was where I spent the next four months, at a phenomenal financial cost which I no more want to go into than the phenomenal pain which was involved in quitting. And when I got back out and Murray Higgins and I put together the band we'd been discussing for so many years, Marisol remained my savior still, coming on the road with us and keeping me a safe distance from temptation in the form of all the drug dealers who'd come to know me so well.

She hasn't been back to Brazil since then. It was the last thing Albert said until they pulled up outside Port Authority. He shifted into park and rested his left arm on the wheel, and they looked at each other. Raindrops drummed against the Cadillac's old body and a sheet of water glossed the unwiped windshield like a submarine portal. Latif choked back his shame and wondered what to say: *I'll beat this*, with halfhearted through-the-tears conviction, and Albert would nod back in the same fake reassuring register?

Or *I'm sorry* one last time, and Albert would do what? Tell him absurdly that it was alright? Or *Thank you for everything*, when everything had come to this?

But it was Albert who spoke. *You're gonna feel pain like you ain't yet imagined*, he said. *But while you're going through it, your mind is gonna clear and you're gonna have a chance to do some thinking. To figure out why—with all the war and hatred in this world, and as righteous-minded as you are—you want to be a musician. How you can devote your life to this.* He popped the trunk. *You come tell me the answer when you can.*

Bonzai Bus Incorporated employed more than fifty drivers on the New York–Boston express route, but it was Eddie who was leaning up against the side of the vehicle when Latif stepped through the terminal door, the same cat who'd been behind the wheel when Teef had redeye-jetted from the Bean.

Eddie was a blues head who defied company policy at the lowest volume possible, the strains of his transistor radio barely audible above the engine sounds. No one could hear it except him and perhaps the person in the seat over his shoulder, usually the last one to be taken. It had been Latif's on the way down to New York, and Eddie had been only too happy to shoot the breeze with someone on the early a.m. run. Their conversation slid easily from music into life, and for the first time Latif had verbalized his plan. Hearing himself say it out loud with the craggy Massachusetts highway cliff slabs out the window made it real, shook loose the stardust crust of fantasy and hardened his resolve.

Eddie gave him the address of a boardinghouse in Harlem and told Latif that in the ten years he'd been driving, so many blank-faced folks had filed on and off his bus, sallow and nonspeaking, that he had started to feel a little like old Charon, the underworld ferrydriver who transported dead Greeks across the river Styx in ancient myths. Eddie hadn't known a thing about music until a year into the job, when the tedium of seeing the same gray highway every day kicked in and his wife bought him a radio to fight it off.

At first Eddie stuck strictly to the news station, but the steady gray monotone recitation of despair and tragedy coupled with the grayness of the road and multiplied the ghoulishness. Then he discovered the blues huddling at the lowrent end of his FM dial, at ninety-point-three and eighty-nine-point-one, significant degrees below normal body temperature. If he was carting a busload of dead souls it didn't matter; he had found a soundtrack for it. He gripped the big bus wheel now with a sense of drama, elbow on the armrest, brow wrinkled, leaning back into the mood and nodding through gutbucket grooves.

So I'm in London last Christmas to see my wife's family, right? said Eddie over his shoulder, bringing the bus back and around and then out onto the road. The way the huge craft cornered amazed Latif; from his perch it never looked like the hulking thing could make the turns it did, but Eddie swung the wheel expertly. *I get off the plane and take the tube to Victoria Station to meet her, only I'd gotten confused and given her the wrong flight info and I'm there twelve hours before I told her to meet me. It's late at night and I haven't been over there in years. I don't even have the right change to use the phone cause like an idiot I didn't get my money switched back at the airport and now everything is closed. All I can do is sit outside the station and hope Gloria doublechecks the flight and shows up.*

So I'm sitting there, humming a tune to myself, and these two white kids come over and start drinking beers on the corner, right next to where I'm at. They're loud and drunk and I'm just kind of watching them; I guess maybe I was even staring, because I tend to do that. And one of them looks over at me, swings his head around and sort of readjusts his weight to follow his eyeballs. I can't quite make out what he's saying, so I lean forward to hear him and what he's saying is Are you alright. *Now, for all I know* Are you alright? *is British for* You got a problem? *and he's leaning at me pretty aggressively, or at least I think he is. I decide to play it off like he's genuinely concerned for my well-being, so I raise up and say* Yeah, yeah, I'm okay. How you doing?

He comes over and gets up in my face. I'm still not sure if he's on some drunken confrontation shit or some drunken friendly shit, and his expression isn't giving anything away. He's straight deadpan, like he might up and hit me with a beer bottle out of nowhere, plus there's two of them and I got all my stuff with me, Christmas presents and the whole nine yards. I decide I've gotta do something to try to flip the situation, so I say, real tough Hey, I got a question for you. *They both look at me kind of curious, like they think maybe I'm gonna kick some kind of one-liner and then take a swing like in the movies. The one kid bobs his head at me like* Go ahead, *and I say* Is there any place a man can get a drink around these parts? *real corny, like a cowboy.*

That was probably the best thing I could have done, because all of a moment I'm their new American drinking buddy. All the pubs are closed already, which I already knew because it's the one thing I remembered about London from last time, but they tell me they've got a pint of whiskey, and they break it out. So I figure what the hell, and I unwrap the bottle of cognac I bought for my father-in-law at the duty-free shop and spend the rest of the night drinking on the street with these blokes. And the funny thing is, I'm still not sure if I almost got jumped.

Latif smiled. Eddie was a low-maintenance conversationalist; he was a good listener, but left to his own devices he could talk for hours with only an occasional *uh-huh* or *hmm!* dabbed in like grout between his words. Latif halflistened as the bus chugged on along the highway, the vibration of the engine underneath him fucking with his tender empty stomach until he closed his eyes and let it lull him into sleep. He dozed on and off and woke up each time feeling worse, sweaty against the fuzzy bus upholstery and itching. He had to take a leak and walked on wobbly sea-legs to the back of the bus, but when he bolted the bathroom door and stood bracing himself against the front wall, cock dangling over the bottomless-looking toilet swishing with blue antiseptic, he couldn't do it. He strained and squeezed the piss muscles and stood there foolishly until finally a weak dribble of yellow urine leaked painful from his dick. Only then did he remeber Sonny Burma emerging from the bathroom at a bar one night wincing and muttering *smack piss* underneath his breath.

Latif walked back up the aisle with his hand inside his

pantspocket, holding his smarting organ. The bus just entering Massachusetts: forty-five minutes until they pulled into South Station and from there it was a short subway ride home. Latif hoped he could still find Wessel at his old outdoor woodshed spot, standing on the street just down the block from Giant Liquor Mart providing Saturday night music all week long to sundry passersby. Wessel stood hunchbacked over his horncase in between the sign of the little storefront church, *Jesus Saves*, and the one that said *Food Stamps*, not caring—or maybe enjoying—how crazy he looked.

Might as well make some money while I'm practicing, he'd told the *Boston Globe*, pointing at the forked-open instrument case between his feet, speckled with change. They'd sent a reporter down on what must have been a slow news week to do a human interest story on him: *Monday through Friday, Wessel Gates teaches jazz to students at Mercer Sparks High School, and as many as five nights a week he plays tenor saxophone at clubs around the city. But in warm weather, residents of Roxbury can hear Gates for free, or for the price of a small donation, right on the street. As the self-proclaimed town crier, Gates has been playing on the same corner for the past twenty-five years, to the delight of many and the consternation of a few.*

Most of those consternated few were just the delighted many on off-days. The storefront church people usually hollered bits of chatter at him: *Mmhmm well well well watch it now come on say it mmhm blow that horn now brother, amen*, a curious blend of bandstand language and the way folks talk in church. Occasionally they would cuss him out *You better git from out front this here building with that racket*, and Wess would usually oblige, tip his hat and take a few steps down the block toward the men playing Beat The Champion timed chess on a dirty card table. People joked that Wessel's yearly reemergence on the block was a more reliable proof of spring that any robin redbreast.

There were a lot of stories about Wess: As a youngster in the sixties, he had gotten down with the ungodly undisciplined slap-switch-twist atonal defiance of The New Music as soon as he'd heard it, back when to play too free was heresy against the faded ghost of bebop and just bringing up the names of cats like Ornette Coleman and Cecil Taylor in the wrong company could start a fight.

Once, Wessel had told Latif, he'd gone to a jam session at Reflections and a whole rhythm section—bass piano drums—had walked off the bandstand in protest over what Wess was doing to the music.

What else could I do? Wess implored when he recalled the story of that night. *What choice did I have, all alone in midsolo with a hundred people in the club and even the bartender evil-eying me? I brought the reed up to my lips and blew.*

That was his last Boston gig for a long minute. Wess stood there alone in the universe, saxophone sweating in the heat of refracted light and hot vowels busting through the metal dome of his horn as he played on and on, filling the room with endurance and belief in his music, which was free, but not of history or musicality or discipline as people said. The liberties it took could be abused just like free speech could be abused, but there was a rambunctious beauty in the new sounds, a yearning scramble of ideas Wess didn't appreciate being maligned by the kind of cats who, if they'd been around twenty-five years earlier, would have been talking shit about this new bebop stuff.

The motherfuckers who'd walked off the bandstand had had no choice but to stand back there and sip their drinks and watch the cat they'd cut so violently refuse to bleed. Wess stood defiant and blew everything he could think to, played tunes straight ahead and picked them apart like fried chicken and laid each sliver greasy on the ground, broke down the bar lines and zoned free.

When he was done he walked still blowing off the stage, through the club past those now-sullen cats, out the front door and into the street, the moan of the horn fading to the rhythm of his footsteps and blending with the honks of cars in traffic.

Wess disappeared for a while after that, was neither seen nor heard for several rotations of the cycle of the city, and rumors flew as rumors do. *I had to be invisible for a minute after that shit,* he said. *I went out to Frisco and gave cats in the Bean some time to marinate and get hip to what was going on, and I'll be damned if those cats who'd walked out on me in April—plus a whole bunch who wished they coulda walked in with me—weren't playing free when I came back next May. Just like all them jazz rags that gave Monk's shit one star when it came out and then had to go re-review it a few years later on some ol'* I don't know what we were thinking. Did we say one star? Sorry, we meant five, jazz classic *shit.*

Eddie pulled into South Station at ten-fifteen. Latif said goodbye and hopped a train to Roxbury with his insides queasing and ready almost to collapse. Dark spots flashed and burned if he blinked too fast, as if brown vinegar had been splashed into his eyes. Latif stepped off the train and walked down the block taking small porcelain steps. He was battling the physical with the psychological, depending on a reunion with his teacher to sate his body's craving. As he walked, slow as an old man, Latif remembered the days when he'd raced up and down this very block in a too-big T-shirt playing freezetag with Jay Fox. His mind lit fondly on the sport they'd invented back in junior high, the Tennis Ball Game, which had replaced football and basketball and ruled the hours between school and dinner for a year.

The rules were simple: If you hit someone from the other team with a tennis ball, they joined your team. The playing field was the whole neighborhood, bound by the highway overpass on one side and Rook's house on the other, and it was a great game because it went on forever, for a whole weekend once. You and your team could hide on rooftops or in stores, waiting in ambush for hours at a time. You could prowl, spy, or even snipe. You could go to somebody's apartment and eat dinner and still be playing the game, leaning together over plates of french fries, strategizing. Eventually there would be some kind of confrontation, and usually everybody would get hit at once, all the hours of tactical maneuvers and counter-reconnaissance dissolving into thirty seconds of attack.

There had been one game, though, when Latif had been the only one to get away, the lone survivor. His team had walked into an ambush at the island near the hilltop. It had to have been Shane's idea. Most kids would have forced the enemy uphill, figuring that the incline would slow their retreat time. But Shane knew that throwing uphill was harder than running uphill; let the enemy stumble downhill, building up too much speed to dodge the missiles raining from above, and it would be over just like that.

Latif got away on pure instinct, dodged Rook's first tennis ball, and cut sideways, jumping Mrs. Heppner's fence and sprinting around to the back of her building. He knew Shane knew that her yard opened out into the parking lot: They'd try to catch him there. He doubled back the way he'd come and pressed flat against the side of her house and tried to breathe soft, already thinking how glorious it would be to win, to outsmart them all, already knowing he would do it. He saw every shadow and flicker of light like a detective on a stakeout, an Indian huntsman, Tarzan.

When he was sure they'd circled to the back, he made a break for it, vaulted the fence and sprinted up the hill and out of sight before they knew they had been tricked. He ran across the yard on tiptoes, arms down and fingertips splayed out like sensors, relishing the perfect self-control he felt, the focus. Latif cleared the fence cleanly, swung both legs over together, and hit the ground running, striding longer and longer until he was whipping past houses and bodegas, slicing through backyards and soaring over shrubbery. There was no reason to stop. He felt the looseness in his limbs, the strength endless in his chest, and sprinted on elated and victorious. He stayed alone for hours, spying, tracking their movements from afar, watching them split up to find him. Sometimes he stopped watching them and just ran through the streets.

Finally the game ended and the others called his name across the blocks to tell him that he'd won. And even then Latif didn't believe them, thinking it was a trick to make him show himself, and wanting the game to go on forever he stayed in hiding, running from safespot to safespot until he finally decided it was alright to emerge. He walked back to Rook's house, homebase, grinning and huffing, to a hero's welcome and a smuggled glass of beer. Even now, Shane always found a way to mention that game.

Latif wiped his nose against the back of his wrist for the hundredth time; the patch of skin was already snotcrusted. He turned the corner, walked midway down the block, looked up, and smiled: Wess was standing in his spot. The tenor had been kissed goodnight and tucked into its case, which leaned against the wall next to him. A tall brownbagged can stood by his feet.

Wessel Gates!

Hey, Latif. He didn't spring off the wall to meet his student in a bearhug as Teef had expected. The months they'd been apart stood like a block of ice between them. But the seriousness with which Wess looked at him melted the time to water.

Aren't you surprised to see me?

Wess ground his hand over his cheek stubble and studied Teef. *I got a call from Sonny Burma earlier today.*

Latif blanched, going ashen. *What he say?*

What do you think he said?

Latif sighed, hung his head. *I know what he said.*

Wessel's eyes and mouth bent downward in torment. He hadn't believed Sonny, Latif thought. He'd been hoping it wasn't true until now. *How could you?* Wess whispered. Latif was quiet. There was nothing he could say. *And then you come here*, Wess went on, shaking his head and staring slackfaced, baleful. *You hardly call your mama for months and now you want to bring this into that sweet woman's home?*

I've only been messed up a week, Latif said. *I'll tell her I'm sick, and I'll stay and get well.*

No, Latif. Wess shook his head. *No. Please. Let me take you to the hospital.*

I can't be around a bunch of junkies, Wess, even if I could afford a hospital. That was the fucking problem in the first place. I've just gotta clear my head. It's only been a week.

Sonny said he felt like this was his fault. Wess jowled his cheeks and looked down. *I feel like it's mine. I never should have let you go down there.*

Latif scowled. *You didn't let me go anywhere, Wess. I went.*

I should have stopped you. If I'd known Van Horn and those cats were still dopers I would have.

Van Horn's clean, said Latif. *And no, you wouldn't. You're not my father, Wess, even if I used to wish you were. You couldn't have kept me.*

Wess pursed his lips, opened his mouth to speak, stopped, and began again. *I didn't want to tell you this when you were young, Latif, but now I wish I would have. I met Van Horn once, in Frisco. He wouldn't remember me. Higgins would, but not by name. They were sitting in a musicians' bar talking about the group they planned to get together. The Emperor had been in town for a run, and when he left, Albert stayed behind. Word around the campfire was that he hadn't so much quit as been kicked out. To hear Van Horn tell it, though, he was good and ready to be on his own.* Wess spoke as if he were being forced, as if recounting something he'd tried to forget.

He and Higgins were sitting with their arms around each other's shoulders, getting drunk and loud, talking about how this was it, this was the moment they'd been planning for, and the shit they were gonna do was gonna blow minds open. Everybody in the joint was shaking their heads like Listen to these drunk cocky bastards talking shit. *Van Horn was doing most of the talking, telling Higgins that he was the only one who understood the mission and so forth.*

Cats who knew him couldn't believe what they were hearing, because Albert had a reputation as a real nice guy, a little on the serious side but always very humble and friendly. After a while Van Horn stumbled into the bathroom, and when I went in to take a leak a little later I saw his legs sticking out under the stall. I figured he had passed out, so I rapped on the door and said Albert! You alright, brother? Wake up!

He didn't answer me. The stall was locked, so I crawled my ass underneath and found him lying there with his eyes rolled way back and this big vein in his neck twitching like it wanted out. Thick white shit was dribbling down the corner of his mouth. And then I saw the needle in his hand. I thought this cat was dying on the men's room floor, and I picked him up and carried him back out on my shoulder. Higgins saw him and flipped, started shaking him and slapping him, trying to wake him up. I had a car there, so me and Higgins took Van Horn to the hospital and waited while they did whatever they do with overdoses.

He looked up with hounddog eyes and Latif realized that Wess was telling this story not for its own sake but because it gave him momentary reprieve from the present, from dealing with Latif.

We sat there in the hall for about twenty minutes before a doctor came out and told us that Albert was alright, he'd shot some bad shit and he was damn lucky we'd gotten him there or he'd be dead. As soon as Higgins heard it he grabbed me and said Come on. *I was too shocked to do anything but follow him. He took the keys and drove my car down to some boxing gym somewhere. Next thing I know three big dudes in*

*sparring gear are packed into my station wagon and Higgins is driving
like a madman.*

*A couple minutes later we pull up to a poolhall. Higgins and his boys
go straight to the back and roll up on these three cats sitting at a table.
Higgins knocks the table over and grabs the dude sitting in the middle by
his jacket. Before the other two can move, Higgins' boys have got them
pinned against the floor. Higgins cracks homeboy hard across the jaw, a
regular knockout punch, and then locks the cat's arm behind his back and
drags him outside.* Pop the trunk, *he says to me.* I'm like, Are you
out of your mind? You're ain't throwin nobody in my trunk,
man. I don't even know what's going on.

*He stares at me for a second and then slams the cat on the hood face
down, picks him up and slams him again.* I should kill you, *he's yelling.*
I should kill you for selling me and my man that shit. *The cat can't
even respond. Higgins flips him over and catches him again across the
face. You could see his nose was broken and probably his cheekbone too.
Higgins hit him with about five body blows, and I mean hard. He missed
once and dented my car with his fist. Homeboy just slid down off the
hood into the gutter. Higgins walked away and the dude's boys ran over
and tried to help him up, and then Higgins spun around and they just
fled. When it was over I dropped his boys back at the gym and took Higgins to the hospital. Then I went home and poured myself one goddamn
enormous drink. That was enough to keep my ass away from dope for
life.*

*I wish I'd told you that story, Latif. But I thought they were clean
now. I figured nobody on dope could play like Higgins has these past forty
years less he was Superman.*

He is, Latif said. *But I'm not.* He shook his head. *I'm so
ashamed, Wess. I just wanted to play . . .*

Wess relented and stepped forward, put his arm around Latif's
shoulders and grimaced when he smelled Latif's body and felt the
rubbery weakness of the return embrace, the limpness of Latif's

arms on his back. *You'll help me, won't you?* breathed Latif. His mind's eye saw Wessel blink and turn away: *You played with fire, you got burned.*

Of course I will. Wess squeezed him harder, then pulled back and eyeballed him, poker-faced. *You're sure it's only been a week? Positive?* Latif nodded.

Alright. Wess sighed. *Let's go see your mother.*

Leda opened the door the way she had when Latif came home past curfew as a kid. She unlatched it an instant before he inserted his key and stood in the hallway with the doorknob in one hand and the other fisted on her hip. It was a reminder of her omniscience, Leda's way of letting Latif know he couldn't get over on her or the world. *Try showing up at quarter past for a noon train and see what happens*, she'd say, holding the door wide as he bailed in sheepish. *Next time you're not getting back in til morning.* It was just a threat, though. Even when he was young, Latif had understood that his mother needed to discipline him as much as he needed to be disciplined and maybe more, that her life was a fight against the statistical likelihood that her young poor fatherless black son would end up dead or in jail like Leda's poor fatherless brothers.

Knowing he was all his mother had and that every time he left the house she fretted over who he was with and what he was doing had been enough to keep Latif on the straight and narrow as a child. He thought his mother so fragile that he never disobeyed, not out of fear of punishment but fear of hurting her. Latif remembered the first Red Sox game he'd been to, with Rook and Rook's brother and father, when he was eleven. A ninth-inning rally had tied the score and sent it into extra innings, and in the bottom of the tenth, with the score still locked and men on base, Latif looked at his watch and left because it was seven-thirty and his mother had told him to be back for dinner no later than eight. Rook had looked at him like he was crazy, and even Rook's dad had assured him it would be alright to stay, but Latif would not be shaken. He listened to the game-winning fifteenth-inning hit on his transistor radio after dinner. Years later, Rook's whole family still fucked with him for leaving.

Hi, Mama. Her hair was twisted into two long braids and

wrapped around the crown of her head. She'd been wearing it natural when he left. Same baby-blue tracksuit, though, looking even paler against Leda's dark, rich skin. She seemed a little heavier; Latif wondered if it was because all the recipes she knew fed two. He stepped forward and hugged her. Leda hesitated for a moment before she brought her arms down over his back and returned the embrace.

Latif, baby, I can't believe you're here. She stepped back and looked at him and Latif saw a tongue of fear flicker across her face, as if his presence in Leda's home alarmed her, and his stomach dropped. Then Latif remembered how he looked.

Is everything alright? She put her hand to his forehead, instinctive. Latif loved the architecture of his mother's hands, long and slender like his own. There was a time when the most highly anticipated feeling in the world had been the light feathery tickle of her fingertips against his naked back, soothing him to sleep.

Everything is fine. He carried her hand down and patted it, hoping too late that his palms weren't as sweaty as they had been on the bus, when he'd had to wipe them on the seat next to him every few minutes. *I'm kind of sick*, he said. *And things have been tough.* He smiled. *And I missed you. I should have come home sooner.*

Well, of course you should have, Leda said, fake scolding, and Latif exhaled relief; his mother was alright now, moving jubilant around her kitchen and beckoning her son to sit down. Nobody had to ask her for some food; Leda assumed you'd make it known if you didn't want to be fed.

You don't look well to me at all, Latif, she said, glancing over her shoulder, brow lifted in concern, as she rummaged for something in a high cupboard.

I've been better. He sat down at the halfmoon kitchen table. There were three chairs and Latif always sat in the same one. His mother sat across from him and the middle chair was for guests. Once, Latif supposed, it must have been his father's. He wondered where Wess sat when Leda invited him over for dinner.

Wess stepped into the room and kissed Leda hello; they both stood over him and suddenly Latif found himself confronting the idea of their relationship, whatever it was. Although he had often thought of Wess as a father, the idea had never conjured any corollary connotation of Wess partnered with his mother. It was something Latif didn't think about, not because the thought disturbed him but because there was no direct evidence to suggest romance aside from an obvious, almost familial, tenderness. They saw each other frequently, Latif knew, now that he was gone. Perhaps they thought as he did, and were drawn together by a parental bond separate from amorous interest.

Sit down, Wess, said Leda. *Take a load off. You look like you've got a bad flu,* she told Latif. *Have you seen a doctor down there in New York?*

Nah. I haven't even taken off from work. As far as Leda knew, he was a waiter at Dutchman's.

Well, I'll call Doctor Wilson in the morning and make an appointment. You might need some antibiotics or something.

Boy's probly working too hard, said Wess, and clapped him on the shoulder. *Bedrest might do it.*

You're one to talk, smiled Leda. *Up at the crack of dawn and out until all hours of the night. At your age.*

My age, frowned Wessel, twisting in his chair to face down Leda's teasing. Her back was to him by the time he swiveled, like she'd said nothing provocative. *Shoot,* Wess chuckled, *you better hope you look this good at my age.* He turned to Latif to cosign or undercut his jive and Wess's face fell as he remembered what was going on. The kitchensounds covered a momentary silence, and then

Leda was at the table with them, pouring coffee into mugs and serving thick wedges of peach cobbler messy on dessert plates.

I know I sound all mothery, but I bet you haven't had a decent meal in months, she said. *Eating dinner at a nightclub.* She tut-tutted and looked at Wess. *He never did let me teach him how to cook.*

He shoulda, said Wess, chewing. His glance danced to Latif, whose head was bent over the plate. He was chopping the cobbler smaller and smaller with his fork and dreading the moment he'd have to put some in his mouth. He imagined it sitting gooey on his swollen tongue. *Women love a man who can sling those pots.*

I broke up with Mona, said Latif abruptly.

Oh, baby, I'm so sorry. Leda reached over and squeezed his arm. *When did this happen?*

Latif could feel Wess staring at him, but he spoke looking at the table. Same old blue tablecloth. *About a week ago. Probably why I got sick.*

Well, I'm sorry about Mona, said his mother. *But I'm glad you're here.*

Latif gave her a sad, rueful smile and said nothing. He knew he was play-acting but he almost believed himself. To miss Mona was invigorating: a normal, human thing to feel, a pain he longed to deal with instead of what he faced.

Is it something you want to talk about with your old mother? Leda asked, trying to make him laugh.

Yes, but not right now. Right now I just want to sleep; I've been on the bus all day. He stretched and yawned. *Unless anybody's got a bedtime story.*

Leda spooned more sugar into her coffee and smiled. She wanted to visit with her son a little longer. *Wessel's got a new saxophone,* she offered. *Or did he already tell you about his latest feat of heroism?*

I don't believe he did, Latif said, turning to Wess. He wished he'd left for bed without providing a prolongation clause; there was no way he could leave now, with a story on the table. Not without appearing sicker or stranger than it was in his interest to look.

Wess smiled humility. *She's making something out of nothing. Do you remember a cat from the neighborhood name of Jajuan?* Wess's cheek twitched. *A junkie?* Latif shook his head, wincing inside himself and wondering whether Wess had said the word with newfound sensitivity or venom. *He used to hang out around Giant and buy fortified wine in there, that real sweet cheap shit the junkies like?* He turned to Leda. *Pardon my language.*

She touched four fingertips to her sternum and batted her eyelashes. *I'm shocked.*

Wess smirked. *Now, as you know, I do enjoy a little drink myself from time to time. And for years, every time I walked past him and into the store it was the same ritual; this cat would ask me if I had any change to contribute to the Save Jajuan Fund and I'd say* I'll catch you on the way back out, Doctor, *come back and sprinkle change over his tattered waxpaper cup, or maybe place a saggy bill in his hand. Cat had hands like catchers' mitts. Elvin Jones hands.*

Wess took a sip of coffee. *I know I could put my money to better use, but I felt I was being kind of neighborly, you know? And then one day, maybe a month ago, after years of this, I was playing my horn on the street and—I say this with a lot of pride, I'm not embarrassed to admit—I moved Jajuan.* Wess sat back and smiled. The soapbubble bluenotes had danced down the block in the wind, popped on Jajuan's grimy cheeks, and stood him up straight as a Sunday churchgoer. He'd loped on over, ass dragging like a skidrow pimp, and dropped all his money in the world into Wess's horn case. *I'm telling you,* Wess laughed, *it might have been the greatest compliment I ever got.*

Anyway, a week later I was passing by the alley in back of Giant on my way home from a gig and I heard screams. I went back there and Ja-juan was curled up on the ground, and two of these young around-the-way punks were kicking him and watching him spit blood. Neighborhood people and businesses and even Jesus Saves had chipped in money after that to help Wessel replace his sax, now dented from the fight and unplayable. He had been grateful and quiet in accepting the donations, really just itching to play his horn again.

What else could I do? Wess asked, sticking a finger in his empty cup and licking thick coffeesugar from his fingertip. *I don't like to put my hands on anyone, but I couldn't just walk by. Anyway, this new horn sounds sweeter than the old one ever did.*

Well, I can't wait to hear you play it said Latif, standing up. Leda glanced at his reconfigured peach cobbler and said nothing. He yawned again, demonstratively. *I've got to catch some Zs, though.*

Things sure change, said Leda. She addressed Wess with a memory all three of them knew by heart. *When he was younger, I couldn't pay him to sleep. He would say* But I'm not tired, Mama, *sitting there all cute and bright-eyed with that horn in his hands. I'd tell him he had school in the morning and turn out the lights, but I knew he'd be sitting up in bed until the sun came up no matter what I did.*

I got all the sleep I needed in science class Latif said, heading toward the kitchen door with a fake sleepy bedtime gait. *I had a deal worked out with Mrs. Ames. She didn't call on me and I didn't ask why we had to do all those stupid experiments that didn't prove anything.*

Wise words from a scholar, said Wess.

Latif chuckled. *Goodnight*, he said over his shoulder. *I'm going to sleep for about fifty hours.*

Your bed is all made up, said Leda. *Sweet dreams.*

Latif closed the door on silent hinges and faced the room in which he'd grown up. He felt strange in its doorway, as if the walls themselves were bitter over his absence and his presumption in returning, as if the bed might shrink from his body when he laid himself upon it. This room was pure, a place of dreams and childhood, and he was dirty, had betrayed it. The world's grime hung on him; the noxious stink of his armpits corroded gentle air. The care with which his mother had made the bed saddened Latif; the quilt was folded carefully and tucked under the mattress tightly, the way he'd liked it ever since he'd been tiny and had delighted in rolling off the bed into the sidepouch of quilt and hanging there, supported.

Leda could have used his room: made herself a den or even taken on a boarder to help pay the bills. The meager salary she brought home compounded Latif's hatred of her job. He winced at the sight of Leda pushing a white baby's stroller, despised the fact that there were a hundred black women pushing white babies in strollers through the park on any given day—some of them pushing their own children in cheaper strollers alongside their charges. Leda could have rented the room and worked part time and gone to nursing school the way she'd always wanted to, but she'd preserved the bedroom for her son. She'd sounded hurt on the phone when Latif suggested renting it, although really he had said it just to hear *But what if you want to come home?* He was too selfish most of the time to think about what his mother did now that he was gone, and Leda was too supportive to ever mention loneliness, but now Latif began to think about his mother puttering through the empty apartment, singing church music softly to herself.

He saw her sitting in the kitchen with his picture in her lap, a framed portrait from class photo day, crying silent tears that fell and splatted melodramatic on the glass frame. Latif imagined how she must have felt when he left, sudden and stealthy like his father. Leda had known that it was coming; Latif's thirst for New York was all he'd talked about for months at breakfast, dinner, all the designated times when son and mother spoke. But still he'd left without goodbyes, denied her the ritual of seeing her son venture off into the world. Called her collect from a Manhattan payphone hours after she'd panicked.

He had apologized on the phone, tried to explain the sudden explosion that had propelled him to the bus, the feeling that there would never be another chance, another moment as perfect as this one, and Leda said she understood he'd had to leave his way. But Latif's mother knew the maternal art of making her child question himself without her ever saying he was wrong, and when Latif got off the phone that day his stomach knew the truth. Most of the hurt he'd experienced in his life, Latif reflected, had ricocheted back at him off of other people; he'd been hurt by the realization that he was hurting someone else. As if only he could inflict injury.

His head swam woozy, and he flushed his mind of thoughts and collapsed onto the bed, and for an instant the room felt right again. The view from the window hadn't changed. Nor had the feeling of the mattress. Then his body knotted. Cramps popped off like solar flares in places where there were no muscles and he knew his jones was coming down and it was tardy red and angry. A nightmare was beginning. Sweat trickled from from his temples, armpits, thighs; his stomach seethed and churned. If there had been a crowbar in the room he would have gladly knocked himself unconscious to avoid what was coming after him, rounding the corner and unhinging its slavering jaws, about to leap. He wondered if Wessel was still in the kitchen with his mother, but he didn't want to stand for fear of jogging his body into illness;

Latif was horrified of what vomiting would feel like, afraid that the experience might kill him.

The only thing he could think to try was smoking the pot he'd taken with him, in the hopes that it might calm him down. *My dro is the illest*, Spliff had bragged; maybe it would even knock him out. With shaking hands he pushed open the windowpane and lit a prerolled joint. The smoke hit the back of his throat and Latif almost threw up just from the contact, but his instinct was to gulp and he swallowed a cloud and coughed it all back up and out the window, then took a longer pull and forced himself to inhale, holding the smoke in his throat for as long as he could, imagining it seeping and wisping through his body and calming the tide of his blood, which seemed now to be crashing in sharp waves against the insides of his veins, rebelling, trying to pound through and saturate everything in him.

He expelled the smoke from his body and felt a slight dullness creep over the pain, a teasing hint of relief, and frantically Latif smoked more, smoked deeper, felt the weed fumes twirling through his body, billowing inside him. He was past the point of worrying about discretion, about his mother smelling the herb and catching him smoking, but Latif was inhaling so deeply and exhaling so powerfully out the window that only a trace smoke-squiggle from the joint itself calligraphed inside the room. He smoked until his thumb and finger burned and felt himself slip down into a muted haze. The beast was still there, ravenous, but it was trapped beneath a poreless thin net, snarling but not yet pouncing. He had bought himself an hour.

But he could move now; in fact, it was more painful to stay still. Inertia allowed the nausea to triangulate his position and move in, but the combination of movement and a constant nicotine smokescreen threw its tracking system off. Latif lit another cigarette and knelt next to the stack of records he had left behind.

He'd taken only a small portion of his collection to New York: albums he hadn't had a chance to study yet and a handful he'd already memorized but couldn't do without. Now he flipped nimblefingered through the LPs with a dexterity honed ransacking Boston's vinyl spots until he found a heavyweight first pressing from 1970, the cardboard cover bowed with water damage from some previous owner's unfathomable carelessness.

Translucence, by the Albert Van Horn Quintet with Murray Higgins on drums, Trey Valenzuela on bass, Lonnie Liston Smith on piano, and Freddie Hubbard on trumpet. Latif leaned against the speaker, legs tucked to his chin and left hand covering his face like a huge spider as the music—what? It didn't begin as much as suddenly exist, spring battle-ready from the womb like Latif's mythological homegirl Athena, goddess of war and wisdom. The record caught the band somewhere on the turbulent road between point A and what they were trying to become, Albert's horn careening and caroming like a rubberroom inmate trying to wrench himself out of his straitjacket, slamming against padded drumwalls and leaping wildeyed at the unreachable pianochord ceiling and falling hard and sweaty on ungiving bassline floorboards. This was Van Horn as pure unruly energy, rogue scientific madman: Van Horn as Latif had first fallen in love with him. Now Albert's sizzling red-blue revolution cries were an absorbent soundtrack, articulating and thus soaking up the pain Latif felt, diverting him even as he wondered whether the fight against dope was exactly what the song was about. He counted backward on his fingers to the time when it was Albert sitting somewhere wracked with torment, waging this same battle.

Suddenly Latif felt part of things again; the tradition slithered toward him, a lethargic black snake, and let him pet its slick head. He thought of all the cats who'd rolled dice with the same demon he was squaring off against: the few who'd hit a lucky seven and found God and jetted with their now-skinny billfolds tucked into a sweatsock, and the many who'd crapped out. And Van Horn blared and jarred, pulling the world apart and holding Teef together. Latif smiled with wet eyes, ear against the speaker, mind floating in a tiny salty warm oasis. Van Horn dipped like a kite in sudden heavy wind and hit a breathy low whole note and Latif bent his head, anticipating the upswing he knew was coming, the hint of resolution in the next strangely pretty sound.

It never came. The stylus jumped the groove like a derailing train, screeched across the vinyl til the needle snapped. The record continued turning, silent, ruined, a scar etched across its face. The broken stylus surfed the platter, detritus on a placid sea. Latif jumped up, teeth grinding, eyes darting raccoonlike. Holes opened in the floor around him; the black snake slithered into one and disappeared with a pop like a spaghetti strand slurped into a child's mouth. The oasis drained away and the rawrubbed holes in his arm, no longer balmed with music, moaned anew. Latif blinked back reality like teardrops and retreated from the room as if it had a gun on him.

He climbed out the window one gangled leg after the other, refusing to let his mind in on what his body was doing for fear that it might try to stop him. It was not yet midnight and there would be cats out, cornermen; he knew where to find them quite nearby. Thoughts ran across the bottom of his brain like film subtitles, free to be horrific because they were ignored. Acts he'd heard of junkies perpetrating to get dope flashed spastic through his brainpan: desperate panicked thieveries, inept robberies, abhorrent acts of prostitution, degradations of all kinds. Latif discounted them and walked until he heard the guttural slogan, so familiar, so revolting, once so intriguing and mysterious, now so hatefully coercive.

Got coke, got dope, got smoke, spoken low without the expectation of response. *Got coke, got dope, got smoke:* words he had never uttered or answered, the lowliest refrain of the dope game. He leered toward the words, toward two dark figures in the shadows of the awning of the closed corner bodega. His eyes keened wildly as Latif tried to decide what he could say.

Whatchu need, man, what's the deal, talk to me, the shadow rapped. A match flared and a cigarette crackled. *C'mon, c'mon, let's take this walk,* and Latif followed, a cigarette dangling from his own lips, as the man looked over both shoulders and sauntered purposefully towards the streetlight. He stopped and stared down the block, standing sideways to Latif, deliberately not looking at his face. *Whatchu need? Dope, smoke, or coke?*

Dope, choked Latif.

The light hit the dealer's face and Latif's cigarette fell from his lips. He gaped in surprise, relief, and dismay.

Shane?

The cornerman scowled and turned; he grabbed Latif by the collar, pulled him into the light, and recognized him.

Latif? Oh shit! Mike, come here! It's T.T.! What's up, baby? He laughed and pulled Latif into a bearhug.

T.T.! The second shadow stepped into the light and became White Boy Mike.

Whatchu doin back from NYC, man? Latif gave Shane a look unguarded in its fear, a look one only dares give family. He covered it expertly, so fast that no one but family would have seen it to begin with, but that instant was enough. Shane's joy at the reunion vanished. *Please tell me you were joking,* he said, somber.

I wish I was, Latif said, eyes flickering shame. *I'm caught up in some shit, man.* He scratched fitfully at his arm. *My jones is coming down, Shane.*

Shane narrowed his eyes, cutting out unnecessary portions of the world. *What happened to you?* He took Latif's face in his hands like a doctor. *You're not supposed to be here. Not like this.*

Latif said nothing; his countenance pled mercy. Shane stared at him for a long moment. Mike stared at Shane. All three waited for Shane to come to a decision, and *Fuck that* said Shane, *you come with us.* He grabbed Latif's elbow and pulled him in the right direction, gathered him in and threw an arm around his shoulders. *I'm taking you to my crib.* He walked faster, elbow locked around Latif's neck in an almost-headlock. *This Shane talkin at you, nigga. We done been through a lot of shit together, and I want you to know that it's been many a night we've sat around and wondered what old Rabbitsfoot was up to down in The Apple. We all knew one of these days you'd be sending us tickets to come and see you play down at the Blue Note or the Vanguard or somewhere. And I don't doubt it to this moment, T.T. You gonna pull through this.* Latif concentrated on walking.

You know why you'll pull through this? Shane asked him a few minutes later, as they sat in Shane's murky secondhand living room and Shane passed him joint and sipped a beer, the walk and whatever explanation Latif could stammer out over and done with, the time line and the mission clear and the process of keeping him sedated underway, *Do you know why you're gonna be back at Dutchman's with Van Horn before you know it?*

Latif inhaled the smoke sharply, winced, and shook his head. *Why?* he croaked, holding his lungs full as he spoke, feeling the cannabis drift through him. Shane had weed for days; *We'll burn trees all night if that's what it takes*, he'd vowed on the way over.

You know why? Because I put years into you, nigga, and I want a return on my investment. I saved your ass from having to go through a lot of shit, and you know why? Because I knew you were talented. I'm smart, but you're talented. You got something, and it didn't just disap-

pear all of a moment like a magic rabbit. That's bullshit. You're gonna get straight and go back and use that blocks of sound shit you were talking about plus everything you already knew, which is plenty, and you're gonna make good on my investment, and Mike's investment, and all your peeps' investment, and that crazy nigga Wess's investment, and your mama's.

Do you know what she told me last time I stopped in to see her? Shane asked, effortlessly keeping both ends of the conversation going. *I go by there every once in a while, because she likes to talk to somebody about you, and she told me a story about when your ass was seven years old and she took you and Rook to see the circus. She said soon as you found the band, some ol greasy no-music-playing circus pit band, that was all you watched the whole damn time, and she couldn't get you to look at the clowns or the lions or the tightropes or any of that shit. Do you remember that?*

Latif fluttered his eyelids and tried to answer Shane. He could see the tent now, the huge fat mustachioed white tuba player and the mammoth mounds of dank elephant shit. And here was Shane, leaning forward in his chair elbows on knees, benevolently and firmly in control. He had always been this way, and Latif wanted more than anything to tell Shane how important he was. Latif struggled to sit up; the chair was overstuffed and cushy and Latif's muscles felt like limp spaghetti ropes; his brain floated in beer and clouds of smoke and pulsed with torments, but he had to muster speech.

The whole time we were growing up, he said slowly, looking at Shane from beneath half-drawn eyelids, *what I wanted most was your respect.* He turned his head to look at White Boy Mike and felt his sinuses screech an objection. *Mike knows what I'm saying. I always wanted to feel like you thought I was legit. I used to wish I would get jumped just so you would jump in to help me and I'd know for sure. I always wondered if you'd fight for me.*

I'm fighting for you now, said Shane, *and I would've fought for you back then.*

We used to talk a lot about respect, me and T. T., said Mike, trying to catch Latif's eyes. They were closed. *I guess because we wanted it so bad. Remember when I first moved to this neighborhood, when I was thirteen? Cats used to let me slide during the daytime, but once the sun went down it was like* Yo, where that nigga Mike at? *Cats was beating my ass every night. You remember that, Shane. I had to fight mad dudes just to get back in my building, and if I knocked one cat out, the next one would step up like* Yo, you knocked out my man, let's go. *That shit went on every day for months before cats was like* Yo, that nigga cool. *I went through mad drama. Running away from cats on my own block.*

I remember you used to tell us you weren't really white, that your father was Puerto Rican, said Latif with his eyes closed, leaning back and smiling despite it all.

Ahhh, screamed Shane, laughing and pointing at Latif, *that's right! I forgot! He used to say that shit!*

Mike laughed. *Only for a hot second. I ain know no Spanish except* puta.

Who was it started calling you White Boy Mike?

It was everybody. There was Black Mike who lived in Jay's building, remember?

Jay Fox, said Latif, and poured the sudsy remainder of his beer onto the rug.

Hey, what the fuck you doing, man? Watch my fuckin rug.

Latif opened his eyes and stared groggily at Shane. *Jay Fox*, he repeated, louder.

Jay Fox, said Shane, solemnly, and wet the rug with his own brew.

Jay Fox. Mike followed suit.

They sat and smoked, and the pauses between words stretched

longer and longer until finally they snapped and snores replaced them. Shane and Mike dropped where they lay, Mike with his feet up on the couch and Shane twisted into the narrow wicker chair frame. Latif drifted off to the muted sounds of A Tribe Called Quest. Shane had thrown *The Low End Theory* on the stereo: implicit tribute to a moment he and Latif had shared years ago, when the album dropped. Latif had hipped Shane to Miles' late sixties quintet only days before, and when Q-Tip, grinning on the outro vamp to "Vibes and Stuff," announced *Yes, my man Ron Carter, is on the bass*, Latif and Shane stood up like *Oh, shit!*

Listen to the way he says it, Latif had insisted, rewinding the tape to re-peep Tip's intonation. *He's wild happy. He knows it's some historic shit.* He and Shane basked all afternoon in the casual alliance of musics, traditions, generations that too often seemed at odds, that came together awkwardly when they were forced to hang out at family reunions. Latif still got heart surges when he heard the joint.

He fell asleep halfway through the next song and woke with a start in total silence, rubbing dreams out of his eyes. An untextured hazy presence, like something from a dream which had followed him back into life, rose and hovered above Latif as he stood up on wobbly legs and pressed a hand against his lurching stomach. He felt watched, oppressed and mocked and haunted by something unidentifiable, something that controlled him that he hated: maybe God and maybe not, maybe the toxin he needed to course through his system that had slowed instead now to an insufferably delicate and sluggish trickle.

His legs were not seaworthy, and the apartment rocked like a schooner in a maelstrom, throwing him off balance. Reluctantly, Latif abandoned the failing dignity of walking and lowered himself to the floor. He shuffle-crawled toward the bathroom, raised his head and twisted it to look behind him at nothing, nobody, flung it back on his neck to stare up at the rainclouds that shadowed his aching trip across the floor, purgatory rainclouds drenching him in nothing.

You got me staggering lopsided through your sketched-in vaguely outlined world, Latif's mind mumbleranted. *Frankenstein Godzilla hobo scratchin out my eyes: Johnny five deuce uno,* if thine eyes offend thee pluck them out. *Can't go to heaven, you won't allow me to believe. If you don't believe in heaven you'll believe . . . in hell. Why don't you just kill me, you incompetent cruel bastard? You call this a life? Does this look like life to you? You made me razor jagged so I claw at you in screams and begging: Do I have a father? Have I been abandoned? Do I pray? Eat? Can I love? Am I you? Is that it? Why do I deserve this? I'm so thin wind whips right through me, or it would if there was wind. I can't think at all: I'm a slapdash vagrant bundle of half-truths anecdotes pisswater scripture and feelings lost in the translation, stabbing myself just to see if I have blood. Unequipt to live but neither is my so-called world yet vigorous enough to kill me: it too is shapeless warmish embryonic mass, and so I huddle with your other failed experiments, clasp my rickety malformed enormous knuckle hands and pray, for what I can't imagine and to who I can't be sure.*

He was almost to the bathroom, pulling himself hand over hand across the floor like a mountain climber battling a sheer cliff face. He sunk his fingers into Shane's grey carpet like pickaxes and saw yellow fluorescence flickering beacon-like ahead. If he dared look behind him Latif knew he'd see a trail of slime such as a slug leaves, a heavy mucus ribbon oozing from his body and clinging to the floor, things inside him that were seeping through his pores. Finally, Latif's hand touched the cool white bathroom tile and he pulled himself all on it and pressed his cheek against the cool, lifted his shirt and slapped his belly down against the cool, flayed open his palms against the cool and lay breathing long and slow and regular.

And when he had composed himself Latif opened the cabinet below the sink, from which Shane had removed the bag of herb. He looked inside and saw three large plastic bags lined up against the wall: *got smoke, got coke, got dope.* There was a box of smaller bags there too, and Latif filled one with smack, pouring from the big bag to the small, replacing everything and pocketing his prize, snorting what he spilled up off his hand. He flopped back over on his stomach and began the long crawl back to his chair as the sun started to creep above the filth-covered windows.

*Good morning, Ms. J-P., this is Shane . . . Yes, ma'am, that's just why
I was calling. Latif saw me going past your building last night and the two
of us went for a walk. He didn't want to wake you by coming back in, so
he crashed here . . . Well, he's still asleep and . . . Alright, hold on . . .*

It was a shame to wake him, Shane thought, looking at Latif's
slack face, mouth open in deep sleep despite the sunshine slashed
across his face. The cat so clearly needed rest. He shook Latif's
arm, eliciting only an unconscious groan. Latif pulled away and
shifted his position.

Yo, T.T. Wake up, man. Your mother's on the phone. Latif!

Latif brought his hand up to his face. *What?*

Phone. It's your mother.

How'd she know I was here? he mumbled, rubbing his head.

Because I called her. Here. Latif was too fucked up to stand and
Shane half-lifted him on to his feet. Latif stumbled over to the
kitchenette and leaned over on Shane's counter, twisting left and
right to pop his vertebra. His legs came slightly into focus underneath him, and he picked up the phone and wrapped the cord
around his wrist.

Hello?

Latif, you've got to come home immediately. Leda was rushed,
hard, shaky all at once; he'd never heard his mother's voice like
this. His first thought was that she had found something in his
room that had revealed him, or that Wess had told her. *Can you
do that? Can you come home now?*

What's wrong, Mom?

Leda's voice faltered. *Here, talk to Wess,* she said. Latif heard
her pass the phone, imagined his mother reaching for a tissue. He
braced himself.

Hello, Latif. Wess was sedate, controlled. *Are you alright?*

I'm fine. Shane and Mike took care of me. What's going on? What did you tell her?

Latif . . . Wess paused. *Sonny Burma called early this morning. Albert is dead.*

What? Latif had never thought that people's knees buckled in real life, but he had to grab Shane's counter to keep himself from falling to the floor. *What happened?* Horror pooled up in him like oil, black heavy and thick. Latif's vision exploded starry and he felt his stomach fold in on itself. The room, the world, went slack. Colors were being sucked out of the universe forever: blue had evaporated into empty space and red was burning its fierce self to nothingness like some distant quasar. Without Van Horn to conjure them into fullness blue and red didn't exist, and yet how could Albert any more be dead than color itself? How could simple neurons firing or not, crude blood pumping or stagnating, how could these horrid scabid earthly technicalities apply to Albert? Van Horn must have died in his sleep; death would never have dared face him with his saxophone in hand.

Latif? Are you still there?

How did it happen? he asked again, not having heard the answer. The words were gray leaving his mouth, as gray as his hand on the phone and the brain clodding in his head. He was surprised they traveled as far as the mouthpiece without disintegrating and scattering in the grayish wind like chalk dust.

They found his body in the East River in Harlem. There was a bullet in his head.

Oh, Latif said dully. That made as much sense as anything. It was no more or less abhorrent than an overdose or heart attack, no more or less surprising than if Wess had told him that the Sun God had swooped down on his chariot of flame and scooped Van Horn up in his arms and carried him away into the skies. The grayness engulfed Latif and he felt nothing, only despair, which was not a feeling but an unfeeling, a numbness predicated on the certainty that hope was gone. He found himself quite capable of speaking calmly, because he gave not a fuck about anything that he or Wess or anyone could say or play or think.

Do they know how it happened? he inquired.

Wess didn't know what to make of the flatline of Latif's voice. *Are you high, Latif?* he whispered.

If there's anything I'm not, Latif said cold, *it's high.*

I'm sorry. It's just that you sound so calm.

Mmm, Latif responded, waiting for an answer.

Wess sighed. *The main rumor is that Albert was cheating with somebody's wife and the dude popped him. People are saying all kinds of shit, though, everything from Van Horn owing money to the mob to drugs to the whole thing being just a stickup that went wrong. Sonny said there's even a rumor that Van Horn took his own life.*

Albert would never do that. Latif felt a tiny bit of color returning to his cheeks, to the world, indignation that anyone had the audacity to think Van Horn would kill himself. *He should have died on stage*, Latif said after a moment, then wondered why he'd said it. What good was it to die on stage? What empty romance, what solace, could be squeezed from the circumstance of any death? Latif found himself wondering what Van Horn's final song had been, what melody had run the final lap around his mind, what thought or color or vibration he'd last released into the air, and soon he found himself in tears. Shame overwhelmed Latif and he slid down the counter and sat crosslegged on the floor.

The music is gonna get played with or without you, Van Horn had told him the second day Latif had shown up on his doorstep, nervous and overeager, a shaky-handed wannabe torchbearer. Albert had tapped him on the knee, smiled; *So just relax and let it happen.*

Latif wondered how the music would get played without Van Horn, through whom it would now gust and whip and bellow.

Despair was melting little by little, and the heat of desperation was the cause. Albert had protected him somehow; how and from what he didn't know, but Latif felt the particular fear that the death of leaders brings, whether they be kings or warriors, gangsters or judges. Such men are not mourned with tenderness and reflection, as men, until the void has been filled either by the emergence of a new leader or by the realization that life can proceed without one. People quaver with self-discovery as the search runs its panicked course, realizing *I must catch the torch before it lies in smolder on the ground,* or *I am not the one,* or *I must now look within because what's without is gone.*

All three awarenesses rumbled in Latif, tremoring his hands. He remembered the day of Jay Fox's funeral; after the service all of them had left their families and walked quietly together to the woods behind Rook's house, twelve darksuited boys of fourteen, fifteen, and sixteen. They stood in a circle on the sparsely stubbled ground, inventing the ceremony as they performed it. Shane had been the speaker because only Shane dared speak. Perhaps he dared speak because the others looked to him to speak, and perhaps they looked to him because he had almost died with Jay himself, and would have missed the funeral if he had not left the hospital's recovery ward against a doctor's orders to be there. Latif remembered what Shane had said then: All the things that made up Jay were in the air now, floating, and it was up to each of his boys to claim them, pull them in, give them a home. That was what it meant to keep Jay Fox alive.

The image had disturbed Latif at the time; he'd pictured them in their dark suits as vultures, hunched together, sharp beaks picking at the dead. But the longer he thought about it, the more comfort Latif culled from this idea of repossession, until he came to think of it as a spiritual will, the passing down of whatever was good, sweet, useful to live on, and the death only of what was nothing, bitter, rotten in a man.

Van Horn was a man, Latif reminded himself, sitting on the floor with his head cradled in the L of his thumb and first finger. Van Horn was a man and he deserved to be mourned as one. The world would mourn him as a genius, a conduit of truth, love, fire, future, history. It was for Latif to remember his cooking, the warmth with which he joked, the walk they'd taken once along the water, around the reservoir in Central Park without speaking, each one lost in his own contemplation yet connected. Like two astronauts floating through space inside their suits but holding hands.

Wordlessly, Shane offered Teef a cigarette. He took it and a light, nodded thank you, puffed, and wondered momentarily why it was that Shane had been by his side for both of the deaths he had experienced. Shane made himself scarce and Latif tried to concentrate on his memories of Albert, to catalog them in some meaningful way, to remember all the crucial moments. Every moment had been crucial; they blurred and vanished and Latif flashed back to one of his arguments with Mona: *You can love more than one thing at a time*, she'd told him. *You can be a musician and a man.* But what would Van Horn have been to him, to anyone, if he wasn't a musician? Would he have been a great man still if he had never played a note?

For the first time Latif wanted to answer yes, but he could not make himself think so. Albert had found truth in music and music in the truth. Music had made Albert what he was, pushed him into what he had become, brought the love out of him because it allowed him to proclaim and probe it. This was how Albert had grown. Just as a plant can only grow as big as the flowerpot in which it lives, a man can only grow as big, as wise, as loving, as the means through which he finds expression. Without the infinity of music Albert would have withered and atrophied.

But by the same nickel, Latif reminded himself, there had to exist some seed of greatness to begin with. A plant destined to be small will not grow simply because it is transplanted to a bigger pot. That he was such a plant was a life-threatening fear only because Latif aspired to hugeness, understood the size of the pot and yearned to fill it with himself. No plant would try to be what it was not, he thought, and hoped he was so wise.

Sonny had offered to drive to Boston and pick Latif up for the funeral, saying he might as well be on the road as anywhere and besides, being confined to the cockpit universe of his whip tended
to help clear his head. Wessel had accepted on Latif's behalf. The
service was the next morning and Sonny arrived late that same
evening.

Latif spent the day sitting at Shane's crib, thinking and shaking
and smoking everything Shane handed him, drifting briefly off to
sleep, returning to his mother's house to say goodbye. She and
Wess bid him a sad, quiet farewell; he heard himself tell them he'd
come back soon, as soon as all of this was over, for a proper visit.
Wessel squeezed his bicep fiercely, discreetly: *Please do*, he intoned
with guarded meaning. Latif nodded. Leda kissed him on both
cheeks and then the forehead, whispering a final condolence; Latif
mumbled his downcast thanks and shuffled backward out the door,
duffel strap slicing his shoulder and horncase weighing down his
arm. The smack he'd stolen from Shane was in his underwear,
plastic knotted, tucked against his balls for safety. Stealing it had
made him sick, but not as sick as not stealing it would have.

A soulfood spot called Bob the Chef's was the only thing in
the area Sonny was sure he could find. Burma was waiting in the
parking lot when Teef got there, leaning back against the hood of
his car and staring vacuously, hat pulled down close over his eyes
against the nonexistent sun. Latif mouthed hello and they em-
braced. Sonny's hug was tight. The first hour passed wordlessly,
with nothing to distract Latif from his thoughts but the metronome click of the blinker when Sonny changed lanes, which he
seemed to do at random. Latif tapped his foot in counterpoint
long after the noise abated. He wished Sonny would scan the radio, cough, sigh deeply: anything. Soon, though, the silence grew
on him like moss on tree bark, soft padding, and Latif found him-

self fretting about the inevitability of conversation. Whatever words shattered the congealing air would not be worth it; the silence was tribute to Albert.

Latif wondered if anyone he knew would ever speak normally again, if in a week or two or six months' time rooms would fill once more with loud casual conversation, chatter, bullshit. How long before Sonny and Amir were twin pillars of discourse again, riffing on each other's jokes and trading tagteam stories? Nothing ever shook the world for long. Jay Fox's death had not stopped them from laughing, and at first that had seemed horribly wrong, but soon it was horribly right. Latif stared out the window at the headlights of opposing cars, wondered what Sonny was thinking, and decided his own loneliness outweighed the importance of the ceremony.

I know this sounds crazy, but I feel like Albert died for my sins.

Sonny glanced over, across his rigid pilot arm. *I feel that way too*, he confessed. *But the truth is, Albert died for nothing. It ain't meant to be, it ain't the Lord working in mysterious ways. It's just some fucked up unfair fucked up shit, and I'm not gonna dignify it with that kind of thinking.*

Without taking his eyes off the road, Sonny opened the glove compartment and dropped the *New York Post* onto Latif's lap. *Look at the shit they write.*

Latif picked it up and turned on the vanity light. The newspaper was folded over and the inside headline read *Jazzman Found Shot Dead.*

They make him sound like a gangster in there, Sonny said. *They don't get to the music until the fifth paragraph, after a whole bunch of there* is speculation that Van Horn's death may be in some way tied to narcotics *bullshit.* Sonny locked both arms, pushing like he wanted to smash the dashboard with the wheel. *Newspaper motherfuckers. Couldn't do him right when he was alive and just as ignorant today.*

How's Marisol? Latif asked.

Hysterical, absolutely hysterical. Keeping herself busy with funeral arrangements, though.

Still the manager, huh?

Mmm. Sonny turned toward him for longer than was prudent, a confidential glint in his eye. *You know,* he said, *if Albert was cheating—and I ain saying he was or he wasn't—but if he was, Marisol would have killed him herself.*

Latif studied Sonny's profile. *And how are you?* he asked.

Not much better than Marisol. He was quiet, face drawn grim. Latif noticed the uneven splotches of stubble prickling Sonny's face and realized he'd never seen Burma unshaven before.

I'm better than Higgins, though, Sonny volunteered after a moment. *He's taking it harder than anybody. No two musicians have ever been closer than them, man. Or pushed each other like that. Albert was his brother and his patron saint rolled into one, and I'll tell you right now: if he finds out who killed him, Higgins' gon live out his days in jail for murder one.* Sonny laughed mirthlessly. *That's his coping technique; he's quote unquote investigating. Anybody so much as gives him a name, Higgins' gonna walk out his front door with a shotgun and start blasting.*

Sonny sighed, tossing up his hands and letting them fall back into position on the wheel. *You know,* he said. *It's horrible, it's a tragedy, it never should have happened, there's not much else to say. You're never gonna go to his house and vibe with him again. I'm never gonna sit down at the keys and listen to him play and do my best to keep up anymore. Even if they do solve it: So what?*

Latif kept still. Some day Sonny would want to talk about Albert's life, laugh, reminisce, smile with remembering, tell stories. But now was a time for simple unarticulated sorrow. Latif thought of the biographies lining Albert's living room and wondered who would write Van Horn's. He had always looked at those books, famous names aggressively emblazoned on their spines, as being authoritative, definitive, official. It was only now, as Latif sat with *Jazzman Found Shot Dead* in his lap, that the absurdity of such an assumption hit him. Why should anything in those volumes be true? Who could tell if the authors had known their subjects, understood them, why they even wrote those books? Latif thought of Higgins with the shotgun, an image he had no difficulty seeing, and felt that he would wring the neck of anyone who distorted Albert's life, miscolored what he was about.

Latif closed his eyes but he was wide awake, thinking. He rolled down his window slightly, just enough for him to snake his hand out and hold the roof and catch some breeze. When he was young Latif had liked to rest his elbow on the bottom of the backseat window of his father's car and cup his hand, letting the moist wind fill it like a sail and push it back. Now, though, he could only bear to let it blow against his fingers, lest the wind play the holes in his arm like a flute.

I'm quitting junk, said Sonny out of nowhere, just as Latif was thinking of the stash in his drawers, the ache to get some in his system mounting, wondering how Sonny would react if he pulled out the bag and offered him a bump.

You're what?

I've been clean since you left. He drove with his wrist casual atop the wheel, shrugging, dangling his hand. *I've been playing with fire way too long, man, telling myself I was cool but never really sure.*

So you just quit, Latif said, flat. *Just like that. After all these years.*

Sonny nodded, oblivious to the jealousy in Teef's voice. *Cold turkey. Everybody said they'd never seen somebody kick so easy. Guess I'm lucky.*

Goddamn fuckin right you're lucky, Latif growled. He pulled the bag out and untied it. *Care to join me? Seeing as it was so easy for you to kick, how bout a little bump with a motherfucker you practically convinced to start?*

Sonny stared out at the highway. *If you want to blame me you can blame me,* he said. *I probably shouldn't have been so honest.*

You think? Latif powdered his finger, held it to his nostril, and glared through bloodshot eyes. His snort was gratuitously loud. Sonny didn't react. Latif leaned back, eyelids humming, wiped his nose and took another hit.

I want you to know, Latif, Albert wasn't mad at you. Sonny spoke deliberately, hard and ponderous, knowing his words had to penetrate a heavy haze. Latif said nothing. His nose twitched.

He saw a lot of himself in you. He told me that.

Well, Latif said, sullen, *I guess that proves even the great Albert Van Horn misses sometimes.*

You think so? Sonny's voice rose, indignant. *How many times Albert leave The Emperor's band?* he asked, shooting the question with pop-quiz velocity.

Latif frowned. *Twice,* he said. *Once to go home when his pops had cancer, and once when he got kicked out.*

Wrong, said Sonny. *Once when he got tossed and once for reasons nobody knows but Albert. He was gone a year and it wasn't Pittsburgh with his father like he told you or India to study with the master musicians like he told me or Africa to learn the tribal rhythms like Amir thought.*

Sonny eyecorner-checked Latif to see if he was listening, saw him toying with the bag of smack and found himself wanting some. *I knew he'd never tell,* Sonny continued, ignoring the craving, *so back when I was the new guy in the band and she still liked me, I asked Marisol. She got real big-eyed and solemn and said* Albert figure out what is musician. *Shook her fist and walked away.*

Sonny looked at him as if he'd proved his point. *Well, more power to that nigga,* Latif retorted. *He coulda told a motherfucker the answer.* He knew it was no way to speak of the dead, but all this had lost its potential to comfort Latif, even if he believed it. Par-

ticularly since Albert had emerged from exile and exploration un-
scathed, and here Latif was jagged and tattered and Albert was
dead. Albert was dead.

Sonny gave up, on comforting Latif and contorting himself.
Gimme the bag, he said. Latif passed it, professionally unsurprised,
and Sonny's mind flinched. Should he toss the junk and stare
you–better–get–your–shit–together eyedaggers at Latif, or share a
moment of sympathetic indulgence with him, a mourners' mind-
erasure solidarity interlude even though the kid couldn't handle
his dope? The bag was in his hand now: Who was he to start playing holier-than-thou? Sonny did a bump, felt better than he had
in days, and passed the bag back. Latif took a small hit and leaned
back, zoning. Sonny tightened his hand around the wheel, and
when Latif awakened they were home.

The funeral was a jazz world who's who. Mournful men filled the aisles of the uptown chapel, unsurprised that another of their ranks had been plucked early from the earth. Stainedglass light rays shined soft and brightly on the tears of matronly women in the front rows of the pews and on the bowed heads of gray distinguished gentlemen standing in a line against the back wall with gray hats atop their folded stridepiano hands. Sonny was the organist, sitting onstage in his black suit amidst the rainbow flowers amassed everywhere: on the dark wood steps, the stage, across the closed oak coffin. Latif looked at the box and could not believe that it contained Albert Van Horn, that he lay inside with arms pressed to his sides, straight as a soldier at attention, his eyes touched closed probably by some white police captain's leather-gloved right hand, a strange fish washed ashore in Harlem.

Latif was paralyzed upon entering the church, unsure where to sit and afraid of violating the unfamiliar protocol with which everyone seemed so ghoulishly conversant. An usher approached on silent feet to guide him to a seat. Latif followed him up the aisle and saw Marlon Burma on his left. They greeted each other with tightlipped halfsmiles. On his lap Marlon held a houndstooth fedora, distinctively cut and unmistakably Sonny's. Latif looked at it in wonder and then glanced back up at Marlon. The painter touched the brim.

Latif walked on. The usher stopped and took him lightly by the elbow, gesturing to a half-empty pew. As Latif shifted to shuffle into the row, he saw Mona sitting on the bench behind him. She beckoned to him, her eyes clear and open, removed her purse from the seat beside her, and patted the pew. He lightstepped past the others in her row and sat to Mona's right. She said nothing, only slipped her arm through his and laid her head across his shoulder. The service was starting. Latif scanned the chapel, noticing faces familiar and famous and registering slight, muted reactions at the sight of curvy, fluid nightclub people pressed and starched and staring straight ahead like automatons.

The preacher's eulogy floated languid and lush over Latif's head, pretty but ignorable. The cat quoted the Bible, a book Latif had never noticed on Albert's shelves, and he half-listened and devoted his attention to the scent and feel of Mona, nestled between his head and shoulder, her hair tickling his neck.

He was grateful for her presence; sadness, memory, hope, and comfort were stirred by the naturalness of touching her. He wondered what they would say to one another when all this was over; Latif rehearsed an apology and stared at the candles on the altar and felt a righteous steadyburning desire to make his life correct and clean and proper, refill his drained hull of a body with better potions. He looked around and wondered how many others were resolving to reform themselves right now. Marisol and Murray were in the front row with Amir and some of Albert's family. He feared speaking with any of them; perhaps he would eschew words and simply hug each one in turn. Words seemed to have no place or power here.

The preacher disagreed and spoke on and finally was finished, and then the worst began. Murray and Amir joined Sonny on the stage, Amir carrying his bass and Murray sitting down invisibly behind the coffin, where his trap set waited. They began to play a delicate, heavy ballad of Van Horn's and it was terrible: terrible because where Albert's horn should have come in there was nothing and everyone in the chapel heard it. There was a hole in the music and that was all Latif could hear, a giant unfillable vacuum. The sight and sound of them brought it all home; sobs swelled to wails and the calm sea of funeralgoers rippled with tiny, minimized motions: handkerchiefs and tissues dabbing eyes, hands clasping more firmly, shirtcuffs and watches suddenly visible beneath suit jackets as men squeezed women tight around the shoulders. Seeing the three of them up there was like watching a broken bird attempting flight, and there was nothing anyone could do but sit and listen. Tears rolled down Latif's face and glistened in Mona's hair and he let them, his hand in Mona's and his body shuddering slightly in silence. He looked down and saw one of her tears fall, felt the dampness seep through the knee of his suit.

A man slid in beside them and tapped Latif's elbow lightly with a finger. Latif turned his head and Larry Calvin moved in closer, conspiratorial, his eyes darting left and right before finally setting on Latif.

Say, bruh, he said. *You think when this is over you and I can take a little walk?*

Loathing poured undisguised from Latif's eyes. He was sitting in a church pew listening to a whispered plea for skag with one ear and the sound of a black hole collapsing with the other. Albert's supernoval collapse pulled all light into its void and Murray, Sonny, and Amir were standing at the edge, feet planted, straining to keep from being sucked into oblivion. Latif wanted to punch Larry Calvin in the face, but instead he lifted Mona's head gently in his soft palms and slid out from underneath its weight. He stood up and brushed wordlessly past Calvin, turned crisply on his heel, strode quick and solemn to the rear.

He looked back for a second, hand on the polished brass-ring doorknob, and took in the whole church: the full rows of people, Sonny hunched over the organ, Murray staring down into his necktie as his brushes swept the snare drum, Mona looking back at him with confusion and concern in her moist eyes, the red carpet and the altar and the coffin buried in flowers, and the stained-glass Jesus on the cross, his arms around it all.

Latif pushed open the immense wood door. A stalactite of pure noon sunshine cut into the church and Latif slipped out onto the steps and let the door creak shut behind him. He lifted his face and stood glaring into the sun, waiting to go blind as Shane had playground-claimed so many years before, scaring him so much that Latif had never dared to stare at heaven since then. His vision dissipated into brightness, and when he heard Mona say his name behind him and turned to face her Latif saw nothing but a blotch of sheer light still. He closed and rubbed his eyelids, massaged the light until it calmed and dulled and he could see her, standing on the top step with her purse between her hands. *Are you alright?*

I guess there are a lot of ways to take that, said Latif. *And the answer to them all is no.*

She nodded and looked down. The doors were far too thick, but Latif could swear he heard the faint strains of Albert's ballad through the wood and stainedglass nonetheless.

Albert asked me once why I was a musician, said Latif. He put his hands in his pockets and looked up the steps at her. *Instead of somewhere with a bomb strapped to me.*

Mona was walking toward him, head bowed in respect like they were still inside. *The only way you can justify it*, he continued, turning sideways and dipping his shoe into the air between his step and the next one down as if testing a swimming pool's temperature, *is if what you create is on the frontlines somehow. If your music pushes people into thinking about freedom and justice and love and what they're fighting for, then maybe you're doing your part. I could live with that, anyway, if that was what my music did.*

Mona stopped and stood a step above him, between Latif and the sun, their eyes level. In the coolness of her shadow, he relaxed his brow. *I used to think fear made me a musician—a musician instead of a warrior. But I'm not scared of what's out there. He tapped his chest. I'm scared of what's in here. Of how much hatred might come out my horn if I let it, how much sadness, and what that might do to me.*

I'm not talking about some friendly-ghost melancholy blues you shoo away, Latif said. *I mean the sadness and the violence that come out of knowing I might make it, and you might make it, but not me and you and Shane and Sonny and Albert and Spliff and Kofi Ogunde and Jay Fox and my mother and my dad and my whole neighborhood. I mean knowing that every day I've gotta deal with things that somebody who looks like you never has to consider at all, even if we're sleeping in the same bed. I mean knowing we're all gonna end up dead as Albert, no matter what we do, and most of us a whole lot quicker and with less to show for it. Knowing we've gotta find love in the midst of all this savageness. What's the beauty of the struggle against the fact we gonna lose?*

Latif paused, momentarily shaken at what he'd uttered in the clean sunshine church air. This must be the moment when some cats find religion, he thought, then went on. *There's some kind of violence deep inside me, Mona, and I'm just realizing it's there. Maybe I'd never need to play at all if I could just kill everybody who looked at us the wrong way on the Reese Beach boardwalk, or every cop in this city, or my dad.*

Mona's hands were folded in front of her, purse dangling by its strap before her knees. She looked like a schoolgirl on the verge of tears. *And if I could treat the people I love right*, Latif added. *And be sad when I need to.* He thought at first that he was saying it for her, but when the words hit air they felt true.

Latif sighed and craned his neck back to look at the whole church, the building unfinished after a hundred years' construction, scaffolding obscuring its face, and the steeple set off against the blue sky, poking God right in the ass. *That's the kind of stuff I should be blowing, but I don't have the strength, the courage, to be the conduit for so much pain. I couldn't do it if I wanted to, because I've got a shutdown instinct that stops me from playing before I self-destruct.*

He retreated another step, spoke looking up at her. *I need to hurt, though, Mona. Not dull and steady and almost forgettable like life, but sharp, all at once, so I can pretend I'm on the frontlines. For a while music let me regulate my dosage of the pain I'm addicted to, the pain that's our birthright. Maybe smack was just a way to get to some pain once I built up an immunity. A way to do it alone.* Mona bit her lip. She wanted to say something, to touch him. Perhaps, Latif thought, she was wondering if being with her had been another way he'd tried to put himself next to some pain. She came down a step, raised a hand to his face, looked into his steady eyes, and let it drop back to her side.

We're all junkies and pushers, Latif said, *addicted to hope and trying to get a fix of beauty, scraping our souls and offering the shavings to each other. Not sharing goes against this whole tradition, but somewhere down the line I decided my shavings were toxic. Everything poison I've ever tasted is buried inside me, Mona. Albert never taught me any alchemy, how to turn that into love or let it out without it killing me. If I override the shutdown switch those snakes are gonna slither out my horn and who knows what they'll do?*

But I can't be scared. I've got to pick up what Albert left me, figure out how he got past all this and made it pure, where he found so much love.

Mona stepped forward and hugged him. They stood together without speaking until the bass solo was over. *I wish I was Marisol,* she said. *I want to be the one to step in from nowhere and save your life.*

I want to do it myself, Latif said. *But maybe that's the problem.*

Maybe it is. They each stared down, intently, and then Mona took his hand. *Come on, let's go back in. It'll be over soon.*

He shook his head. *I can't. It's too much. I've got to go home. Will you come up after it's over?*

Mona closed her eyes and nodded, squeezed and released his hand. Latif let it swing to a standstill.

If that's what you want, then I will. She turned and walked back to the church, pulled open the door and disappeared inside. A gush of piano bass and drums escaped as she entered. Latif watched the door close, gangled down the last few steps, and plodded uptown to his room with the sun on his back and hip hop blasting past him. He gathered up his saxophone in aching buckled arms, cleaned it inside and out, warmed the cold reed with his tongue, and tried to play.

ACKNOWLEDGEMENTS

Love and thanks to my entire family. To Elvin and Keiko Jones for showing me the music and the world and making me family. To Delfeayo Marsalis, Sonny Fortune, Cecil McBee, Robin Eubanks, Greg Williams, Carlos McKinney, Antoine Roney, Frank Foster, Eric Lewis, and Steve Kirby for breaking it all down in words and notes. To Andre C. Willis for ten invaluable years of guidance. To my peoples for their love, interlocution, spirit, support, time, collaboration, guidance, and energy: William Upski Wimsatt, Tricia Rose, Douglas McGowan, Eugene Cho, The Apple Juice Kid, Vernon Wilson, Mark Hanson, Jason Santiago, Robert G. O'Meally, Dave Cohen, Kevin Aquaboogie Glenz, Rachael Knight, Sarah Suzuki, Katherine Aaron, One*9, Petra "Treek78" Richterova, Jimmie Williams, Lucas Carlson, Sophia Wang, Gerald Cyrus, Michael Eric Dyson, Bonnie Hiller, Gil Scott-Heron, Cary Broder, BOM 5, Adam Lazarus, Andrew Bujalski, Michael Heppner, Ricardo Cortes, Lethal, Dan Bailis, Jon Caramanica, Eli 173, Danny Rudder, Adam Levine, Mercer Sparks, William Fisher, Jamel Brinkley, Jason Fifield, Silo Grainbomb, Chicago Joe Hundley, Manie Barron, Frankie Hernandez, David Miguel Gray, Phase 2, Special K (Treacherous Three), Jack Kaplan Trent, Aura, Keith Gessen, The Five Thousand Pound Man, Cee Justice, Shane Sweetwater, Gnomad, Steeples, DJ Frane, G'Brey Milner, Kenneth Reynolds and the Darkside Crooks. To Alan Ket, Vee Bravo, Clyde Valentin, Ray Acevedo, Jessica Green and all the original *Stress* magazine heads for keeping me covered back in the *elementary* days. To Michael Cunningham, Binnie Kirshenbaum, Nicholas Christopher, Wallace Gray, Ann Douglas, and Tim Taylor for being my teachers. To all my tennis ball game cats for growing up with me. To all my hip hop and writing